Dearly Beloved

Dearly Beloved

a novel

HARRY SYLVESTER

Foreword by Sean C. Hadley

Angelico Press

For information, address:
Angelico Press, Ltd.
169 Monitor St.
Brooklyn, NY 11222
www.angelicopress.com

PB: 979-8-88677-080-3
Cloth: 979-8-88677-081-0

Book and cover design
by Michael Schrauzer

To write a novel of a country where for three hundred years the names have been Camalier, Mattingly, Duke, and Tennison, and to call the imaginary people of that novel Harrington, Jones, or Smiley, would be to impose a strange handicap. To call the people of this novel by the old names is merely to give needed strength to the method of implication. The use of these names does not mean that the imagined people of this work portray or are related to in any way, any person living or dead bearing the same or similar names, or to any person. Nor does the town of Calverton in any way resemble any actual town or place.

H. S.

MEET HARRY SYLVESTER

Harry Sylvester's writing career began in 1926, with his first published essay appearing in the Notre Dame *Scholastic*. That essay, an exercise in sports journalism, which would be Sylvester's primary vocation for many years, put his skills on display. The elements which would shape his career into some of the most promising Catholic fiction in the twentieth century showed their earliest manifestations in the undergraduate Sylvester. For the next fifty-five years, Sylvester wrote journalistic pieces, short stories, novels, letters to the editor, radio scripts, and book reviews that covered a wide range of the human experience. Alongside these writing endeavors, the life of the author was likewise varied and tumultuous, with broken relationships and the pressure of constantly moving weighing heavily upon him. And Sylvester seemed keenly aware of how biography shapes a writer's legacy. In one of the only autobiographical pieces of writing Sylvester authored during his career, he explained: "The real landmarks in anyone's life lie within. A man's birthplace and travels are meaningful only in that they may have helped shape and mark him."[1] Though the external "landmarks" of a writer's life do not provide a

---

1 Stanley J. Kunitz, "Sylvester, Harry (January 19, 1908–)," in *Twentieth Century Authors, First Supplement: A Biographical Dictionary of Modern Literature*, ed. Stanley J. Kunitz (New York: The H. W. Wilson Company, 1979), 977.

secret code with which to unlock meaning, the shaping and marking which such experiences exert on an author should not be overlooked.

A key element in understanding Sylvester's works comes from his contribution to Kunitz's *Dictionary*: "the Catholic Church has been the central theme of almost all of my serious writing, I cannot write of myself as a writer without making clear my relation to that Church, past and present."[2] Of course, the Catholic Church is larger than Sylvester's singular experiences. Thus, when trying to place his fiction in the lineage of American Catholic authors, it is important to articulate what this means. If all his "serious writing" is directly connected to the Catholic Church, how might this claim shape a reader's interpretation of his texts? What constitutes Sylvester's serious work, as opposed to his unserious work? And how do these distinctions give the reader a better understanding of the Church and the moral tradition of literature that grew alongside it for two millennia? These questions are the proper starting point for understanding how Sylvester's writings serve as an historical witness, capturing the wholeness of the human experience. And one of the best ways to dig into such concerns is to pick up one of his novels. *Dearly Beloved* is a great starting point.

FINAL WORDS, STARTING PLACES

The title of Sylvester's second novel comes from the closing lines of the book. There is a circular idea working here that should encourage readers to constantly recall the familiar priestly invocation: "Dearly beloved." Sylvester's writings contain important elements of study and research. *Dearly Beloved* marked his first genuine

2   Kunitz, 997.

foray into the realm of fiction based upon a researched topic, with societal criticism clearly in the background. The story follows two Jesuit priests who hope to bring orthodoxy and orthopraxy to the rural area around the fictional Calverton, Maryland. These men, Father Cornish and Father Kane, attempt to establish parochial schools of the poor Negro population, start-up fishing cooperatives to compete with the bigger companies further North, and provide catechetical instruction to the white and black Catholic populations. An enthusiastic young man, John Cosgrave, comes down from Georgetown to help them after the first cooperative is bombed. But Cosgrave finds himself embroiled in local controversies of his own when he falls in love with a troubled young woman, Jane Saunders. The novel contains sexual failings, outbursts of violence, and the dogged determination of its priests, all culminating in a chaotic scene which reveals that right actions sometimes come from the most unlikely of actors.

Sylvester spent time in St. Mary's County, Maryland, where he befriended Horace McKenna, a local priest who had founded the Seafood Cooperative to help rural fisherman bargain with companies in Baltimore. Sylvester's fiction reveals careful observation and keen understanding in portraying the area's character, dramatized into an imagined world. Sylvester had previously praised the work of Ernest Hemingway for its focus on "people, not...ideas of culture," and *Dearly Beloved* showed that his own writing was moving in the same direction.[3] These efforts meant that the characters, debates, and sin present in the novel took on the same kind of complexity one would find in real life, something also true of other Catholic authors like J. F. Powers and Flannery O'Connor.

3 Harry Sylvester, "Ernest Hemingway: A Note," *Commonweal* (October 30, 1936), 12.

Dearly Beloved showed that Sylvester could write a Catholic novel that was true to life. A story of segregation and the Church that remained faithful to the real world, while fictional, struck too close to home for many. As he shopped around for a publisher, Sylvester encountered numerous publication roadblocks. In his letters, he complained that *Dearly Beloved* was "apparently too liberal for the Catholics and too Catholic for the Liberals."[4] But his novel of Christianity and racial reconciliation remains relevant over eighty years later. Sylvester's novel confronts readers by reminding them that the Catholic Church requires a particular way of life. And the reader is invited, like the audience at the closing of the book, to consider that ancient invitation from Paul's letter to the Church at Philippi, "Dearly beloved . . . be of one mind in the Lord" (4:1–2, *Douay-Rheims*).

Sean C. Hadley
Fayetteville, Arkansas
January 2024

4 Harry Sylvester to Donald Powell, August 8, 1941, in Donald Powell Papers 1 (Washington, D. C.: Georgetown University Libraries, Booth Family Center for Special Collections), https://findingaids.library.georgetown.edu/repositories/15/resources/12304.

Dearly Beloved

1

FROM the wide end of the triangular square around which Calverton is built, a short road goes steeply down to the waters of St. Clement's Bay, an arm of the Potomac. In the long summer, pleasure fishermen take their boats along the three or four miles of the waterway and out into the great estuary of the river. Blackistone Island is then visible, but few of them notice it or the white stone cross on it, and most of them have forgotten that the island once bore the same name as the bay.

Although the cross was used frequently as landmark by boats headed for St. Clement's Bay or the Seventh District of St. Mary's County, almost no one knew why it stood there. A group of men from England had come to that country three centuries before, seeking sanctuary, and it was on that island that one of them, a priest named Andrew White, had celebrated the first Mass in that part of the new world. Later, White was taken back to England and killed for performing his priestly functions, and still later a generation somewhat mindful of these things had erected the cross where he had celebrated his Mass.

Calverton emerged each day gradually, even reluctantly, from the night. George Blair had once seen an appropriate significance in this, but now he saw, or thought he saw, little significance in anything. Six bars, to serve the town's seven hundred people, edged the square like jewels in a ring, and they alone were open early to catch rivermen on their way to work or drummers leaving the Calvert Hotel on their way back to Washington and Baltimore. Raley's Bar had the best location, being almost in the middle of the south side of the square and not far from the hotel.

The bartender, young Jimmy Gordon, had opened the place this morning and now stood watching his employer coming across the floor of the bar. He noticed with satisfaction the red dullness of John Raley's eyes, the half-hearted rubbing together of the hands in an attempt to convince their owner that he felt well.

"Why don't you tuck in your shirt?" Jimmy said.

Raley was sleepy enough to obey anyone, and he stood by the bar arranging his clothes and waiting while Jimmy poured two drinks of cheap rye whiskey. Raley drank both of them, shivered, and moved to look out over the half-curtain that delicately shielded the bar from the square.

A car was pulling up outside. The first morning light of soft red touched Mrs. Dolly Morgan as she stepped out, a wide smile on her face. Joseph Tennison followed her from the car, the double-chin under the insurance man's face more apparent than ever.

"Guess they been in Washington all night," Jimmy said, stretching to see from where he was washing the glasses. "Joe sure looks it."

"So would you or I," Raley said. Pleasure had begun to touch him flutteringly, like a bird's wing. Staring at Mrs. Morgan and her escort, John Raley came full awake.

4

"I'd shoot Joe if I was Dab Morgan," Jimmy said.

"You just talk big," Raley said. "A little piece here and there ain't that important."

"You talk like you been getting around some yourself."

"No sir," Raley said. "Those two girls upstairs, that wife and little two-year-old daughter of mine—that's all the women I want. Time was when I refused nothing, black nor white, but that time's gone. Yes sir."

He returned to the bar and poured himself another drink. Feeling better, he thought that he might even be able to eat breakfast. He drank the whiskey quickly and tried to get out on the sidewalk before Joe Tennison and Mrs. Morgan went into Clement's Restaurant next door to the bar. Raley was just too late. Perhaps he should follow them into the restaurant, he thought.

The April sun was warm on his hands as he hesitated, a look of pleasant thoughtfulness on his face. A quadroon shuffled by, his swollen jaw ridiculously encircled by a crude bandage tied under his hat. The pale negroid face was marked by a long scar that ran diagonally toward the jaw and pulled one corner of the mouth into an apparent cruelness. Raley stared at him with the faint, easy curiosity someone's else pain often gave him, and thought he recognized the Negro as Loker Abell from down-county. Pain had distracted the man and he did not see Raley as he went by, offering no sign of recognition. Raley grew annoyed and then even alert, as the Negro turned into the driveway that ran between the hotel and the small building block in which were the bar and Raley's apartment. Raley took a few quick steps, enough to enable him to see the Negro about to turn into the side entrance that led upstairs to the apartment and three offices, one of them occupied by a dentist.

"Where you going, boy?"

"Why, Ah got a bad toothache and Ah wants to see the dentist heah. Ah—oh, hello, Mr. Raley, I didn't see you coming by."

"Well, it was certainly time you did know who you were talking to," Raley said, not unpleasantly.

"Ah guess dat's right, Mr. Raley. Anyhow, though, Ah got this bad toothache and Ah wants to see the dentist—"

"You're not seeing any dentist in this building," Raley said, still not unpleasantly. "There ain't no niggers allowed in this building except they work here. You down-county niggers will have to learn that the same as anyone else."

"Yes suh," the Negro said. "You see, suh, Ah been coming up all night from Dameron. Ah couldn't get no ride up. This tooth—"

"Why don't you see Dr. Adams? He's the County health officer and a nigger-loving son of a bitch if there ever was one."

"Ah know, suh," the Negro said. His soft manner, softer than usual, was in odd contrast with the vicious twist of his mouth. "Dr. Adams ain't no dentist, though. He say whenever we got tooth trouble we got to go see a dentist, not he. This tooth—"

"Well, you aren't seeing anyone in this building, Loker. Now run along." Raley had started to turn away so that he wasn't looking at the Negro as he finished speaking. These half-white ones were the worst, Raley thought.

"Yes suh—" Loker said, made aimless by pain.

6

Raley turned into the entry. Mounting the stairs he could smell the eggs and grits frying. He felt all right now, he told himself. The whiskey was warm in his belly and his mouth was running. He felt fine.

Slowly the square became active, took on color and movement. School buses, some orange, some blue, swung around in it and stopped to pick up segregated groups of children. A blue bus stopped for Negro children for the Catholic grammar school down the road near Medley's Neck; an orange bus picked up white children for the public high school up the road toward Loveville; and another orange bus took on colored children for their high school across the County near Pearson.

Victoria Lea, the pretty cashier in Clement's Restaurant, smiled at Mrs. Morgan as she went out, while Joe Tennison lingered to talk insurance to Mrs. Clement. On the street Mrs. George Blair, a large, kindly woman, walked slowly home from week-day Mass. A stake-truck loaded with cattle swung around the square, just missed a bus loaded with Negro children, and was kept from turning without pause into Route No. 5 by a span of oxen lumbering up the grade to town and driven by a Negro. The truck-driver cursed all niggers.

At the cash register in Clement's Restaurant, Joe Tennison paid his own and Mrs. Morgan's check, turned on Victoria the smile that had launched a thousand policies and told her she was looking mighty sweet this morning. She counted his change, avoided without effort his attempt to chuck her, and smiled without looking at him, thinking what a faker he was.

The big, blue mail truck from Washington came into the driveway between the hotel and Raley's Bar. It had

7

hardly stopped moving before poorly dressed Negroes, messengers for the town's two banks and for its wealthier citizens, began to converge on the post office. They were followed more gradually, and as if in response to the warmer sun, by the town's more substantial citizens. George Carroll Blair, immaculate in dress, came slowly along the south side of the square in front of, consecutively, the Calvert Hotel, Raley's Bar, Clement's Restaurant, a grocery store, and finally, on the corner, Clement's Drug Store, soda fountain, and juke emporium. Blair was a tall, slightly stooped man with a lined face that seemed gray. He wore a tailored suit of medium gray and his new, slouch Stetson hat varied just enough in shade from the suit to be in good taste. A black ribbon with his eyeglass attached to it, hung from his neck. The eyeglass he used whenever he safely could and he thought of it as a monocle though he referred to it always as an eyeglass.

He paused on the corner in front of the drugstore as a black Cadillac sedan came up the grade from the south and stopped before him. Henry Saunders stepped out of the car. Once an outlander, Saunders was now, by virtue of his money and his marriage to a Calvert, Assistant States Attorney for the County.

"You're right early this morning, Mr. Henry," George Blair said. Without waiting for a reply, he turned to the car, bowing and smiling a curiously skeletal grin. "And how are you this morning, Mrs. Saunders, and you, Miss Jane?"

The worried-looking woman in the car smiled feebly back and the girl opened her mouth slightly but did not speak. She was blonde and extremely pretty. Her face had an elusive, almost furtive quality and her eyes followed George Blair as he turned away to address her father. The big car moved on to turn into the other side of the square and park.

"Why, Mrs. Saunders is taking Jane to the doctor's this morning, Mr. George," Henry Saunders said, without looking at Blair. "Up to Chaptico to see Wathen McKay."

"No need to go way up there," Blair said. "Wathen'll be at the hospital here at ten o'clock. We all see him there."

Henry Saunders began to walk slowly toward the post office and still did not look at Blair. "For some reason he wanted to see them at his office," Saunders said. George Blair did not speak again until they were in the post office. There, men greeted him with off-handed respect; were somewhat more formal with Henry Saunders.

Blair took a sheaf of mail from his box, including *The Washington Post, The Baltimore Sun, The Annapolis Capital, The New York Times.* There were a number of releases from state bureaus and business houses, one renewal of a subscription to his own paper, *The Torch,* a check for three dollars for an advertisement, and a badge for the spring race meeting at Havre de Grace. The badge made him wonder if he should go to Bowie today. It was Wednesday, the day before press day, and there would be work to do. But Martha, his wife, could do it, he told himself one more time; indeed, she might feel badly if he didn't let her do it. And he hadn't been to the track in three or four days.

Ezekiel Mattingly, a Jesuit priest, dressed in traveling clothes, entered the post office and everyone in it bowed to him. He was a tall, lean man with a long, thin nose.

9

No one bowed lower to him than did George Blair. Henry Saunders shook the priest's hand effusively and the priest looked embarrassed.

"What are you doing down in this part of the County?" Blair said.

"Why, looking for a couple of good lawyers to give me some advice," the tall priest said. "Don't know of any, do you?"

Since he and George Blair were lawyers, Henry Saunders knew that Father Mattingly must be joking. Blair smiled; the smile was like a grimace on the lean and creased face. He had begun to want the black coffee the doctor had forbidden him and which his wife refused to serve.

"We could all repair to the drugstore," he said, "and have some coffee."

The three started out of the post office and people parted respectfully to make way for them. Henry Saunders was pleased by this, but Ezekiel Mattingly dropped back to follow the others, badly embarrassed by obsequiousness. George Blair, his eyes slightly fixed, failed to see the people stepping aside.

As they entered the drugstore, they did not notice Mrs. Saunders and her daughter coming out of a dry-goods store across the square. The quadroon, Loker Abell, was sitting on the outer edge of the long wooden porch that ran in front of the store. Pain had glazed his eyes and he stared ahead. Passing him, Jane Saunders veered slightly away from him in a vague motion of fear and disgust. Her mother noticed it and felt oddly relieved. Looking up, she saw her husband entering the drugstore. She felt inordinately pleased to see him with Father Mattingly, and wondered if she could make up some excuse for joining them. Like her own family, Mrs. Saunders thought, the Jesuits had been three hundred years in the County. And Father Mattingly was doubly distinguished, in that he was the first native of the County to have become a Jesuit and return to it. He was in charge of the community house and mission at Chaptico, and it was generally though unofficially recognized that he was the superior of all the other Jesuits in the County.

Mrs. Saunders stepped off the curb and started across the square. "Mother, it's nine o'clock," Jane said, "and Dr. McKay is expecting us right now."

Mrs. Saunders turned on her daughter in well-controlled anger. The girl's face was mysteriously pitiful, the eyes uncertain, the mouth almost petulant. Because she did not understand her daughter's face, now or any other time, Mrs. Saunders was angry. She literally swayed in indecision. Memory of Wathen McKay's anger when she had visited him about Jane last week, decided her.

"I find you impertinent, Jane," she said, "along with a great many other unpleasant things." She got into the car and Jane followed her with blank, veiled eyes. The quadroon stared dully at them, not seeing them.

2

EXCEPT that they were both members of the Society of Jesus, commonly called the Jesuits, the two priests had little in common. Before the younger one's assignment to the mission parish in southern Maryland, they had met only once before, in the seminary at Woodstock on St. Ignatius Day, July 31. The younger one, now the Reverend James M. Cornish, S.J., had been a scholastic there, and the older one, Laurence Kane, had visited the seminary for the mild festivities Jesuits indulge in on the feast day of the founder of their Order.

They were sitting now in one of the rooms on the upper floor of St. Patrick's rectory at Ridge, a room with a large desk in it and several hundreds of books. It gave onto a porch in the rear, and both the room and the porch overlooked the wide, angling waters of that arm of the Chesapeake called St. Jerome's Creek. Father Cornish liked to call the room his study and nobody bothered to gainsay him.

They were at home and relaxed now and neither looked particularly priestly with his coat, clerical vest, and collar removed. Father Cornish even looked a good deal like the fine athlete he had been up to ten years ago.

"Of course," Father Kane was saying, "it isn't an easy parish. That is," he added quickly, "the white parish isn't." His own parish was the colored one at Ridge. He stuttered at times from nervousness induced by overwork and undernourishment, caused chiefly by his forgetfulness of meals.

"I'd been rather prepared for that," Father Cornish said. "Any place where the Church has been unmolested for so long is bound to have a certain amount of laxity, what with not going to Mass and so on."

"They go to Mass all right," Father Kane said. "The letter of the law doesn't trouble them. It's the spirit of the law. You'd think there wasn't any such thing as the doctrine of the Mystical Body."

"Oh, the Negro and so on," Father Cornish said. "Of course, it's the South. It'll take centuries to eradicate that feeling. I come from Washington myself. You people from the North," he went on, smiling to show he was not entirely serious, "have a time realizing the complexity and whatnot of the matter."

Obscurely and suddenly troubled, Kane surprised himself by the insistence in his own voice. "The doctrine of the Mystical Body," he said, "that all men, regardless of race or any other delineation, are part of one another in Christ, does not admit of different interpretations in different places."

"Of course not," Father Cornish said, hastily. "It's not, of course, a doctrine that's been well promulgated until very recently, when people have stirred up that sort of thing. And this being a border state, the whites perhaps feel a little more concerned about maintaining their position than they would farther South. It's easily explained."

"A true Christian never worries about his position," Father Kane said. He spoke in an undertone, almost mumbling. He looked worried and his face was turned slightly away from his colleague. He spoke humbly, too—as humbly as he could—as though not wanting to judge any particular person.

"Well," Father Cornish said, "these things will be taken care of in time." He rose and stretched his stocky body. "The thing to do now is to bring to these people down here some measure of economic independence."

"The whites, you mean?" Father Kane said, almost absently.

"Now, in Antigonish," Father Cornish went on, sitting down again, "they've been doing wonderful work with co-operatives and so on. There's no reason why we shouldn't do something of the sort here."

Kane looked at the floor thoughtfully. Watching his almost gaunt, wide-eyed face, the bones sharply marked, the skin weathered under the graying hair, Cornish felt sorry for, and perhaps scornful of, the man who was his superior here.

"I've got three groups studying credit unions," Kane said.

"Negroes?" Cornish said.

Kane nodded. "I don't know what will come of it. It took them so long at Antigonish."

"Long?" Father Cornish said. "I didn't know it took so long. Why, we've only heard of it in the last few years."

"It took them the best part of twenty years to lay the groundwork."

Father Cornish whistled. Kane rose, fearful of having embarrassed his colleague, and looked from the window at St. Jerome's Creek, below them and half a mile away. Fishing boats were coming in along the channels. The evening light, the sprawling, irregular shape of the so-called creek, with its many points and small headlands, the white and umber houses on them, gave the appearance of unreality. Craning his neck from where he sat, Cornish could see the boats. "I wonder how they made out with the herring today," he said. "They've not been getting a good price for them. The buy-boats come from Virginia and the Eastern Shore and there's a pretense of open bidding but actually the price has been fixed in advance and the fishermen don't stand a chance."

Kane knew these things but gave no evidence of it now. "I wonder who runs the buy-boats that do come here?"

"Jews, I imagine," Father Cornish said.

The silence that followed had a quality of which Cornish was not aware. Kane looked out to where the dusk covering the Chesapeake rose from the Eastern Shore. Presently he said, "Let's not forget that it's Saturday and we've got confessions to hear."

"Here at Ridge," Father Cornish said, now standing, looking raptly into the darkening light, "one can be quiet and away from things. Although I've only been here a few months, when I go up to Washington or even to Calverton I can hardly wait to get back here. It should be good to sit here on a winter evening with walnuts and a bottle of port–" He gazed fondly into the gathering dark. Culture had come to him late and very suddenly.

Kane was experiencing a feeling he did not know was one of awkwardness. He cleared his throat and put on his clerical vest. At Ridge, as at all the mission parishes, they had little opportunity to wear a soutane. The bell for supper was ringing below them. "You'll eat here tonight, won't you, Laurence?" Father Cornish said.

"I guess I'd better. The nuns have already eaten at the convent."

Frequently Kane ate his mid-day meal at the convent, served by the Negro nuns who taught in the Negro parochial school, a mile away from the white rectory and nearer the main road. But since the white rectory also served as a community house for the two Jesuits, Kane ate there more often, although he had living quarters over the new brick church he had built for the Negroes near their school.

The meal they sat down to after saying grace was well cooked and poorly served by Melissa Maddox, the shapeless and good-natured wife of a fisherman. She cleaned and cooked for the rectory and kept her own house; she felt ashamed when she took each week the six dollars Father Cornish gave her for her part-time work. Her supper this evening consisted of hard and soft crabs, country ham, potato salad, and hot cornbread. Father Cornish ate heartily, Father Kane more sparingly, less through choice than necessity. Infrequent and hurried meals had shrunken his stomach so that in a curious way asceticism had almost become a necessity with him.

Cornish talked steadily throughout the meal about co-ops for the fishermen. Kane tried to listen politely, but his mind was on other things: whether the archbishop would give the Institute twenty-five hundred dollars as he had the previous year; where he, Kane, could get a horse for Johnny Barnes. Johnny had inherited some land and was now one of the few Negroes in the County to own property. And what, he wondered, shall we call Minnie Jordan's new baby? The third and no marriage. She loves them so. Really, I should see she gets married.

"—a small group," Father Cornish was saying. "Just a small group to start with. I'm getting to know these people."

"They're awfully independent," Kane said and immediately regretted his words. He did not want to say anything that might discourage Father Cornish. There was so little zeal today. He wished he had some of Father Cornish's zeal.

"I know they're independent," Father Cornish said. "And I'll stress that angle of the thing. When they understand that co-operatives will make them *really* independent, they'll fall in line." He nodded his head once, vigorously, for emphasis.

Kane wanted to say something about first having study groups but he told himself that that could be said later. Zeal was too rare a thing to hinder in any way. At least in the beginning.

The house of Fenner Ridgel stood on one of the numerous points that jutted into St. Jerome's Creek. Water was on three sides of the little point, and the weathered, sound, but rather ugly house was surrounded by a litter that included a tobacco barn, a corn crib, a hen-house, turkey roosts, a hand-pump, a battered Ford sedan, a meat-house, a privy, an empty crab-car—half out of water, a skiff, a rickety wharf to which Fenner's powerboat was moored, and some farm machinery.

Ridgel himself was a tall, stout man with a round, sullen, querulous face and powerful arms and hands. He sat now with his back to the afternoon sun, mending a net, and thought of the evening. His wife was away, at the bi-weekly meeting and card-playing of the Ridge, Scotland and Point Lookout Rural Woman's Club, and even so brief an absence as that could make him think of her and of the evening.

A new, black coupe jounced through the mudholes of the road that led deviously to the house through scrub pine and cleared land. Fenner squinted at the car, trying to recognize it. The car stopped nearby and Father Cornish got breezily out. Fenner rose, puzzled but looking sullen, the net draping from one hand with unconscious effect.

"How are you, Fenner?" the priest said, taking the diffidently offered hand.

"Right good, Fawther, thanks. How are you?"

"Just fine, Fenner. Sit down. Go right on with your work. Don't let me disturb you."

"That's all right, Fawther." The big man stood there, the sun in his eyes giving them a slightly pained expression, the net still a wide cone depending from the hand.

"No, you sit down," the priest said and sat down himself on a chopping block. Fenner eased his two hundred and fifty pounds onto the log from which he had risen.

"How are the herring running, Fenner?"

"Herring running right smart, Fawther. Price ain't so good, though."

"I know that. What's to be done about it?"

Fenner looked at the net in his hands. Like most of the fishermen and farmers of the County he was not given to shrugging. "We go to the buy-boats with the catch," he said, "and they each got a man comes on the dock and bids. But it ain't no real bidding. They fix that price among themselves each day and no one goes higher. They just take turns, kind of, each day, for each boat to get the herring catch. And we send the other stuff to Baltimore, the shad and hard-head and rock-fish, and we send a box with maybe two hundred thirty pound of fish in it and they tell us when it gets there it got only a hundred seventy pound of fish in it. We got no way of checking. We can't run up to Baltimore every week."

Fenner liked to talk and drew a breath to continue.

"That's what the others have been telling me, Fenner," Father Cornish said. "I've been talking to them." He paused, he hoped impressively. "Foley Raley, Havenner Maddox, and John Mattingly. They all say the same thing."

Fenner nodded, blinking, his face grave and sullen; he thought one more time that he didn't like Foley Raley.

"And what's more important," the priest went on, "they're agreed that there's something we can do about it, and pretty soon."

Fenner shook his big head. "Like to know what."

"All right, I'll tell you. The buyers are organized against you, so to speak. You just organize against them. Pool your herring catch, promise it all to one buyer. In return make him promise you, say, fifty cents or a dollar a thousand more than the market price for that day. He'll do this in return for the assurance of having herring every day."

The big man frowned thoughtfully. "Been a long time since we got the market price for any fish."

The priest went on. "Then you could get a real cooperative going. You could buy together as well as sell together and get the advantage of your collective buying power." Fenner bit his lip in attempted understanding and the priest explained. "You can buy net for five men cheaper per man than you can buy net for one man."

"Who's going to run this, Fawther. I won't stand for no Foley Raley running it. That no-good, big-mouth—"

"John Mattingly will manage it or be president of it, or whatever you want to make him." It was Father Cornish's trump card and, he told himself again, he had played it successfully here, too, as he had with the other fishermen. It had been Father Kane's idea that his colleague should first get the consent of John Mattingly, a respected salt-water farmer and fisherman, to head the co-op.

"John Mattingly a right nice man," Fenner admitted slowly, looking out over the water. "Be a good manager. But I don't see how he'll have the time with his own work on the boat and in the tobacco fields."

"If he hasn't, we'll hire an assistant. What about the idea otherwise? What do you think?"

Fenner scuffed one foot on the ground and looked thoughtfully at it through the arch of his arms. "Don't like the idea of working in anything with Foley Raley. That man—"

"Now, Fenner," Father Cornish said, prepared, "we've got to be true Christians. The Pope and the best Catholic thought want people to have a better economic life, and they specify that co-operatives of one sort or another are among the means to be employed. Now, for the sake of a better social order you ought to be willing to work with someone whom you dislike. Not only for that reason but to help yourself. It's the only way you'll break the organization of these Jews that run the buy-boats."

Fenner was confused, did not even know some of the terms the priest was using. "Only one buy-boat run by a Jew," he said, absently, because 'Jew' was the last term he remembered hearing the priest use. "Worst one of all, name's McCarthy, carries a cross in the cabin of his boat. It was his idea, I hear, about the fixing a top price."

Fenner was a man incapable of subtlety and now was embarrassed and confused to see the priest flush. To end it quickly, he said, "All right, Fawther. Guess we ain't got much to lose. I'll try it for a while." He raised his great fist and shook it. "But if that Foley Raley starts running off at the mouth, I'll twist it for him right around the back of his head."

Father Cornish smiled, partly in relief. Having been an athlete once himself, he was fond of saying, he knew the psychology of men of violence. "I think it'll be all right, Fenner." He rose and the big man followed him ponderously.

"We'd right like for you to stay for supper, Fawther."

"Some other time, Fenner, some other time. I've got to get going on this thing right away. We've got to draw up papers and incorporate, you know. Guess the best lawyer in Calverton for us would be George Carroll Blair, eh?"

"Cousin George'll do," Fenner admitted, "if he ain't away at the races or something. Wish you'd come stay for supper, Fawther. Mary'll be right mad when she gets back and finds I didn't keep you. She'll be back 'fore edge of dark."

"Edge of dark," Cornish repeated. His expression was rapturously thoughtful. "Edge of dark. What a wonderful phrase for evening."

Fenner scuffed the ground. "Wouldn't rightly know, Fawther."

"Well, goodbye, Fenner, and God bless you. We ought to get this thing started in a couple of weeks."

"Yes, Fawther. Goodbye, Fawther." He watched the priest drive off and then sat down, puzzled at his feeling of relief. His big fingers began to move at last deftly through the twine. "Co-operatives," he said, slowly. It was a long word for him. "Sound like it might be a good thing," he said, aloud.

3

THE brick church for the Negroes at Ridge had been built by Father Kane himself. He had built it after their wooden one had burnt down, shortly after he had come to Ridge to reopen the Cardinal's Institute. The church's inward arches were Romanesque, the outer pointed gently to the sky. The altar was wide, low, and simple, the brick walls unadorned but for the Stations of the Cross, simply carved in wood. On the altar only the tabernacle possessed elegance, with its domed top edged with filigreed bronze and gold, and the heavy, silken curtain that hung before its grooved, rounded doors.

Great beams, hand-trimmed by axes, broke the ceiling, leading Father Cornish, when he first saw the church, to suggest that it was unfinished. (Kane had stuttered more than ever and said that there did remain a little work to be done on the altar.)

Over the left arm of the transept Kane's sleeping quarters were built. In the wall of the bedroom, just over the floor, a small window looked down into the sanctuary. Thus, Kane could make a 'visit' to the Blessed Sacrament each morning as he woke.

Benediction on Sunday night he usually allowed to be as elaborate as possible, restrained only by the number of cassocks and surplices available for the Negro acolytes.

The pews, widely spaced in the church, had been made at an orphanage and were half-filled now with Negroes, who clattered dully to their feet as the first acolytes came out onto the altar, swaying slightly from the studied slowness of their walk.

An even dozen of them, of various ages, preceded Kane, arranging themselves symmetrically on either side of the altar. The priest followed them, looking almost frail under the heavy, embroidered cope. He placed the pyx in the monstrance and knelt at the foot of the altar. Behind him the voices of the Negroes rose in a rich tide of sound, at first slow and even a little uncertain, then gathering swiftly confidence and volume.

Like all Negroes, they sang well in a group. Their voices set up an answering tone in Laurence Kane, his body being suddenly not weary. It was something quite apart from, though experienced simultaneously with, the mental ecstasy he felt kneeling before his God, exposed there on the altar in the monstrance under the ancient form of bread.

The voices died and rose again.

Tantum ergo sacramentum.

An acolyte placed the veil around his shoulders and another took the censer from his hands. Laurence Kane ascended the low, wide steps of the altar. Holding the shaft of the monstrance in the ends of the veil, he turned to the Negroes. Three times he elevated the Host and the dark, gleaming faces bowed before it. If only their God were all they had to bow before, he thought. He put the thought away, almost automatically. He would bring no bitterness to the altar.

The southwest wind came over the fields that dropped

to the river, carrying some of the freshness of the new-turned ground into the church. The Host held overhead, Kane prayed again that his people might find their salvation in the land. The wind blowing, the toning of the struck gong, the smell of the fields and the incense were in all of them. To Kane it was, briefly and blindingly, as though the land were coming toward them in a long turning.

He lowered the monstrance more quickly than usual. As with most Jesuits he was skeptical of anything resembling a vision. A miracle would have embarrassed him badly. He wondered at times if he and his colleagues did not carry their intellectuality too far, were not in occasional danger of missing a supernatural manifestation. It was, he always recognized, part of the heavy price they paid for the title of The First Legion of the Church. Other priests and other orders would have to have the honor of discovering miracles. These others, too, would make the far more numerous mistakes.

He would not give a sermon tonight. They were talked at enough. With them he finished the Divine Praises in partial reparation for the blasphemy which rose continually in the world. The acolytes swayed off the altar, the yellow faces and the black.

After he had removed his vestments, his body was tired again but his mind remained clear. Some of them would be waiting outside in the darkness to speak to him. He would stay here tonight. Jimmy Cornish probably had work to do. And the Negro nuns could serve him breakfast here in the morning. It gave them, he knew, a disproportionate pleasure to do so.

Outside, the men were waiting for him, the deep

tones of their speech hushing as they saw him. In darkness they seemed always to huddle. Or was it that the darkness just accentuated this? he wondered. The steadiness of the wind pushing off the river was heartening. And out of the hush his presence had induced, a strong murmur, "Evenin', Fawther."

"Hello," he said. "Hello, men." Isn't there some less banal salutation? he wondered again. In a mental gesture of almost simultaneous recognition and withdrawal, he saw that as they were now, they would always shame and embarrass him. As they should others, he thought, and put the thought away. "It's been a fine evening," he said, his voice almost cracking. There was still light behind the Virginia shore, over the Nomini Cliffs.

"A mighty pretty evenin', Fawther." Their voices had some of the quality of a trained chorus. So much talent, he thought again. The thought had become almost automatic in him. He stared for a moment at the light. The tall, lean figure of the young Negro dean of the Institute, Samuel Raife, showed against the light. The others were diffident and no one spoke.

In a group they found it difficult to make small talk. "How many of you will be coming to those new meetings?" Kane said. "The ones about the credit unions?"

There was an indefinite murmur which he could not —even after three years here—understand. He must have communicated his small dismay to them, for Bernard Hebb spoke briskly. "All go, Fawther," he said. "All go. They getting smart around thisaway. Heh." He managed the farm the Institute stood upon; a tall, spare, heavy-boned, yellow man, sixty years old and looking about forty-five.

"I hope you're right, Bernard," Kane said. "Look,

26

men, we're having one group meet in Scotland, another up at St. Inigoes, and one here at the Institute. Now, why couldn't we have meetings at Wynne and Dameron and Point Lookout. You all need things for your farms or your boats, and by forming credit unions you can get them."

Their silence told him that they didn't believe it, and for a moment he didn't believe himself. "How many of you ever tried to borrow ten dollars from the bank in Calverton to buy pigs?"

The answering murmur was mostly an unpleasant kind of laughter. No one thought it worth while to offer specific comment.

"This way," the priest went on, "you own your own bank. You borrow from it and when you pay interest you pay it to yourself and the others in the union with you."

He had mentioned it to them before, but their silence continued to say that they did not believe it: that they did not disbelieve him, his intention, but simply doubted that such a thing could be accomplished among them. He thought that this might be his own fault. He had tried to surround the project with the air of allurement certain parish priests used to cajole parishioners into attending the next church fair or bingo party. It had been a mistake; poverty was too close to them, too bitter. A Jesuit should know better, Kane thought. But that was pride, he thought immediately. And as an Order, their sin was pride, he remembered an old Jesuit saying.

"You explain to them at these here meetings, Fawther," Bernard Hebb said in his brisk, hoarse voice. "These men here take a lot of explaining."

The others laughed a little.

27

"Maybe we could have the St. Inigoes group meet at Johnny Barnes'?" Kane said.

Johnny shuffled. "Guess so, Fawther."

The silence again. A silence out of a long and terrible darkness. Kane wondered where such thoughts came to him, what vision brought such phrases to his mind?

"Will all the St. Inigoes men try to be there?" he said.

The murmur again. "Try to, Fawther." "Yes, Fawther."

"How about every Wednesday at seven?" he said.

"Wednesday courtin' night, Fawther," someone, not Bernard Hebb, said.

It was good, a sudden relief, even, to hear them laugh aloud.

"None of them goes courting that early, Fawther," Bernard said. "Wednesday be good time."

"All right, I'll be at your house Wednesday then, Johnny."

"Yes, Fawther."

In the silence Kane noticed again that there were almost no young men among them. The young men were in Calvert County, shucking oysters at twenty cents a gallon. They would be home in May, their carfare, perhaps one night in Washington, taking all of any money they had saved. If they could have a shucking house here. . . . He was too hasty, Kane thought; he must exercise prudence. His predecessor, Father Edward Latain, who knew these people better than anyone else, had said, "If you can even lay the groundwork in your lifetime it will be more than we could hope for."

They were going away now, murmuring their indistinct, their pleased goodbyes, the old cars wheezing, walking forms becoming quickly part of the night. Only Bernard Hebb and the tall young dean remained.

"They take some moving, don't they, Father?" the dean said.

"They'll be all right. It's so new to them."

There was some light from the stars, to which their eyes had now become accustomed. Kane could see the dean's features. They were frankly negroid but lean and even fine in the long face.

"I guess it is new," the dean said. "I still haven't become used to their being so backward this far north. When I came up at the beginning of the school year last fall, I expected to find things different here from the Deep South."

Bernard Hebb laughed without sound. In that light they couldn't see his eyes and Kane thought that it was best so, was even grateful for it. He knew he was fortunate to have Samuel Raife as dean of the Institute and he knew that St. Mary's County was a place where a man might easily become discouraged.

"The South," Kane said, "like New England, is principally a state of mind." His voice was tired and he had no wish to pontificate. "And there's no denying southern Maryland is the South. It's something all of us have trouble getting used to when we come down here, although St. Mary's County has been a Jesuit mission for over three hundred years, and our own annals should warn us." What they had to get used to was a lot worse than that, he thought. What they had to *avoid* getting used to.

"They despair so," the young dean said. He was a comparatively recent convert to Catholicism and had not gone to a Catholic college or high school. "Their

Catholicism seems to mean so little to many of them. I've frankly been disappointed to find that so in a place where so many, almost all, the Negroes are nominally Catholic."

Kane thought of the lengthy answers, thought that the end of the school year was finding the dean a bit on edge. He should see to it that Samuel got away to summer school at some Catholic college. It might even be best if he went to one that was not run by Jesuits; he had to work with a Jesuit all year. But that was a problem, too, for the University of Notre Dame did not admit Negroes, Kane knew, and he had not even heard of any non-Jesuit Catholic college that did. Although there might very well be one that did, he thought quickly, and there were some of their own—Georgetown, for example—that did not admit Negroes.

"That priest," Bernard Hebb said. The briskness had become an almost incongruous mutter. "They still remembers about him. That's what help do it."

In the almost stricken silence he had induced, Bernard said good night and walked away, toward his house just below the Institute on the long slope that dropped to the Potomac. The two he left did not know that they had not wished him good night in return.

"Just what is it he means, Father?" Samuel Raife said, evenly and respectfully. "I hear the people make the same reference at times."

Kane had a feeling that he should be dismayed and at the same time a strong joy that he was not. After all, it was not a thing that they had ever sought to conceal, however much they might be shamed by it. "It goes back almost a century and they have no written record of it," he said, not knowing he had paused before speaking. "Although, naturally it is in our own annals. Yet, even among them it has not become apocryphal or in any way distorted. If they have not left the Church by now because of it, they likely never will."

The dean waited for him to go on. They were both facing the river below them, a mile away, and saw the light of a steamer passing.

"We own a lot of land down here," Kane said. "And a hundred years ago we owned more, too much, perhaps, for an Order of priests to own in one place, although at the time there were justifying circumstances. We'd been left land that we couldn't sell by the nature of the deed. We had community houses and churches so situated on other land that the parcels, if sold, would be badly broken up and the land would be ruined for the ordinary farming of the time. Not being able to sell it, we worked the land that we owned. And the only way to work it in those times—we've never had enough lay brothers, anyway—was with slaves."

Kane was aware, as he paused, of the dean's stillness, in which there was neither agreement nor comment, perhaps not even understanding.

"Apart from the fact of their slavery," Kane went on, "they were well treated. And if they had been given their freedom in that time—the 1850's—it would have been both imprudent and a disservice to most of them.

"The times were troubled, as you know. People saw the war coming. A new provincial of the Maryland-New York Province of our Order felt that we should not raise any more crops than were needed for our own food down here, and ordered that our slaves should be sold.

"Looking at his letter in our local annals, I think that

31

principally he was concerned that we should not own slaves, but of course the letters of a provincial are sometimes studiously lacking in implications. He was a Northerner, who apparently overlooked the fact that the Negroes were better treated by us than they would be on many plantations; and he didn't seem to know much about the character of the man who was superior of the house at St. Inigoes—our community house in this section then—the man the people here call 'that priest.' "

Alone, with one or two people, Kane rarely talked at such length. He wished now, as he paused in his stuttering, that Samuel would speak. But the dean remained quiet.

"I think the man may have been ill," the priest went on. "So many of our Order become so, trying to lead two lives virtually, one in community and one in the world. He was to be transferred, he had never liked it here—we know from the annals—and he was in a hurry to be gone. He sold the—our Negroes to almost the first bidders, plantation owners from the Carolinas, and in doing so he separated, or allowed to be separated, families. Some remained here, in the northern part of the County, in Charles and Anne Arundel, while their wives or husbands were sold into the Carolinas." Kane added the last almost aimlessly, as would a man distracted by some pain, secret, prolonged, his own.

He wished desperately for Samuel to speak, say anything. He himself, it seemed, had never been so uncontrolled of gesture, had never stammered quite so much. Waiting now, in the darkness, he heard with gratitude Samuel finally speak.

"He must really *have* been sick, Father. But I guess

it's hard for us to achieve—understand, I mean—the mental attitudes of a time a hundred years gone."

"Christianity as an idea wasn't any different then," the priest said wearily. The stutter was almost gone from his voice and for once he did not question his own uncharity.

The light of the steamer was almost gone, toward the Chesapeake. Again, he wished for Samuel to speak, but the dean seemed tired, suddenly a little stooped. He wanted to go, Kane could see.

"Well, good night, Samuel," Kane said.

"Good night, Father," the dean said respectfully.

Walking alone toward the door of the church, Kane stumbled. Tears were at the back of his eyes. He had never in his adult life allowed himself their luxury. And now he wondered why they came so strongly. Anger at a dead man dismayed him, as though he had discovered and committed a new sin. His weariness grew so terrible that he felt sure it was intended to prevent his praying for the man, and like a diver walking through water, Kane forced his way through darkness to the altar and knelt there.

4

LAURENCE KANE woke at ten minutes to six in his brick-walled room above St. Peter Claver's Church. He rose with almost automatic promptness and dropped to his knees, midway between the brick wall and his narrow bed. The small window just flush with the floor looked into the dimness of the church he had built for the Negroes. Through the window could be seen almost nothing of the body of the church and little of the transept, but a direct view of the altar. On the altar was the domed tabernacle, containing the body and spirit of his Lord and Savior, Jesus Christ, mystically entombed there, by Laurence Kane himself, in unleavened bread. The priest contemplated the mystery briefly, regarding with a curious mixture of awe and tenderness the bronze and gold tabernacle that held his dependent God and sorrowing Master.

Stripping off his cheap, white pajamas, Kane stood naked for a moment in that first, washing light of the morning. His body was the hue of dirty ivory and the casque of his ribs showed clear, every bone. He was badly underweight, the muscles of his abdomen sagging evenly forward and sideways from his ribs. His knees were large and bony and the whole body looked even more ridiculous under his tanned, corded neck and serious, quiet face. The skin of the face and neck was

34

weathered and vaguely lined; the lines were not deep because the skin of the face was drawn tight, particularly over the high cheekbones, and Kane was only a year or two over forty.

He dressed quickly in traveling clothes of black suit and clerical vest, and went down to the sacristy to say his morning prayers. From the prie-dieu upon which he knelt he could see part of the church, its details growing into outline as the shifting blue light became quickly full morning. Separately, Samuel Raife and two Negro farmers came into the church, an old Negress, and two girls of about eight and eleven. The nuns came last, in two neat pairs, preceding their superior, Mother Mary Benedict, and Kane knew that it must be nearly half-past six and time to invest himself.

He felt a separate pleasure whenever he saw Negro nuns. The dark faces under the stiff, white wimples seemed to symbolize so completely the synthesis of race and people in God. He wondered one more time and now almost idly if there might ever be a Negro priest here; and recalled the story, almost legend, of the Negro Jesuit from Jamaica who had visited Ridge decades ago, and how the Negroes had knelt to kiss the dumbfounded man's hands, and how they had wept in terrible sobs.

Kane put these thoughts away to say the specified prayers of his investment. The little wind the chasuble made as he dropped it over his neck like a yoke—had he read or thought of the phrase: the oxen of the Lord?—was pleasant, for already the day was warm and he felt the heat in his heavy vestments. It would soon be time to use the summer vestments. He wished he had the money rather than the summer vestments, but they had been a gift from a comparative stranger and he could not very well have asked for the money in their stead.

He said Mass, slightly preoccupied with his plans for the day. His acolyte was eight-year-old Kezer Washington, open-mouthed and wall-eyed. Kezer had come from Virginia a year ago—rowed across by kinfolk where the Potomac was eight miles wide—to live with relatively better-off kinfolk in St. Mary's County. They had promptly had him baptized and Kane had christened him Michael but had never had the heart to call him anything but Kezer.

In the little dining room they had partitioned off for him at the Negro convent Kane ate bread and coffee, refusing almost automatically the cooking sister's usual suggestion of ham and eggs. Her principal joy in life— she did not teach as did the other four nuns—was that Kane ate many of his meals at the convent and, knowing this, Kane sometimes ate special dishes she had prepared for him even when he had no appetite for them.

Outside again in the white light he saw Samuel Raife waiting for him, carefully dressed, his bags at his feet. Two other Negroes in old, black suits stood near. The three of them talked diffidently, almost as though embarrassed. Kane wondered if not the least of Samuel's troubles was that the older, local Negroes were puzzled at his learning and misunderstood his quietness. Right now, Samuel seemed embarrassed, something he never was in class or with white people.

"Good morning," Kane said. "Everyone ready?"

"Looks that way," Samuel said. The others mumbled and shuffled. They were going to Annapolis to a funeral and then to look for jobs. The funeral had been scheduled for yesterday but they had not been able to get a ride until today; so they were going now, hoping that

36

somehow the funeral had been postponed. They were cousins, Tom Whelan, a fisherman out of work for the summer, and James Washington, Kezer's uncle, a farmer who could cultivate no more than a garden patch because he had no horse.

Kane and Samuel sat in the front, the cousins in the back of the light, three-year-old sedan. Kane would have liked to see one of the cousins in the front and Samuel or himself in the back. But it might have embarrassed Tom or Jim. A diffidence that was little short of morbid lay on most of the Negroes of the County. As a thing to be overcome, Kane knew, it was second only to the deeply rooted and now unreasonable hatred of the whites for the Negroes.

Kane swung the car away from the small group of buildings composed of the Negro grammar school, the convent, and the church, and along the dirt road that led past the Institute. The long building of weathered stone looked blank now that it was closed. Its blankness caused the priest an almost indefinable pang. Perhaps, he told himself, it was because he alone knew it might not open again.

On Route No. 5 the car was less noisy. For a mile or two, heavy woods, almost forest, rose to either side, then fields began to break into it. St. Mary's City, on the nameless demi-lune of a bay that was part of the St. Mary's River, was hardly more than the Episcopal Girl's Seminary, the replica of the old State House, the statue of Tolerance at the fork in the road. It was hard to believe St. Mary's City had once been the capital of Maryland. The statue whisked by on Kane's left and he didn't turn to look. It was a pretty poor piece of work, anyway, and a mockery, too, now in a place where neither

37

Protestant nor Catholic was overfriendly and both hated the Negro.

Then Park Hall, with its half a dozen houses and stores; and Great Mills, pathetic under the burden of its mighty name. He should stop off and see Rose Camalier, Kane thought, but it was too early for her to be at the school in Great Mills, where she was principal. She was a tall, homely, intelligent girl, one of the few people in the County to have attended college. Kane thought of her father, David Camalier. He had been a County Commissioner. At seventy he was tall and spare and his face had acquired—as some old people's do—a translucent quality; he seemed, Kane thought, a man who shed evil, who even disregarded evil, walking in his own separate air and light.

He must visit David and Rose soon, Kane thought, now that summer would give him more time for amenities. The priest would have been shocked to know that David Camalier was the only white man in the County whom he respected other than as a creature of God.

The car was coming up the long slope to Calverton. Kane thought that instead of swinging left into the upper square, he would go right and out of town. An early fallacy of his own had been that if the whites saw Negroes with himself or other priests frequently enough, it might soften their hearts. When Kane had come to the County three years before, Father Latain, his predecessor, had given him very little advice. As the months had passed Kane realized that it had been because the older priest, unwell as he left, had not wanted to discourage him or seem cynical.

But he would have to go into the upper square, where the stores were, to get gas. He swung completely around it to be heading out again on No. 5. Signs of morning had begun to show in Calverton. John Raley was opening his bar and Victoria Lea was going into Clement's Restaurant. The faces of Negroes nodded to Kane with what might have been furtiveness. Raley turned his back so that he would not have to greet the priest. Faces peered out of stores and upper windows.

It seemed so to Kane. . . . And then, catching himself, he thought that he was just imagining these things, that he was developing a persecution complex. Martin Combs came out from his hardware store to fill the car's gas tank. "Mawnin', Fawther, mighty pretty mawnin'."

"It is, Martin. Are the children well?"

"Yes, Fawther." Combs, a tall, portly, white-haired man, continued to fill the gas tank with almost studious concentration. Bucky Maddox strolled thoughtfully along in front of the stores on the south side of the square. Three of the town's many fox-hounds saw him. He was on the way to the beer truck he drove for Charlie Combs but the hounds thought differently. He was a wiry, handsome, young man who blew the conch shell at the fox-hunts attended on foot by the local devotees. The fox-hounds, Big Girl and Charles County, stopped and watched him. The fox-hound, Patuxent, sniffed his hand.

"Go 'long, you," he said, raising his arm in aimless dismissal. "This ain't no time for runnin'. You'd never run no whelpin' vixens, anyways." Resignedly, the hounds turned and moved away. "G'mawnin', Fawther," he said to Kane. Bucky didn't know why he suddenly felt embarrassed, unless it was because of what he had heard others say about the priest.

Joe Tennison and Mrs. Morgan, back from another

39

night in Washington, saw the priest as their car came into town from the north, and Joe began to drive around the square until the priest should have gone. Mrs. Clement, short, stout, with a fresh, rosy face, hurried out of the restaurant. "Just noticed you standing there this minute, Father. None of them in the restaurant would think of telling me. You come right in and have some coffee and old ham and cornbread. How are you, anyway?"

She was tugging at his arm and it set him stammering again. "R-really, Mrs. Clement. R-really. I'd love to, but I can't. I've got to be in Baltimore by ten-thirty and its five after eight now."

"Oh, you can get coffee, Father. You come on."

"I'd love to, really." He would have liked to, but something deep in himself that he hardly recognized, something stubborn and almost perverse, wouldn't let him leave the Negroes to wait in his car. Not here and not now.

"You don't get up here often enough, Father," she said.

"Oh, yes, I do. I sort of ease through town. I'm so thin, you know; it's an advantage in avoiding my creditors." It was his idea of a joke.

Leaving town, Kane felt better. He was grateful to God for the consolation of Mrs. Clement's invitation, and sorrowful that he had been so little trusting in God's mercy and the incidence of His grace as to need consolation.

"You know, Father," Samuel said, when they were up the road past Morganza, "I could drive faster than you, and you could be saying your office."

"So I could." They changed places.

40

"You don't want to stop at Chaptico now, do you?"
Samuel said.

"No, I'd planned to stop there on the way back. Get
supper there and save money. Have lunch at Georgetown."

Samuel Raife smiled. "Maybe the archbishop will ask
you to lunch."

"I'll be lucky if he doesn't throw me out when he
hears what I want. He's a fine man, though," Kane
added hastily, lest he give the others scandal.

"So I hear. Sometime I should like to meet him. He
must be a great man."

"I think he is. He's very outspoken, though. That's
why he's never been made a cardinal. That's a terrible
thing to say, though, isn't it? Imagine the implications
people could read into that. I'd better say my office."
He opened the book and did not see the slow smile on
Samuel's face. It had just occurred to the young dean
that Laurence Kane was the first person he had ever
loved.

The four drove in silence to where the Annapolis road
bore east. Kane had almost finished his office when the
car stopped for the cousins to get out. "I'm sorry we
can't take you right in," he said.

"This is fine, Fawther. That was a good ride."

"You got any money?" He tried to make his voice
humble.

They shuffled. "We got some, Fawther," James
Washington said.

They had silver, Kane knew. He gave James, the
older, two dollars. The men, standing outside the car,
looked down, thanking him. Kane had, as so often before, the sense of a great sullen chorus in the wings of

a tragic play. The answers, the results were always known, were almost formal. But the tragedy was happening to the chorus. . . . To the chorus, *too*, he amended. That was more accurate and more terrible.

In Baltimore they drove directly to the chancellery and the archbishop's residence. From there Samuel would go to get his train.

"Until the fall, then, Samuel," Kane said, "unless I happen to see you at Fordham summer school."

"I hope you get up, Father. You need a vacation."

"I never thought in the old days that I'd go back to New York for a vacation."

"I didn't know you were from there."

"Brooklyn," the priest said. "A strange place, but doubtless some day some good will come out of it." He was trying to be funny again, because Samuel was apparently feeling bad about saying goodbye. "I'll write to you as soon as I have any definite word about the Institute. I'm sure that by the grace of God we'll be able to open it again in the fall. And now goodbye and God bless you, Samuel," Kane went on, not giving the younger man a chance to speak. "A safe journey."

Kane turned and quickly went up the white steps. A porter answered his ring but he was not made to wait. There was no one in the archbishop's office and the porter led Kane through a narrow, connecting corridor to the residence. The wide doors of a living room were open and the porter left Kane there. It was a long room whose windows, giving on a kind of courtyard, made it one of many subtle lightings. Two sides of it were lined with books to the height of a man, and there was a rich but simple carpet on the floor. The carpet was apricot in color and seemed to glow where it crossed the direct light from the windows. There were no religious ornaments in the room. Treading with ponderous silence on the apricot carpet, came now to greet Laurence Kane the Archbishop of Baltimore. He was a heavy man of about sixty with a round face that would have been bland but for the eyes, at once shrewd and deep. He was dressed in the summer, silken cassock or soutane of a monsignor, the piping and buttons of ecclesiastical purple startling against the black. His hands, like the man, were blunt from certain angles; they had done manual labor in their time and it was easy to believe that the hands held a certain attitude of readiness and strength.

"Well, Laurence," he said, a hint of mock resignation in his voice, "I see you've finally ferreted me out. I give careful orders that you are not to be admitted but it's no use."

"You know I wouldn't bother you, Bishop, unless it were necessary and unless I thought you were interested." He stood, more slender than ever in his black near the archbishop, knowing that the other man was joking, but himself making the obvious, the almost prescribed answers. His face was a curious mixture of laughter and diffidence.

In the second of silence that followed, Kane started to kneel to kiss the archbishop's ring, but the other man stopped him with a small, sharp gesture. "Don't be foolish, Laurence. Sit down, sit down, man." The archbishop turned away in embarrassment. Seated now, the two men looked at each other, uncertain laughter at the edge of Kane's face as he waited for whatever the archbishop would say.

"Sometimes," the big man said, "I think you're a faker

43

like the rest of your Order, Laurence. There are very few Jesuits one can trust." He settled himself comfortably to watch the effect of this on Kane.

It would please the archbishop, Kane knew, if he took the words seriously and broke into stuttering argument or protestation. But he smiled in spite of himself and the older man began to laugh quietly.

"You—you see, Bishop," Kane said, "I don't rise to your bait as I used to."

"It must be that I am getting old and losing my skill," the archbishop said with the appearance of thoughtfulness. "Time was when I could bring a Jesuit out of his chair foaming at the mouth. Like when Zeke Mattingly came here last winter with that long nose of his blue with the cold, to beg some money to heat that barn of a house you people have in Chaptico. I told him that I'd heard they'd been doing enough drinking down there to keep warm. Ha, that fetched him. How is Zeke, by the way? It would do him some good to take a drink now and then. I think he has an ascetic streak in him that'll bear restraining."

"Zeke's about the same. I haven't seen them at Chaptico in weeks. I'll probably stop off there for supper tonight."

"And Georgetown for dinner," the archbishop said. "You're a regular beggar, Laurence. You should have been a Franciscan instead of a Jesuit."

"Oh, we have to do as much begging as they, Bishop. Only we don't make so much fuss about it as they do."

"Ha, that was a good one," said the archbishop, who had been a Franciscan before being made a bishop. "That was a good one. Right where it hurt."

44

Kane regretted his remark and hoped that he looked as suddenly humble as he felt.

"Of course," the archbishop said, "you people, unlike us Franciscans, are always after big stuff. No alms or a dollar here and there for a Mass; you're after endowments and such. Well, Laurence," he said, raising himself in his chair, "here you are, wasting my time, and you haven't even mentioned what you want. Although I know it must be money you're after. You should know by now that I haven't any money."

"It's about the Institute, Bishop," Kane said, leaning forward. "We'll need five thousand dollars to run it next year. I think I can get about twenty-five hundred of that from various sources but it won't be enough."

"And so you think I'll come through with the rest, eh? The archbishop is a soft touch. That's what all you Jesuits think. Well, some day I'm going to fool you. Where do you think I'm going to get twenty-five hundred dollars?"

"Of course, if you haven't got it, Bishop—"

"The Institute," the archbishop went on. "What a terrible name! It's a wonder my predecessor, the cardinal, stood for it."

"It was named after him, Bishop. The Cardinal's Institute. Institute wasn't a bad word to his generation. It was even fashionable, I imagine."

"It was, indeed," the archbishop said. "Tell me, Laurence, do you think the Institute really does any good? I mean, teaching Negroes handicraft and American history is all very well, but teaching them scientific farming when they haven't the land or the equipment— and all the while the whites down there falling away

45

from the Church. Or worse, becoming merely nominal, like the Italians and Spaniards."

"I suppose any country that's been Catholic a long time will have a certain amount of nominalism," Kane said. "And they've been Catholic down there since 1634. At least they were Catholic when they came here, then, and had been for centuries before then. But about the Institute—our hope is to make, in the vicinity of Ridge, with the Institute as its center, a Negro craft and agricultural group that will be economically self-sufficient or nearly so. We—"

"I know," the archbishop interrupted without impatience, even absently. "I know. Latain gave me the same line for years when he was down there." He paused, staring darkly at the apricot carpet. "They'll be calling you Communists and worse—if there is any worse." He paused again, still staring downward, and Kane moved a little, uneasily. "How is Latain, anyway?" the archbishop said.

"Why, he's in New York, at Loyola House. He's not well, of course. Hasn't been in years. But you know. He's one of the editors of our magazine, *This Country*."

"That horrible little paper," the archbishop said, without heat. "Written by and for semi-literates. What do they put a man of discernment like Latain in with a bunch like that, who think with their intestines?"

Laurence Kane was now very nervous and thought it best to be silent. But since the archbishop was actually waiting for an answer, Kane simply said, "I don't know."

"It was bad enough to bounce Willie Bartlett," the archbishop went on. "He was making it a good magazine and was respected by non-Catholics for his intelligence. It was bad enough to bounce him because he took the side of the elevator boys in the strike and the borough-hall Catholics who owned the apartment houses didn't like it and complained to the chancellery office in New York. Ha," he said, parenthetically, "I wish they'd come to *me* to complain. I'd have curled their hair for them." He stared again moodily at the floor. The face remained bland, only the narrow eyes creating the feeling. "It was bad enough to bounce him, but to put that bunch of lightweights in his place. Really, I haven't been too pleased with the way the provincial of your Maryland-New York Province has sometimes handled his men. Of course, in a way, it's none of my business. On the other hand the Jesuits have many enterprises in my diocese and I can help them or not, as I will."

He paused and finally noticed that Kane was so uncomfortable as to be sweating. "I tell you, Laurence," the archbishop said, his tone changing. "Not quite a month ago I was left sixty-five thousand dollars. Not by a relative or through any merit of my own but simply because I happen to be Archbishop of Baltimore. Out of that sum I now have thirty-five hundred dollars left."

He paused and the priest said, "The d-drain on your resources must be terrific."

"I have thirty-five hundred dollars left," the archbishop repeated. "I give you your twenty-five hundred and then I have a thousand left."

Kane relaxed so abruptly he feared some sort of collapse. It seemed for an instant that he had never been so happy. "That's awfully good of you, Bishop. We'll all pray—"

The archbishop waved him quiet. "So you can go

47

ahead with your communistic credit unions and what-not."

Kane flushed slightly. He had not known the arch-bishop knew of that part of his work. "You see, Bishop, the credit unions are part of the parish work, not of the Institute. You see—"

"*You see* I know about them. I keep in close touch with all of you." He stood up and turned away from Kane. "Putting the banks out of business," the arch-bishop said, almost inaudibly. "Ha."

Kane had stood, too, and the archbishop, turning back to face the priest, was afraid that Kane would again try to kiss his ring. He drew himself up straight, his heavy, workingman's hands at his side.

"I don't know how to thank you, Bishop—"

"Never mind that, Laurence. We'll give the thing an-other try for a year. Goodbye and God bless you and give my best to Willie Bartlett if you see him at George-town."

The archbishop didn't want to talk to him any more and so Kane bowed and left. Outside the hot air seemed sweet and dry. He started the car and went unknow-ingly through a red light. He remembered that one of his reasons for coming up here was to suggest to the archbishop the inadvisability of Father Cornish's start-ing the co-op without more preparation for it, and to suggest that no money be given Father Cornish until later when he and the fishermen were better prepared. Now that he had forgotten to mention this to the arch-bishop, Kane could think it was best so. His own good fortune had made him quickly sanguine about the co-op.

Kane stopped at a large house whose mistress occa-

48

sionally collected old clothes for him. He found that he was grateful she wasn't home; and after carrying to his car the large bundle of clothes she had left with her maid for him, he drove the car to Washington, arriving at Georgetown University by noon.

5

THERE were only a few days of school left. In the white sunlight the almost formal campus had many people on it. The students showed as odd, over-diffident youths, caricatures of the Yale and Princeton under-graduates whose caricatures they saw and admired in the clothing ads and who in turn were caricatures of something or other. Seeing them as he went across the campus, Kane thought again that a Catholic university that was even tacitly a school for rich men's sons was something like a contradiction in terms. And yet, he knew, his Order found its excuse for conducting schools for the offspring of the rich in the fact that such off-spring would go to non-Catholic schools if there were no Catholic schools which were fashionable. Such thoughts wearied him further, he knew, and he must not waste his time on them. He had his own work.

Passing the gabardined, tweed-ed, linen-ed, be-slacked youths, he was looked at curiously. They had little or no respect for most of the priests connected with the university, and for an outlander such as this one, with his drawn, disturbing, and distracted face, they had only the same lukewarm and aloof interest they would have in a curious bug, save that this feeling now was mixed with a touch of disdain.

Kane passed them by, sorrowing for them.

Brother Anselm, major-domo of the faculty dining room and as much of a guest-master as the university possessed, had seen Father Kane from the top of the main building steps, and was hurrying down them to meet him. "Very good to see you, indeed, Father; very good, indeed." He bobbed and gesticulated and was really glad to see the priest. He was a tall, bald, and slender lay brother who had subordinated whatever wit and intelligence he had ever had to the weary business of being a menial in the Society of Jesus. He was one of the many people who, for greatly divergent reasons, embarrassed Kane. Speaking in an undertone, for some reason he could not understand, Kane followed the man to the faculty refectory.

Some of the Jesuits there Kane did not know. The president of the university felt the weight of his office unduly and shook Kane's hand with quick politeness. Other priests who would have liked to speak there and then to Kane, waved or nodded greetings. There was a curious strictness among them concerning the promptness with which a meal should be started. So they stood and nodded to Kane and waited for the president to say grace. He said it in a loud despairing voice, "Bless us, O Lord, and these Thy gifts which we are about to receive from Thy bounty through Christ Our Lord, Amen."

They sat down and William Bartlett came in, late but hurrying. He stood still, 'or seemed to stand still, in the doorway for an instant, so completely and in such a brief time did his glance pick up the entire room and its people. Kane, watching for him, had sat in the empty place next to his. Unconsciously, he had been looking forward to seeing Bartlett. People were too sentimental these days, too fond, and Kane had wearied of it and had thought of Bartlett, as always in the time of that weariness.

William Bartlett's kind is why the Jesuits were once called The First Legion of the Church. His mind automatically, indeed, unconsciously, stripped things of their nonessentials. He did not forego sentiment; he simply felt that if a person trained himself to be as objective and truly discerning as it was possible to be, that person would still have enough of sentiment in him. His belief in the tenets of his Church was based so completely on his intellect that he periodically knew a kind of spiritual ennui: the thing—to him—was so obvious, the arguments so logical. Yet so frequent were his contacts with intelligent non-Catholics and so wide his reading, that the errors of his time were constantly assailing him. He found it easy—too easy, he sometimes feared—to understand the point of view of those whose ideas were opposed to those of his Church. He was bitterly mindful— his only bitterness—of the defections in his Church as an organization, just as his mind gloried in the perfection of his Church as an idea. The corruption of the Church in Europe, the slackness and pedestrianism of the Church in the United States, were always in his thought; and he had long before had to decide that he must be a realist and accept the fact that it would take generations if not centuries to correct these things. If he could not accept such a view, he would soon become a nerve case.

The face went with the man. It was wide across the cheekbones; his eyes, under the wide and high forehead, were of some light, indeterminate color. The full mouth was drawn straight; his chin looked heavy. There was a quality of flatness about the whole face under its tan, and people were sometimes startled into thinking they had seen it before and in a strange place; but it was only that they had seen its like in reproductions of medieval engravings. The body was short and slight although the wide shoulders under the belted soutane of the Jesuits were deceiving. The low, slightly rasping voice showed emotion at times but the face almost never. He came very close to being what Ignatius of Loyola, who had thought to build a religious order along military lines, had wanted a Jesuit to be.

Needless to say, William Bartlett was not greatly liked by most of his colleagues. None of them spoke to him as he entered the room and those who glanced at him did so almost furtively. He had the reputation of being a strict disciplinarian when he periodically held authority; he was supposed to verge on unorthodoxy (meaning principally that he favored trade unions). But mostly he shamed them, and for this they could not forgive him.

Laurence Kane half-rose to meet him and stuttered a greeting. Bartlett's hand on Kane's shoulder unobtrusively kept him from rising. "How are you, Laurence?" Bartlett said grace hastily to himself. "You come at odd times, Laurence," he said, sitting down. "When no one can talk to you. We're right in the middle of examinations. I bet you want money."

Kane almost choked on the food in his mouth. "I—I know better than to come here for it. They always give me a lot of fine talk about it but all I actually ever get is a meal with dessert. Dessert always overwhelms us country boys, they figure."

Bartlett smiled. "I don't suppose there is much about us here that pleases you. But you ought to be glad we ran a course in co-ops this year."

"That was your fault," Kane said. "After they tried to bury you down here. Although I suppose it was a concession on their part to allow such heresy as co-operation to be taught here."

"You talk like Savonarola, Laurence, be careful."

"It amounted to financial heresy, teaching co-ops here," Kane went on. "The only kind of heresy that matters to them any more." He was tired and Bartlett had known quickly that that was what made him talk this way. "It's a wonder the Chicago and New York lace-curtain Irish didn't snatch their sons out of here."

"It was added to the curriculum late," Bartlett said, "and didn't get into the catalogue. Although it's also likely that the borough-hall Catholics don't know what co-ops are or what they imply."

"How I talk, though!" Kane said, finally noticing his own strangeness. "I sound as though I'm disloyal to the Order."

William Bartlett finished his soup before speaking again. "How is Cornish making out down there?"

Kane didn't answer for a moment. "Not so good. I think his co-op is going to fail unless he educates them first."

"I've been afraid of that. He's started them off without any preliminary education or—"

"It's his zeal," Kane interrupted, something he rarely did. "It's so hard to find someone with both prudence and zeal."

Bartlett let his silence express his opinion of James Cornish.

Kane said, "Of course, he's so keen on getting money to give them equipment, an oyster-shucking shed, and so on." But Bartlett did not speak.

They finished their meal almost in silence. After it, Bartlett said that he had about half an hour to spare and the two men went up to his office. Walking along the corridor whose outer arches looked on the antique chapel of the inner campus, Kane turned from the chapel —it held his God—to look at the oil paintings of past presidents of the university on the opposite wall. They seemed, most of them, severe, he thought; but perhaps it was the fashion of their times—the eighteenth and nineteenth centuries—in painting.

William Bartlett's office was simple and not too orderly. His secretary, a rather plain young woman, sat in an adjoining office, typing.

"You have a girl now for a secretary," Kane said. He smiled and attempted one of his jokes. "You see so many government people that I would imagine you'd give them scandal."

"They take scandal easily," Bartlett said. "Official Washington is like big-business New York. If a man has a female secretary they naturally assume that he's committing fornication or adultery, as the case may be. If he has a male secretary, it's a *prima facie* case of homosexuality. I prefer to be accused of the lesser of two evils."

Kane was depressed by these remarks. Bartlett noticed it and said, "How does your own work go?"

"About the same. With luck and an okay from the government I may have the first of the credit unions going by the fall."

"Have you had any opposition from the whites?"

"I don't think they even know about the credit unions."

"What about the local banks?"

"What do you mean?"

"You're going into competition with them. Although I don't suppose you depend on them for any financing."

"I took a thousand-dollar mortgage out last year on the church to get certain equipment for the Institute. I suppose I was foolish, considering the people lack food as well as equipment."

"You do manage to complicate things, don't you, Laurence?" Bartlett smiled a little.

The secretary looked in and said that Mr. Cosgrave was here to see Father Bartlett.

"Ask him to come in, please."

"I should go," Kane said, rising.

"Wait a minute. It may do this youngster good to meet you."

Kane sat down, somewhat bewildered. The young man who came in was well dressed. He moved with a strong, easy grace that the subtle strain in his face seemed to belie.

"This is Mr. Cosgrave, Father," Bartlett said. "Father Kane."

The young man seemed honestly surprised. "I've heard of your work for a long time," he began. "It's been an inspiration—"

"Listen to him, Father," Kane appealed to Bartlett. "Where does he get such stuff?" To the young man, "I remember you or your name. Weren't you one of Georgetown's great athletes?" A vague irony had come into Kane's voice without his willing it.

"I was a runner here," Cosgrave said. His face reddened a little. "It was a great waste of time. But I've been at Harvard taking my master's degree this past year," he added by way of apology.

"He's a thorn in our side," Bartlett said, with his wry smile. "He wants to take his doctorate here in non-capitalist economics. I don't know where he got the term although it's a good one. He'd like us to institute courses especially to please him. The truth is he knew he couldn't get it here, but he came and asked for it to embarrass us."

"Not at all," Cosgrave protested. He smiled, but it fooled neither Bartlett nor Kane. All three of them were harassed, Kane felt, but he and Bartlett were better equipped to stand it.

"Not at all," Cosgrave said again. "I don't want special courses."

"In effect you do," Bartlett said. He spoke with a kind of pleased resignation. It gave him pleasure that now, after generations, an American Catholic should ask an American Catholic university for something it was not prepared to offer. He had not expected to see it happen in his time.

An odd silence had come among the three men. Bartlett, with his usual distrust of such moments, broke the silence. "Well—" he said, somewhat loudly. His voice rasped more than usual.

"Look," Kane said hastily to Cosgrave, "theory is good but it's a relatively simple thing. Supposing you were offered something practical to do?"

Cosgrave looked at him so oddly that Kane grew startled. "For example?"

Kane had spoken at first on impulse and in an unconscious effort to simplify all that he had suddenly felt he must say to Cosgrave. He had seen Cosgrave as someone potentially tragic, more so than most people are, and he wanted to speak to him of a frightening number of

57

things: of the difference between the Church as a radical idea and the Church as a conservative organization; of the Church immature in America and now coming of age; and of how a man might be ground between the millstones of the idea and the organization. Of how the first—and Cosgrave was one of the first, here and now—would be bitter and impatient and misunderstood or understood too well. But all Kane had managed was his impulsive question.

"We have, or we think we're going to have, a co-op down in southern Maryland," Kane hurried on. "Not I, but Father Cornish, who works with me. He—well, he may need a manager."

"My God," Cosgrave said. "I'd work for nothing at it. I—"

"Of course," Kane said, "it's more or less theoretical. I—I'll write you—" He felt badly, seeing something like joy fade from the young man's face.

"I wouldn't be too sanguine, John," Bartlett said crisply. "The apostles of non-capitalist economics are going to have more misses than hits for a long time to come."

"You are probably right," Kane said, rising again. "Well, I must be going. Goodbye, Mr. Cosgrave. I hope they get you straightened out. I will write to you when, and if, I have any news of Father Cornish's plans."

"Goodbye, Father," Bartlett said. Kane turned to him because Cosgrave seemed nervous saying goodbye. "Don't forget to keep us posted about things down your way," Bartlett went on. By 'us' he meant himself, not wilfully but because that was the way it was.

Outside on the campus again, Kane saw two Jesuits he had known in the seminary at Woodstock ten years ago, looking into his car and laughing. Seeing Kane approaching, one of them said, "I see you're still collecting old clothes, Laurence, just like the St. Vincent de Paul Society."

"Got to keep people warm somehow," he said, rather feebly. He was tired and could not think of one of his jokes.

"I bet your Negroes sell the clothes and buy gin," said the second of the two. He was running to fat and taught Christian Doctrine at the University. When a priest connected with a university is incapable of teaching anything else he is always set to teaching Christian Doctrine.

"Well, they can keep warm with that, too." Kane laughed to show that he was not serious, as with these two he had a fear of giving scandal.

They smiled slightly, showing their teeth. Kane had laughed, so they knew it was a joke. They smiled, then, to show that they knew it was one, too. They felt considerably superior to this priest who—they felt—had not been urbane or intelligent enough to be assigned, like themselves, to a university.

"Well, Laurence," said the one who taught Christian Doctrine, "someone must do the field work."

Kane nodded, starting the motor. Lately, he had found himself growing irritable at times. Like others of his kind, he could bear with fools, quite without conscious knowledge that they were fools. But now, he was aware only of the new irritation. He supposed it might be due to Father Cornish. Without meaning to snub anyone, since he had almost forgotten about them, Kane let the clutch in and drove away in the middle of a sentence of banter coming from the teacher of Christian Doctrine.

Kane supposed—driving—that the Father Provincial would hold him responsible, in part, for the failure of the co-op. Wherever two or more Jesuits were gathered together they constituted a community, and one of them was officially its superior. When Cornish had been assigned to the white parish at Ridge, the provincial of the Maryland-New York Province had written to Kane about the new priest.

"He possesses considerable vitality," the provincial had written, "for he was once a fine athlete, and he has great enthusiasm. As you know, he was out in the world for several years after he had finished college and before he entered the seminary; part of that time in the advertising business. He is lacking in prudence and patience. I am sure that you will be able to supply the necessary control until such time as he has matured."

It had been strange, Kane thought, that a man who had been an advertising copy writer (who was still boastful of it at times) should have become such a proponent of radical economics. And yet he knew the answer. Father Cornish's devotion to the principle of co-operation was superficial; he had read the encyclicals and, as a new priest, felt constrained to begin something fresh and startling, a novelty. It was not that he appreciated the principle or even realized its implications. He himself, Kane thought, had hinted at things Cornish should have done more slowly or not at all. He supposed that he might have been blunt instead of subtle and yet it was not in him—he thought it a weakness—to command, to be a superior. As though to relieve him, a sentence of Bernanos' came into his head, ". . . the mediocre priest is the most impenetrable of beings."

It shocked Kane back into his usual state of mind,

which was perhaps what it was intended to do: a state of mind whose very air was charity as the air of the mind of the ordinary businessman is acquisitiveness. Who was he, Kane thought, to think such things of his colleague? With a single wrench of his mind he almost convinced himself that it was not of Cornish that he had been thinking.

And yet he knew that it was so. He had spoken to James with care, subtly, about the Jews, about haste and prudence. Kane was subtle, not for subtlety's sake, but because scripture spoke that way usually, because it was the way of the Holy Ghost, and if it was His way it must be the best way, a way that would get to a man's mind gradually and surely, without offense to pride. Pride was the wall; subtlety the water that could seep through it.

But it had not seemed to affect James, Kane thought. And if James was mediocre, what of himself? Certainly he was no more than that. Probably less. And what had he himself accomplished? So very little—and that only by the grace of God and the archbishop. Although weariness was his normal state, extreme weariness always puzzled and betrayed Kane. It would take him days to realize that it was weariness clouding his thoughts, bringing to the surface the uncharity that exists in the mind of every man.

He stopped the car before a quietly pretentious house of brick on Pennsylvania Avenue. He had hoped that Mrs. Carteret would not be at home, but she met him at the door, a tall, fleshy woman in her fifties who, in her loose, beaded dress, seemed to smile all over.

"And how are you, dear Father Kane? It's so good to see you. Come right in." Clasping his bony right hand in both of hers she virtually pulled him into the house. Venetian blinds were drawn against the afternoon sun and the living room was quite dim. Kane was relieved to find another person there, a Mrs. Widdecomb, a counterpart of his hostess except that she was shorter and her hair was dyed blond. She was more restrained than Mrs. Carteret, who unconsciously explained this by volunteering the information that Mrs. Widdecomb was not of their "faith" but was greatly interested in the "work." Kane murmured something about that being fine.

"We had hoped, Father, that you would arrive in time for lunch," Mrs. Carteret said. "And now we hope that you will stay to tea."

Since it was not yet two o'clock, Kane was freshly dismayed at the idea of waiting here until tea-time. "I-I'd love to, Mrs. Carteret, but it's impossible to do so." He couldn't, he thought rapidly, tell her that he had merely other engagements. She would be immediately jealous of other, mythical hostesses. He would have to be specific. "I m-must get back to the university," he said. Reference to the university always placated people like Mrs. Carteret. It was as though they felt included in some way in the allusion.

"Ah, yes, of course," Mrs. Carteret said. "The university." She seated herself comfortably while her friend surveyed the two of them silently and with a sort of strained approval. "You look well, Father," Mrs. Carteret went on. "I suppose the work is progressing?"

"As well as can be expected." He had long ago accepted the fact that the Mesdames Carteret reduced all things to a common denominator. What he could never quite resign himself to, though, was his taking advantage of such a situation. Yet he did so often. "Money, of course, is our big obstacle." He paused to let Mrs. Carteret and Mrs. Widdecomb, too, nod gravely.

"Naturally," Mrs. Carteret said. Her voice and face contrived to be at once servile, understanding, and proud. Kane had seen her manage this before but it could still make him gasp inwardly. He had the feeling that in coming to her for charity he was giving her distinct pleasure. He didn't like it, but he was willing to do it.

"And we're totally dependent on outsiders," he said. "The whites down there are pretty poor."

"Even if they wanted to help," Mrs. Carteret parroted. Her face had taken on a superficially pained look and her eyes squinted a little.

"Of course, I believe that the Negro should be kept in his place," Mrs. Widdecomb put in.

"Well, I do, too, Evelyn," Mrs. Carteret said, turning hastily to her friend. "But that shouldn't prevent us from aiding them. I'm sure Father Kane—"

"We'd just like to make them self-sustaining economically," he said. His voice betrayed nothing. The anger in him was an old anger. It was the most terrible thing that was his; it was also, whether because or in spite of this, the most controlled. He had never released it; he never would. For fifty dollars to buy them pigs, it was a small price to pay.

"Of that I approve," Mrs. Widdecomb said flatly in the little pause Kane had made. "Even though I doubt that you ever shall."

He nodded, blinking rapidly. It was safest, he had found, not to think, to blank his mind in such times. "It will be difficult," he said. His voice sounded so small that he was disturbed separately by it.

"Of course," Mrs. Carteret agreed, almost enthusiastically. "But you, like brave soldiers of the Church, march ahead."

Something choked in him. It was not vomit but it might have been. Mrs. Carteret was beaming. It was as though she had planned this, leading up to her statement, the meaningless cry she had uttered so often from the platform of the Catholic Daughters, of sodalities. Kane nodded in self-defense. He had known it would be bad but not like this. It was always worse than he expected.

After a half-hour he rose. "Oh, must you go, Father?" Mrs. Carteret said, rising too, her forearms raised like a seal's flippers.

"I r-really must get to the university," he said. "I-I'm sorry—"

"Yes, of course, the university."

"If my late husband, the congressman, were alive, he would be greatly interested in your work," Mrs. Widdecomb pronounced in her almost masculine voice.

"Oh, yes," Kane said. He wondered why she had waited so long to let him know she was the widow of a congressman.

"And now, Father," Mrs. Carteret said, "I have some things for you." The entertainment was over, now she would pay. "Some clothes, which the maid will bring, and a little donation."

While the maid brought in a wicker hamper stuffed with clothes, a green evening gown prominent near the top, Mrs. Carteret wrote a check. The maid, having brought the hamper into the room, now took it to the car.

"Possibly, *Doctor* Kane," Mrs. Widdecomb said, "you may think from what I have said that I do not approve of your work. To prove differently I shall match Mrs. Carteret's donation." She rose ponderously, even sinisterly, Kane could not help thinking.

"That would be—" he began.

"Oh, Evelyn, you don't have to," Mrs. Carteret said in a pleased voice. "I'm sure Father Kane—"

"No, Gracyn, my mind is made up. What is your check for?"

"Oh, not much, I'm afraid. Only twenty dollars. The way the market's been—" She giggled.

Forty dollars, Kane thought; he had figured fifty. He felt better, though. Perhaps it was the prospect of getting out of here.

His feeling became one almost of exhilaration as he left the house, and he went down the front steps two at a time. He drove down Pennsylvania Avenue, swung south and past the Navy Yard and into the scant suburbs of Washington. Silver Hill, Camp Springs, Clinton seemed to have still upon them the feeling, like a faint stink, of Washington. It wasn't until he had passed T.B. and the junction with the Baltimore road and finally Mattawoman Creek and Swamp and was in Charles County, that he felt free and in his own country. Some of the weariness left him and he looked forward to supper at Chaptico and talk with the other Jesuits there, most of whom he had not seen in a month or more.

Their house at Chaptico was a large, square, white building that had once been the manor house of a recent plantation. It was set on one of the few hills in the County and served as a community house for the five priests whose mission parishes lay in the upper reaches of the County. It was neither new nor old, handsome nor ugly. Its distinction lay in the manner its whiteness rose above the surrounding country. Mindful of this, Ezekiel Mattingly, the superior of its community, had it painted regularly every spring, even if it meant leaving the house cold in late March.

The house was cool in the long summer and chilly and drafty through the winter, being built, like most of the houses in the County, to withstand heat rather than cold. Its rooms had many large windows. From its eminence the house looked out on Chaptico Bay and, when the weather was clear, that other bay, called the Wicomico River, an arm of the Potomac. In the winter, from the porch, they could see the great rafts of ducks on the surface of the bay, blackheads and canvasbacks, and their mysterious risings into great, ragged wedges. Now only a few gulls and one or two fishhawks hovered over the brackish water.

Driving west on the road that led off No. 5 to Chaptico, Maddox, and the entire seventh district of the County, Kane had the sun in his eyes, not directly but diffused off the tar road. He saw the house later than usual. It came on him suddenly and his heart lifted. This was their stronghold in the County, the wooden and exposed acropolis of their *civitate Dei*.

He swung the car up the rising, square driveway. There were two light cars parked under the second-floor porch and Kane knew who was home, Father Mattingly and Father Daniels. There was also a rather expensive coupe parked in the drive, Dr. Wathen McKay's.

The refectory was in the front of the house and level with the ground. It ran the width of the big house and was only partly finished. At the farther end of it Ezekiel Mattingly and the doctor were nailing up pine paneling. The tall priest was in a long duster such as mechanics sometimes wear, and the doctor, a short, wiry man, in shirtsleeves and old pants. They were standing on a low bench and turned as Kane entered the room.

"Well, look who's here," Father Mattingly called. He strove consciously at times for the banal word or phrase. It was part of his strange humility. He stepped down and came across the room to shake Kane's hand. "How are you, Laurence?"

The doctor followed more slowly to greet Kane. He looked tired; at thirty-eight he seemed older; there were triangular shadows under his eyes. "Hello, Father, haven't seen you in a long time."

"You haven't been here when I have, Wathen. And I've somehow contrived to miss you at the hospital in Calverton. You're usually there mornings, while I rarely get in before afternoon or evening. I've got a lot to thank you for, for what you've done for some of our people."

"Don't talk that way to him," Father Mattingly said. "He's here doing penance."

The doctor colored and Kane grew confused. It was like Zeke Mattingly to mention something that was true as though it were a jest. They all had to have some release, Kane knew, and most of them were pretty poor jokers.

"Don't know what you're talking about," the doctor said to Kane.

"All this false modesty floating around," Kane said.

"I suppose you've stopped off to bum supper," Mattingly said.

"Why else, Zeke? I know there's no chance of getting any money here."

"He called that one, all right," the doctor said. He sat down wearily after Kane.

"How about some of that blackberry wine?" Mattingly said. "The stuff we made last fall."

"I will if I have to," Kane said. "If I don't get a meal otherwise. But it's vile stuff. It gave me the runs last time."

"Take it for a penance," McKay said. "That's what I do."

"The trouble with you two," Mattingly said, "is that you've foregone the simple life. Civilization has sophisticated and ruined your tastes."

"Listen to him," the doctor said.

"Once a farmer always a farmer," Kane said.

Father George Daniels came into the room. He was young, ordained less than a year. Like all the young Jesuits he liked and respected Kane. Father Daniels was an odd mixture of piety, alertness, naivete, and what he thought was worldly wisdom. He had entered the seminary at sixteen. After three years as a priest there is no apparent difference between those priests who enter the seminary young and those who spend some time "in the world" before doing so. But Father Daniels had been ordained less than a year.

He sat with the others, a slightly foolish grin on his wide, intelligent face, and sipped the bad wine as though it were fine and he a connoisseur, but really because he disliked it. Mattingly regarded him a cold, affectionate eye.

"How are you making out, George?" Kane said.

"Oh, he's doing all right," Mattingly said, "considering he's an expert on the Eastern Schisms and he's been sent here to handle a mixed white and Negro parish."

"You see," Father Daniels said to Kane, "I don't have to answer, they answer for me."

"What the hell are the Eastern Schisms?" the doctor said, in his sharp, hoarse voice, rough with weariness.

"You see, in the Orient," Father Daniels began, with perfect seriousness.

"Stop, George," Mattingly said. "You mustn't take people seriously. Especially people like McKay."

Father Daniels colored, partly in anger. "Oh, all right, if that's the way you feel."

"But I really want to know about the Eastern Schisms," the doctor said.

"Oh, no, you don't," Mattingly told him. "You're a faker, Wathen. And you're a bad enough Catholic without our giving you the Eastern Churches to think about and try to justify yourself."

"There you are," the doctor said. "Just like in the dark ages. The Church repressing knowledge and whatnot. I know. I read about it in a book." Father Daniels had left the room. "Here I am," McKay went on, "trying to make him feel good by having him tell me about his specialty in the seminary, and you spoil it."

"What do you want him to feel good for?" Mattingly said.

"Oh, I know that stuff," the doctor said. "It's an old Jesuit trick. Only you ought to reserve it for the seminaries, when you're teaching the youngsters patience by irritating them." Mattingly's thin face colored slightly, and he sniffed. "I want him to feel good," the doctor said, "because he's been feeling bad lately.

Hardly anyone but the blacks in his parish will talk to him."

"That's another one of your exaggerations, Wathen," Mattingly said.

"If it is, it's not much of a one. The first Sunday he was there he saw the Negroes crowded into the four rear pews and he thought they were just shy, so he told them to move on up in the church. Wow! Some of them did."

Kane smiled faintly in the silence. "He knows now," Mattingly finally said. His lean face and hawk-nose were a carefully made expression of indifference.

The doctor had not eaten since breakfast. The wine on an empty stomach was headier than whiskey. "Sure," he said, "we make the niggers sit in the back of the churches, and the Protestants don't let them in at all. I don't know who's the worse but I think maybe they're the more honest."

"I always felt you were a Protestant at heart," Mattingly said. His irrelevance was purposeful; like himself the doctor knew the weary answers.

McKay shook his head mournfully. "If and when I leave the Church it'll be to become nothing. Remember what James Joyce wrote about not forsaking an absurdity which was logical and coherent for one which was illogical and incoherent. Boy, that was a honey."

Now Kane colored slightly but Mattingly remained undisturbed. "You talk too much, Wathen," Mattingly said in his dry voice. "Go home to your wife and children. We can't have you wasting your time around here boozing."

"That's nice talk, isn't it, Father," McKay said to

Kane. "I give up a spare afternoon to help try and make this barn livable, and that's what I get."

The doctor rose tiredly just before two more priests came into the room. The stocky one, Father Edward Steiner, was a doctor as well as a priest. He had taught for a long time in the medical school at Georgetown, but wearying of Washington and the university, had asked to be sent down to the County. The younger one, Father Arthur Doran, was marked by extreme fatigue on his young face. All young priests seemed to get marked in that way when they first came to the County. Father Daniels was the current exception. His naivete had been his armor; it would not last long.

In the little stir and talk of their coming, the doctor slipped away. Kane enjoyed the meal with them, the good talk, embarrassed only by the frequent apologies of the crippled Negress who cooked at Chaptico, that she had nothing more "special" for him.

Leaving shortly afterwards, Kane was happy. Community life was good at times, he thought. The happiness sustained him for a while, but the weariness came back in a kind of swift gradualness and was almost terrible as he neared Ridge. He was glad that he had finished his office for the day, and grateful in memory to Samuel Raife for having reminded him to say it that morning.

He passed the road to the Institute and his church, having decided to sleep at the rectory that night. His mail would be there and possibly Father Cornish would have messages or news for him. He drove past St. Patrick's and between the row of holly trees that led to the rectory. A single bulb burned in the reception room. To its right the red spot of the sanctuary lamp showed where the chapel was in the darkness of the house.

Kane hurried toward the house from the garage. The dry leaves of the holly rustled stiffly in the wind. They were a diffident kind of tree. He wondered why such thoughts occurred to him in passing when he knew an emergency might be close at hand. The light in the reception room meant people waiting for him, although they had been told no one knew when he would be back that night. The wind, coming from the river, smelt richly of the fine, the untilled land.

Two Negro men rose as Kane entered the reception room. "George, John, how are you? What's the trouble?"

"Martin Bennett, he dying, Father. He want you right bad."

"But why didn't you call Father Cornish? He's here, isn't he? In an emergency like that, any priest can come. I'm surprised you don't know that. I've told you often."

They shuffled and looked down. "Father Cornish, he say that, too, when we come here, and he come with us, then. But Martin, he won't go to confession to no one but you."

Kane hurried to get the essentials for extreme unction. Sorrow rose fitfully in him for James Cornish. That this should happen now to the other priest upset Kane. Cornish would take it personally when it was not intended so. Kane wondered how much he was himself responsible for Martin's feeling that way.

He hurried outside again, stumbling once over nothing. They were on either side and caught him as he fell, moving with him through the odorous darkness toward the car.

6

THE certificate of the Sons of the Confederacy, with his father's name on it, hung over the desk of George Carroll Blair. The office gave evidence of his dual, though largely theoretical, professions—those of journalism and the law. Blackstone and the Laws of Virginia and Maryland filled the bookcases, and the rear door of the narrow office opened on the pressroom with its one linotype machine and surprisingly large press. This room in turn gave onto a hall that ran into that portion of the large wooden house that was his mother's and his own home, and where dwelt with him his wife, Martha, and his widowed and partly deaf mother.

Other frames in George Blair's office held rare American butterflies, most of them caught by himself, while the frame nearest the certificate from the Sons of the Confederacy contained both a newspaper clipping and a letter. The clipping was that of the lead editorial from the St. Mary's *Torch* for August 30, 1925, and consisted principally of about four inches of white space under the caption: WILLIAM JENNINGS BRYAN IS DEAD. In the middle of the white space in six-point italics was the legend: *De mortuis nil nisi bonum.*

The letter in the frame was on the stationery of *The Baltimore Sun*, and was from Mr. H. L. Mencken, briefly congratulating Mr. Blair on his appropriate editorial. Both the clipping and the letter had begun to yellow slightly at the edges.

Having risen at about a quarter-past eight, breakfasted, walked to the post office, drunk at Clement's Drug Store the forbidden black coffee, George Blair sat now in his office, looking at the precision of the dead butterflies, wondering if he would take a field trip this year. He felt slight and although but fifty-one, somehow old; he thought he would not take a field trip. Anyhow, he should spend more time on the paper. And even practice again. He recalled vaguely that he had some sort of engagement this morning, but could not think of what it was. He supposed Greg Fenwick would be going up to Laurel today and he didn't know but what he might go along. He had won last time—making two-dollar bets—but he had lost lately making five-dollar bets. He recalled, as he inevitably would as long as he lived, the horse, Tertiary, coming in at 8 to 1 at Bowie, just galloping, five lengths in front, with a thousand dollars of his money on it. His mouth had begun to water slightly, and he began to think of the good days when his mornings had been spent in the Attorney General's offices in Washington and his afternoons at the track. "One of the Attorney General's bright young men," *The Washington Star* had called him. The term had been just coming into use then, had been still devoid of irony.

A blocky figure in clerical black cut off the light from the open doorway. The square body of the Reverend James M. Cornish, S.J., still seemed egregiously athletic. "Well, George," he said, "have I kept you waiting long?"

"Not at all, Father. I've just been sitting here, reading up—or trying to find to read up—something on the laws governing co-operatives." He rose and went directly to the book he wanted, pulling it out of the case. "I'll have the papers of incorporation drawn up tomorrow. You just sit down and tell me the facts."

"It's awfully good of you to go to this much trouble, George, especially when we can't pay you anything, not a dime."

"That's all right." He did not look at the priest. His voice had already taken on an absent note as he started to page through the book. "The Carrolls and the Blairs are used to serving the Church." He smirked a little, conscious that whoever among them had served the Church—and some had done it well—he had not been one of them.

He arranged paper and pencil before him and faced the priest. "Now, how many of these down-county boys are in this and who are they?"

"Five," the priest said. "Willie McKay, John Mattingly, Foley Raley, Fenner Ridgel, and Havenner Maddox."

"It's not many, is it?" the lawyer said, almost absently. "Has that cousin of mine learned to read and write yet? Never thought to see him in anything with Foley Raley."

"Oh, they'll get on," Father Cornish said. "We've got a new spirit down there."

He sounds like a Baptist revivalist, Blair thought. "I see you've even got a Protestant in it," he said.

"Purposely," the priest said. "Purposely. We want to show that it's for everyone, that it's non-sectarian. Then, too, Havenner Maddox is the husband of the woman who cooks for us at the rectory. He's all right. Melissa will up and convert him one of these days."

Thinking he shouldn't say it, even telling himself so, George Blair heard himself say, "Don't suppose any of the local Jews are in it?"

Father Cornish drew in his upper lip and snorted. "This is for fishermen. Later on we'll have other kinds of co-ops, groceries and so on. And let me tell you that I expect the main opposition to come from Jews when that time comes." He spoke with quiet vigor, to let George know that this was something he had thought out well.

I shouldn't have done that, Blair thought, with something of real regret; practically causing the priest to commit a mortal sin. "I suppose Father Kane will have something similar for the niggers?"

"Oh-h, I imagine Laurence will. He moves so slowly, though. But a great man, though, a great man."

The lawyer moved his lips as though an unpleasant taste were on them. If Cornish really thought Father Kane was a great man, Blair knew, it was probably for the wrong reasons.

"Now, look, Father. You sure these boys know what they're getting in for?" He smiled a little, showing his teeth, almost hiding his eyes. "St. Mary's County has never been known for its co-operation. Rather, the reverse."

"They know, they know." Cornish was glib. "They know that there's only one way out. The buy-boats have been gypping them, the wholesalers in Baltimore have, even the company they buy their twine from."

"Them most of all, if they're smart," Blair said softly.

76

"You've got to have nets to catch fish. Now"—louder—"how much is each of these boys putting into this?"

"They're each putting up twenty-five dollars for one share of stock. Then I've been able to get four hundred dollars from individuals and the Freeland Foundation, and the shack and wharf we build with that will be held in common. That'll represent sixteen shares held in common."

"I suppose John Mattingly will be chairman or president or whatever you call it?"

"That's right."

"You know, this kind of thing is going to need someone who will devote almost all his time to it. I know you won't be able to, with your parish work, and I don't see how John can, either, with his fishing and farming."

"Oh, we've thought of that. That's all taken care of. It'll be a chance to keep at least one young countryman from going to the city. John Mattingly's boy, Leslie, is going to manage the shack and take care of the gas pump and supplies for party-boat fishermen."

"Nepotism, already, eh?" Blair said, writing with a pencil.

"I wouldn't look at it that way. Almost all the boys who have had high school go up to Washington or Baltimore, to say nothing of those who have had any college. We're lucky to get Leslie, in a way."

"I guess you are. I wasn't really serious. Don't think I recall him. John's had a lot of children, like most of those down-county boys. Will Leslie have to do much?"

"He's a good boy. Besides what I've already mentioned, he'll handle soft crabs, which we intend to buy from the Negro crabbers. We hope to work a cycle that'll provide employment all year 'round. In the winter there'll be oystering, in the spring and fall, commercial fishing. Then in the summer, when the seaweed fouls the nets too much to fish with them, we'll have party-boat fishing. We'll carry a line of supplies for party-boat fishermen down from the city. And a gasoline pump to sell gas."

"Sounds good, all right," Blair said. He didn't think it was going to work. He wrote steadily.

"You know, George," Father Cornish said, thoughtfully, "I've been thinking. Why couldn't St. Mary's County be developed as an art colony? We could stand to have more writers here."

"The County is in bad enough shape without having an art colony here," Blair said. "And art is like the revolution—it's always getting mixed up with fornication. You people wouldn't like it."

The priest smiled thinly, thinking that George Blair must have his little joke. "But Catholic artists, George. They, surely—"

"There is no such animal. And art is amoral. All artists are neurotics, anyway, and they think up fancier sins than most people do. They'd have you boys looking up your moral theology the first thing you knew."

Father Cornish smiled again. Sometimes it was as though George were making veiled criticisms, he thought. "Well—" Father Cornish said, and let it go at that.

After a moment of uneasy silence, Blair said, "I don't suppose there's anything more I need to know to draw up the incorporation papers." Lately people wearied him, and now he wanted Father Cornish to go.

The priest, too, was slightly uneasy and rose. "I guess

there isn't," he said. "No need to tell you how grateful we all are, and—"

"Don't think of it." He opened the door.

The priest gone, Blair felt tired. He supposed he should write something for the *Torch* about this damn co-operative. Although, in one way, the less said about it, the less trouble there might be from the banks and so on. The County, he considered, was about the one place in the whole damn country that had not had a Communist scare; but this could very well give them one. Well, not with a priest involved, he thought, smiling. But they'd be against it on some grounds, even though probably not the right ones.

His wife, Martha, a large, fair, quiet woman, came into the room. Her face, as usual, was deceptively bland behind her glasses. "There isn't a great deal of copy for tomorrow, George. Not much more than the boiler-plate."

"I know, I know." He adjusted the eyeglass and began to read *The Baltimore Sun*.

"Why don't you write an editorial? You haven't done any in a long time."

"Oh, what is there to say?"

"Hospital week is coming up. And you could say something about this new business of Father Cornish's."

"All right. All right."

"I hope you're not going to the track today?"

"It's too late, I'm afraid." He might as well make the best of it, he thought, and get in a day's work. Feeling his wife still waiting near him with her curious, hopeful, unshakeable resignation, he said, "All right. I'll get right to work. I've got to draw up some papers, too, for Father."

She left him then, as she had left him so often before, with the butterflies, the certificate of the Sons of the Confederacy, and *The Baltimore Sun*.

Leaving George Blair's office, and walking now in the warm, dry light toward the square, James Cornish felt at peace with the world, as he was fond of putting it. His plans were going along splendidly. He couldn't think of a single possible hitch in his plans. What it had taken them twenty years to accomplish at Antigonish, he was going to accomplish in twenty weeks. Of course, on a smaller scale, to be sure, and the Antigonish thing *had* provided an example and an inspiration to all of them; and he certainly recognized that the Antigonish movement, through its literature, would save all kinds of time and mistakes for groups like his own. In only one respect did he feel that the leaders of that movement were wrong. They had written that a long preliminary period of study and education was necessary. He was showing that that wasn't necessary. He would educate his people even while the co-op was functioning. Of course, he had been hurried into it, too, by the need of the fishermen to combat the buy-boat arrangement and the dishonest Baltimore dealers. But he had made a virtue of necessity, he told himself again.

"Hah're you, Father?" John Raley greeted him as the priest passed Raley's Bar, in front of which the owner was getting the sun.

"Just fine, John. And yourself?" He would win John back to the Church yet, Father Cornish had determined some weeks ago.

"Right fine, Father. Don't suppose you'd want to slip into the backroom and have a drink?"

The priest flushed as he smiled his winning, hearty, restrained, athlete's smile. The big bones of his face showed clearly. "Now, John, you know I'm in uniform, so to speak. Couldn't very well do that, you know."

"Sure, Father, I know. Looks like the hot weather's setting in right early, don't it?"

"That'll bring the fish up the bay and the river. That's the Lord's way of taking care of the fishermen."

"Brings the seaweed growing on the nets, too." He laughed. "No offense, Father."

The priest smiled tolerantly. The thing to do with people like John was to go along with them a little way, he considered. He had never heard the real reason for John's having left the Church. Father Cornish was quickly mapping a plan of campaign for this preliminary skirmish, as he thought of it, when Jimmy Gordon came along in his Ford to take the late shift at the bar. Opening his car-door, Jimmy accidentally kicked a crumpled silk stocking out. He flushed and let it lie where it fell, draped from the running board, and hoped that the priest had not noticed.

The fire siren, marking noon from its skeletal stand in the middle of the square, drowned out Jimmy's greeting.

"Right on time, I see," Father Cornish said, smiling. "That's the way to be, Jimmy." This boy was another one he would have to work on, the priest thought, although he himself had seen Jimmy at Mass in Calverton and even down at Ridge when he had been there hunting on a Sunday. Jimmy was a good athlete, too, so Father Cornish, by a dexterous though largely unconscious gyration of his mind, reduced the matter of the silk stocking to nothing at all, an old one that Jimmy had

81

borrowed from his mother or aunt to wipe the dust from the dashboard of the car.

"That's the way I am, Father," Jimmy said.

"You're looking pretty fit, Jimmy," the priest said. "Going to play first base for the town team this year?"

"If I got the time, Father." He swung his hands, loosely bunched, backward and forward, in arcs that met in front of him. He was twenty-four but despite his obvious good looks—the high color, the full mouth, and large eyes—looked in his thirties.

"He don't take care of himself, Father, that's the trouble," John Raley said. Jimmy flushed again.

"Why, you're the one that's looking fat, John." Father Cornish laughed.

They all laughed together, and Jimmy, seeing some farmers go into the bar, was glad for the interruption and followed them in.

"Jimmy's a good chap, all right, isn't he?" Father Cornish said.

"He's sure a nice, young fellow," Raley said.

Charlie Combs, a fat, stolid young man, drove up in his beer truck before the bar, saw the priest, and did not get out. Neither he nor Father Cornish knew each other but Charles felt uneasy near priests or any symbol of authority. Not knowing of his own effect on Charles, Father Cornish still felt that he must go along and not be seen talking too long before a bar. "Well, I've got to be going along down-county, John," he said. "I want to see you sometime soon, though."

"Anytime, Father. Always around."

As he started his car, Father Cornish noticed Charlie Combs get out of his truck and walk toward John Raley, and another fat, but older man, Luke Havenner, come around the corner of the bar nearest the Calvert Hotel. Doubtless, the priest thought as he drove away, he had embarrassed the poor fellows, who had probably all wanted a drink and not dared get one in his presence.

Luke Havenner was squat, ponderous, fat but very strong, more sullen than ever now that middle life was finding his virility slackening. He had never married. The flesh of his great moon face hid his eyes and was marked with the grease of his mechanic shop. He moved, because of his hard fat, in a kind of burlesque of a strut.

"What the hell did he want?" Luke asked Raley.

"That's a nice way for a Catholic to talk about a priest," Raley said, with patent insincerity.

"You should talk, you damn Protestant," Luke said.

"Looked like he was giving you a sermonizing, John," Charles Combs said, with a kind of giggle.

The farmers, lean, poorly dressed men, with thin faces, came out of the bar.

"Got your tobacco transplanted, Willie?" Raley called to one of them.

"Sure have, Mr. Raley," the farmer said. With his companion he got into a model-T.

"Mr. Raley!" Luke muttered. "What—does he owe you money?"

"Why, no, he just recognizes a substantial citizen when he sees one," Raley said. As a graduate of William and Mary and a law school in Washington, Raley liked at times to kid his local friends.

Jimmy Gordon came out of the bar and joined them. "Wonder what Father Cornish wanted up here in town. Up to some more nigger-loving ideas, I guess."

"He knows better," John said. "He's a Washington boy. It's that Laurence Kane down there. That's the one

83

you've got to watch. Why, first thing you know, he'll be campaigning for a nigger County Commissioner from down that way."

"That's the one that really ought to have his ass kicked," Gordon said. He felt pleased with himself when he shocked people, although neither Raley nor Havenner seemed particularly shocked and Charlie Combs had merely turned a little away.

From his apartment overhead, Raley's wife called, "You better come up, John, lunch is ready."

"Damn it," Raley said. "I bet she heard you two. I'll catch hell when I go up. That's what I get for marrying a Catholic."

When Raley had gone, Luke said, "She'll probably be the one that catches hell," and they all laughed.

Joseph Tennison, man of insurance, came out of Clement's Restaurant, chewing on a toothpick. "Afternoon, gentlemen, afternoon. I can see this gathering is up to no good."

"Lookahere who's talking," Luke said.

"We were talking about some of these nigger-loving priests around here," Jimmy said.

"They sure are a few of them," Tennison said. "Fourteen Jesuits in this here County and I bet you half of them are nigger-lovers. They tell me one of them run off at the mouth something terrible last Sunday at Valley Lee. One of these new ones they sent down. Kind of on the nervous side. Looks like they don't send the County nothing but young or nervous ones. Too bad it ain't like the old times. Whenever we got bored or wanted to put any priest in his place, we could just up and cut ourselves a nigger."

There was a slight pause in which Tennison stretched

84

luxuriously, flattening his double-chin against his chest and smiling at the effect of his words.

"What'd this one down to Valley Lee say?" Luke said.

"Oh, something about how we all ought to be ashamed of the way we treated the niggers. Imagine—the son of a bitch. Name's Schneider or something like that."

"I just don't go to church no more," Luke said. "And if they wants to know why, that's why." He dashed to the ground a small piece of metal he had been twisting in his hands, and walked away again with his heavy caricature of a strut. He was given to these fits of sudden rage and the others paid no attention to this one.

"There you are," Jimmy Gordon said. He turned to Joe Tennison with a sharp, judicious look.

"Well," Tennison said, tolerantly, "up here it's not so bad. I got to go to church anyway because I sell policies to all the mission parishes. And old boy Grantham here at St. Aloysius' knows enough to confine himself to sermons on fornication and bingo." He laughed, pleased as always at his own command of words. "I even get a real kick out of hearing him evade issues."

"There's the oddest of the lot," Jimmy said.

"He's all right," Charlie Combs said, a little sullenly.

They all turned to watch where, some distance down the square, near Clement's Drug Store, Zeke Mattingly got out of his mud-splashed car. From around the square he felt the eyes hard on him. It irked them curiously that one of their own people had become a priest and had returned to administer to them. It puzzled the priest as it might, in some future and more thoughtful time, puzzle them.

The Negro called Green Apple, with large head,

brutal jaw, and kind, inquiring eyes, was moving barrels of apples in front of the grocery store. He tipped his hat to the priest and mumbled.

"How are you, boy?" the priest said, almost without looking at him, passing on with the brave, bright appearance of disregard, of even unconscious scorn—and praying, "That they all may be one in Thee, Father, as Thou in me."

Joe Tennison spat after his retreating back.

7

FROM the rise above Ridge that gave the place its name, St. Jerome's Creek often seemed unreal. Its waters angled with wide sharpness inside the narrow creek-mouth, so that it was really a kind of bay made of what might be called the estuaries of several creeks. There were a few houses on the many little points of land scattered inside the creek, and the water was often quiet enough to reflect accurately these and the sky. The high ground to the west protected it from the prevailing southwest wind, so that it was disturbed only when squalls blew in from the Chesapeake or on the rare occasions when the wind shifted to the east. Beyond the creek-mouth lay the great bay of the Chesapeake and on good days the line of the Eastern Shore showed, a dark, low strip across the bay. Because on good days, St. Jerome's Creek did have some of the quality of a Maxfield Parrish bar decoration, Father Cornish was fond of showing it to visitors, and had urged any number of them to buy land on the rise overlooking it.

The outer edge of the neck of land, whose tip marked the northern end of the creek-mouth, bulged with gradual bluntness into the Chesapeake, and a generation not consciously subtle had called it Point No Point. The inner, point-and-creek-marked side of this neck was heavily indented with brackish waterways, the little boats of fishermen moored in them next to the lonely houses. Today almost no activity showed in these houses under the hot light of the June afternoon. Offshore the fishermen could be seen, taking down the net from their traps, and beyond them the smoke of the freighters going up to Baltimore.

From one of the points in the creek projected a new wharf and where it met the land was a sturdily made little building painted a bright umber. Over the wide doorway hung a new sign: *St. Jerome's Creek Co-operative Fisheries.*

Leslie Mattingly sat just inside the door, his chair tipped back against the wall as he read carefully the comic strips in *The Washington Post.* He was a pleasant-looking boy of twenty whose high, smooth coloring and slightly waved blond hair made him seem better-looking than he was. His work bored him, but the eight dollars a week and the small sense of power the position gave him held him to its letter if not its spirit.

Row-locks sounded, the noise almost intolerable in the heat. That would be Loker Abell, Leslie thought. The other Negro crabbers usually sculled their skiffs instead of rowing them. And a hell of a time for that goddam nigger to be coming around with his crabs.

The skiff rubbed against the new poles of the wharf with a smooth, quiet sound and this annoyed Leslie. The Negro's scarred and sardonic face showed over the edge of the wharf. His age was hard to tell, except that he was not young. "Mighty pretty evenin', Mr. Leslie."

"What you want? Get rid of some crabs?"

"That's right. Father Cornish, he tell us this here place of yours is going buy crabs from now on."

"How many you got? It's awful late in the day for them. Probably half dead."

"No suh! Been in a crab-car all morning. All peelers. Sold my soft ones this morning, 'fore I heard 'bout this."

"How many peelers you got?"

" 'Bout six dozen."

"That's a hell of a lot of peelers. What you been doing, robbing someone else's crab-car?"

"No suh. No suh. Represents two mornings' crab-bings." Loker grinned. Leslie could very well be joking and Loker hoped that he was. But down here you could never be sure. What began as a joke, where whites and Negroes were involved, often became a serious thing; and what began seriously could easily become a joke if it was to the whites' advantage.

"All right, let's have them."

Loker turned and lifted out of the water the crab-car he had been towing alongside the skiff. Water ran out of the holes bored in it and he swung it heavily toward the wharf, the lower edge of the car just failing to clear the edge of the wharf. Loker's stagger rocked the skiff but he recovered and slid the car onto the wharf. Leslie stood watching. He had made an unconscious, a spontaneous gesture to help Loker as the crab-car hit the wharf's edge, but had caught himself. It was, although he did not realize it, virtually a matter of duty with him that he give no aid to a Negro.

Loker climbed onto the wharf and opened the car from the top. The last of the water was running out of it and the gray-green backs and bright red and blue claws of the peelers were showing. Peelers are hard crabs getting ready to shed in their process of growth, and to become for a few hours soft crabs.

Holding peelers until they shed and become soft crabs is a delicate process. Hard crabs, which peelers technically are when caught, are worth about a dollar a barrel to the crabber, whereas soft crabs are worth around thirty cents a dozen to him. Once a peeler has shed and become a soft crab it must be quickly taken and kept out of water, as an hour or two in its native element of salt water is sufficient to harden the new shell again and reduce its value abruptly to that of a hard crab.

Carefully, so as not to break the shells, Loker dumped his crabs onto the dock and counted them with a stick as they slowly scrambled. He then held them, one by one, delicately against the surface of the wharf with the stick and nipped them with thumb and forefinger at the thickened base of one of the hind fins; then he lowered them carefully into the crab-car belonging to the co-op, which Leslie had opened in the water under the wharf. There were five dozen and seven peelers.

"Thought you said there were six dozen?"

"Said 'bout that."

"Like hell. You thought I wouldn't count them."

"No suh. I knowed you were going to count them."

"Sure," Leslie said, turning away. "Oh, sure."

Loker followed him into the new building, where Leslie wrote slowly in a rough ledger. "You get a dollar sixty-seven."

Loker had been counting on his fingers. "Dollar sixty-eight, I figures, Mr. Leslie."

"Goddam it, I say a dollar sixty-seven! Thirty cents a dozen and five dozen is a dollar and a half. And half dozen more is a dollar sixty-five, and one more is two cents and that's a dollar sixty-seven any way you figure it."

"It comes two and a half cents apiece, Mr. Leslie. They always gives a man three cents when a thing's two and a half cents."

"Look here, Loker, you're pretty lucky to be getting thirty cents a dozen. Those Baltimore dealers'd only give you fifteen or twenty cents."

"Yeah, I know," Loker said. "But Father Kane, he say they do wrong. You people doing what's suppose be right."

"Jesus Christ!" Leslie half-yelled and said, not without a certain humor he could not avoid, "Jesus Christ and Father Kane! If one more nigger comes in and talks Father Kane to me I'll throw him in the creek!"

Loker looked at the white boy and blinked slowly. He wasn't at all sure Leslie could throw him in the creek. The thought frightened him and he put it away. He watched Leslie count out a dollar sixty-seven, and then Loker picked it up slowly. "You better be sure you get those peelers out of the water right after they sheds," the Negro volunteered.

"You're not telling me anything. Now go 'long." Leslie sat down with his comic strips.

"I wanted buy hooks," Loker said.

Leslie got up. The Negro got a hardly realized pleasure from having made the white boy get up right after sitting down.

"For hard-head or perch?"

"Hard-head," Loker said. "Coming on for summer now and they losin' that iodine taste they got in the spring."

"Hell of a lot you niggers care what fish tastes like."

"I knows I don't like the taste of iodine."

Leslie was silent to indicate that he wasn't interested

in such inanities. Loker Abell sat in his skiff and Leslie sank deep into his comic strips. The motors of the returning boats made him raise his head. A tremendous mauve light was lifting over the Chesapeake out of the Eastern Shore. It grew not quite perceptibly although the sun still touched the ridge behind the creek and would not be gone completely for an hour.

John Mattingly's boat, the *Susie M.*, drifted alongside the wharf and Leslie walked out to help moor it. Loker got out of his skiff again to help.

"How did things go?" Mattingly asked his son.

"All right. Sold gas to Willie McKay and Foley Raley and a stranger that put in in one of those fancy outboard motor affairs. Look like it cost more than a real boat. Fenner Ridgel started over to get gas and he sees Foley here and he shies off again. Three more niggers in with crabs, mostly peelers."

"How many does that make?" John said.

"We got maybe ninety dozen soft crabs and nearly as many peelers."

"You watch them peelers," his father said. "You cost us money two days ago. Don't know where you were that evening but you let close on to forty dozen peelers shed and get hard again."

The boy, a faint color rising in his cheeks, did not answer. He saw that his father was neither observant nor pressing and had not noticed his flush. "You stay here this evening," the father said, "and get out all that sheds; and them that sheds after the truck gets here, put on ice. I'll send some supper over to you."

"All right." A kind of confusion and sheer pleasure came over the boy. His throat was dry and only by an effort did he keep his voice normal. He saw Loker Abell looking at him wisely and he wondered if Loker suspected. Loker had one of those queer-looking ageless faces like a real nigger's, Leslie thought. He wondered if it was true that his own granduncle, Bart Mattingly, had gotten Loker out of a mulatto girl? He watched resentfully while Loker asked for and got permission to tie his skiff to the motorboat for a tow.

The boat drifted away, its motor breaking suddenly into the now violet silence. Leslie waited, unable to read even if he had lighted the kerosene lamp. Once he exclaimed formlessly at his own urgency; it had come up in him, surging like something uncontainable at such a simple thing as his father's instruction to stay at the co-op.

When he heard her step on the wharf he wanted to spring up but did not. That much he had learned recently. In a way, he realized dimly, it gave him pleasure to restrain himself. Jane Saunders stood in the doorway. In the last light he could see the faint, mocking smirk on her mouth, while the eyes preserved the appearance of calmness and even quiet depth. Such things were beyond him, though, and as much in confusion as in passion he dropped his glance to where the outline of her thighs showed against the last of the light coming off the ridge. Her ash-blond hair came back in a careful wave to her shoulders and the ripe mouth mocked the high forehead, the gray eyes and firm chin. The breasts were high, their nipples showing clearly against the light cloth.

"Hello, sweetie-pie," she said. "They're always leaving you alone."

While he tried to speak from his dry mouth she was walking past him, the high heels giving her a faint mince, an almost imperceptible switch to the white, expensive, sharkskin dress she wore. The way it was he felt he would have choked if he had not seized her, and he moved with as little conscious volition as it is possible for a man to move and be that definite in his actions.

He remembered mostly her laughter and her eagerness—such always was his memory of her—and how there was no laughter in himself, but a terrible joy, one he would always think filthy. And the quietness, finally, and the gradual feeling of the rope coils they were on.

He could never understand how she did not seem to feel remorse as he did. He was still young enough to feel defiled, even to dislike her briefly after each time he had been with her. He was sullen now, but he knew—confused and puzzled—that he had been that before, too, and part of his sullenness this time was because he now knew finally that near her no resolve of his own could long last. He rose without looking at her, although a more sophisticated taste than his own would have taken a separate pleasure in the disarray of that much youth and beauty. He stood looking out the doorway to where the violet had deepened and the last red gone from the ridge. Riding lights dotted in pairs the gloom where they rose above their own reflections in the creek.

She came and stood near him, easily. She even looked fresh and, in the white, virginal. "You're one of the least grateful people I can imagine," she said. "And I don't know why you get so upset and gloomy."

Not knowing why himself he could not speak. A car's lights sabered wildly over the bad road leading to the co-op and he said, "You better get in the back there. Someone's coming with my supper."

She moved away, without comment or haste, into the shadows of the storeroom behind the counter.

James Cornish got out of his coupe and Leslie felt suddenly weak and had begun to sweat. "Not much light here, is there, Leslie? How are you?"

"Ain't apt to be no one wanting gas or tackle this time of night, Fawther. Thought I'd save oil."

"I was at your house when your dad came in and I volunteered to bring your supper over to you. How have things been going?"

"It was a pretty good day, Fawther." He told him of the sales and purchases.

"That's good. That sounds very good, Leslie. I hope you're not finding the work boring. I know there must be long periods when there's nothing to do. But patience has to be part of this work, too."

"Yes, Fawther."

"You don't know who it was came in the outboard motor?"

"No, Fawther. Some stranger. Looked the place over kind of queer. Young, light-colored, rough-looking feller. One of them Eastern Shore buy-boats went up the bay a while before. But that was the only big boat that was near and that he could have come from."

"We've been expecting people from the Freeland Foundation down to look over the co-op as well as some of Father Kane's projects. There's also been kind of warnings from the buy-boatmen."

Leslie was silent at the mention of Father Kane. The nigger-loving bastard, he thought. Then, in sudden fear: Wonder if it really is wrong to keep the niggers in their place?

"I don't suppose it could have been one of the Free-

95

land people," Father Cornish said, absently, when Leslie didn't speak.

"Wouldn't rightly know, Fawther."

"I'm glad you're waiting for those peelers to shed tonight, Leslie. We can't have any more losses on them like last time. And I was thinking that nights when you have to stay here like this, inventory might be taken. I don't see any reason why we couldn't even take some tonight."

"Well, the only lamp here, Fawther, is a kind of weak one. I got a stronger one home I been meaning to bring down."

"I haven't looked around in the storeroom in several weeks," the priest said, stepping tentatively toward it.

"See it better in daylight, Fawther." The sweat came off the boy in little streams. Something in his voice caught the priest's attention.

"Are you well, Leslie? You're sure you're feeling well. Not been out in the sun too much or working too hard?"

"Just warm, Fawther."

The priest sniffed. In the smell of rope, tar, and fish there was another, more delicate odor, the scent Jane Saunders had on her.

"What is that smell, like flowers, Leslie? It's really lovely."

"Wouldn't rightly know, Fawther. Hadn't noticed. Must have a cold."

"It must be one of those night-blooming vines. Didn't know there were any this far north. Well, good night, Leslie. We'll get a cot for you here for these nights you have to stay late."

Leslie stood in the doorway, watching the car jounce

away. The luminous darkness, his hidden lust, but mostly the priest's word, "night-blooming," moved in him.

"Night-blooming," he repeated to himself. It was like, it even was, a newly discovered aphrodisiac. He turned, almost gasping. He hardly realized that he was expecting that she would be there when he turned.

She was, in white, and he held her a moment, repeating the word, "night-blooming." She seemed even to understand why he said it, which he could not understand, and laughed a little, meeting his mouth.

Later, from where they lay, they could see together the brightness of the stars. He had felt less remorseful than ever before, though still defiled. They had hardly spoken since becoming quiet again and now, in amazement, he saw that she was crying.

"What's the matter? Did I hurt you?"

She shook her head and did not speak. He was annoyed and when she did not answer his repeated question, he shook her slightly. Jane stood up and walked toward the doorway. He moved after her and touched her arms. She shook him off without much effort and was gone in the dimness, now suddenly his love, his young love, going away into darkness.

He was tired, but most of all quickly grown very stupid. Wondering what he'd done, he sat down. Sometimes he felt that it was Jane who was using him, not he Jane; and that had seemed odd to him, because like most boys he had been made to believe that in having a girl, she had been humbled and defiled while he attained a kind of evil triumph.

He passed thoughtlessly into sleep, waking quickly in the dawn, mindful instantly of his neglected work. He dipped a net into one of the three large crab-cars and brought it out. It was full of sheddings and live crabs. He picked a crab out with his fingers. It was able to nip him slightly. The shell crackled and was the texture of thin celluloid. Already, like most of the others in the cars, it had passed the soft stage and was a paper-shell, scarcely more valuable than a hard crab, which it would shortly be.

The dealer's truck from Baltimore, which should have waked him during the night, he thought angrily, was only now coming along the road to the co-op.

8

THE noise of a powerful outboard motorboat awakened James Cornish. He had not slept well lately. The noise was that of no familiar boat and for some reason, possibly because strain had made him morbid, he rose and went out on the wide second-story porch that overlooked St. Jerome's Creek. Set in its points and little headlands, the creek lay like a frosted sheet of blue-gray glass. The noise of the motor had stopped by the time the priest had cleared his eyes and could see the creek below him. No movement seemed to break the surface of the water, the light too tenebrous yet to show any wake. He stood there, leaning heavily on his arms, braced against the porch rail. That light on this water gave him a kind of consolation, a curious peace which he unconsciously enjoyed and unconsciously knew would not last.

While he stared into the blueness, imperceptibly lightening, the noise of the motor began again, and he could see a shape moving on the surface of the water. It came out from under the co-op's wharf and moved with surprising speed toward the creek-mouth. It was dark in color and moved like shadow but for its noise. It went farther away as the light increased swiftly, so that Cornish could see no more of it than when he had first noticed it near the wharf. He followed it with sleepy perseverance until it was only a blur on the Chesapeake, disappearing toward Point No Point. He dressed in pants and shirt, still watching.

At least he gave the appearance of watching. By doing so he justified his own apprehension, a thing amorphous and fearful but sudden in him. A very few people—Kane or the Negro, Samuel Raife—would have had an instinct that evil was near, and it is no reflection on James Cornish that his feeling was less certain. It was principally that lately many things had been able to disturb him. He kept telling himself that it was just someone off a yacht anchored in the Chesapeake, come in for fishing tackle or bait.

The sun, red and without radiance, came out of the Chesapeake. Detail sprang from the shadow. All the world was light, clear, pervading, without heat or glare. The priest could see everything now: the lettering on the sign above the co-op, the first fishhawk, Leslie Mattingly walking slowly toward the co-op, early now that the co-op was failing and he was partly responsible for it.

Leslie stood with his back to the pump, unlocking the padlock on the co-op. The pump leaned oddly toward him and a column of vapor shimmered a hundred feet into the air. The vapor became flame and the whole landscape seemed to shiver. The shock went through the rectory, passing into Father Cornish through his arms. The gasoline pump rose in the air, the lower, heavier base traveling more rapidly than the lighter top. It turned slowly in flight, giving the impression that its flight, too, was slow.

Cornish did not see it fall. He was running down the stairs and cursing. He had played college and semi-pro baseball. "The sons of bitches!" he kept saying. "The sons of bitches!" Then: "The dirty goddam sons of bitches! Wasn't it enough for them that we failed as it was!"

He was the first one there, driving crazily over the rutted lane that led to the co-op. Only one corner of the building was burning, but the whole thing sagged out over the water, every joint sprung. The little gasoline that had been in the tank—if it had been full it would not have exploded—was burning on the surface of the nearby water, but Leslie had not been burned. He lay where he had been thrown, on the coarse, brown sand of the water's edge. His back was broken and he could not move anything below his arms and them only a little. A slight white froth from his mouth lay sharply against the skin, blackened by the explosion. His eyes recognized the priest and rolled toward him. Father Cornish turned toward the water and saw little fish— black perch, Norfolk spot, young hard-head—floating in it, killed by the explosion. There was nothing on his stomach but it kept retching. By a strong effort of his will he made himself realize that Leslie was dying and that it was more important that he be shriven than to avoid vomiting on him. He knelt by the boy; he was still retching and had not noticed the Negroes who had appeared silently. Leslie was trying to talk.

"Bah . . ." he said thickly. "Bah wi'h girl . . . been . . ."

"Yes," the priest said, "what else?"

"Mamma . . ." the boy said, almost clearly, seemingly without emotion.

"I'll get her," the priest said. "Now go on." He himself was calmed and noticed the Negroes. "You boys go away a little ways," he told them. "I'm trying to hear this man's confession." They backed slowly, with the appearance of sullenness, but really in fear.

". . . name . . . vain . . ." Leslie said.

The priest nodded. How superficial, he thought, some sins appeared at a time like this.

"Bah . . ." Leslie said, ". . . oo . . . nigs."

"I know it's tough, Leslie, boy," the priest said, growing calmer. "And it's all right if you can't be clear. But try to be."

"Bah . . . oo nigs . . ." The boy's eyes were afraid of a lot of things.

People were near again, not too near, though. Suddenly Kane was beside Cornish and the boy. Cornish felt weak. It was as though with someone else there to take responsibility, his body was no longer willing to bear it. "I'm trying to confess him before I give him extreme unction. But I can't understand him. He can't move and I imagine his back's broken."

"Shock, too," Kane said, almost absently. His face was calm except for the slightly twisted mouth, the skin around the eyes wrinkled as though to hide the eyes, then the eyes suddenly, wide and assured.

"I'll give him extreme unction," Kane said. "You try to understand him. It doesn't matter, though. His intention is good."

Cornish nodded. He had forgotten in the excitement. "Bah . . ." Leslie said one more time, even less distinctly. He seemed weaker. ". . . oo . . . nig . . ."

Kane interrupted his own subdued Latin, seeing Cornish's face. "It might," Kane said, gently. "It might barely be that he was trying to say he'd been bad to the Negroes."

Cornish bit his lips; he didn't believe it. "Maybe," he said. "Christ," he broke out in sudden emotion, "in this damned place they think it's a duty to hate niggers!"

"You mean you were bad to the Negroes, Leslie?" Kane said. Leslie's eyes rolled and he managed to jerk a shoulder. A spasm shook him and the eyes turned up slightly. "*Absolvo te.*" Cornish choked, and sobbed into his hands. Kane finished the Latin and stood up, his face unreadable.

Cars were bouncing along the lane. Fenner Ridgel's great body pushed towards the boy and the priests. Then Kane saw John Mattingly coming, moving slowly and evenly, as if he suspected what had happened and was saving his strength for when the full knowledge of it should come upon him.

Now it was mid-morning and most of the people had left the place of the explosion. John Mattingly had gone with his son's body; most of the Negroes had gone, too, as much from a presentiment of evil to come as from evil which had already occurred. The odor of burned gasoline was still heavy near the broken wharf and building, and the little, dead fish had drifted ashore and were scattered on the brownish sand. The day was warm and clear. Father Cornish had let someone drive him to the rectory where he had shaved and dressed and swallowed some coffee before returning to the co-op.

Kane was still there when he returned, and right after Cornish, came three cars carrying, respectively, Henry Saunders, Sheriff Bucky Briscoe, and the lone state policeman assigned to the County, Corporal Edward Small, who like Saunders was originally an outlander.

"Well," Saunders said, smirking quietly, "looks like we had an accident."

"No," Cornish said, "it wasn't an accident."

"Why, what you mean, Fawther?" Bucky Briscoe said. He was a great, heavy man with much loose flesh on his face. "You don't mean that someone come along here and did this ahere on purpose?"

"That's exactly what I do mean."

"Probably some drunken niggers," Henry Saunders said, easily, smoothly, almost indifferently, hardly moving his upper lip. "If anyone really did do it on purpose."

"Someone did do it," Cornish said, "and I don't think it was any Negroes. I think it was someone sent here by fish dealers in Washington or Baltimore."

Saunders' face broke into a laugh. "That's pretty strong talk, Father," he said, not looking at the priest.

"Looky here, Fawther," Briscoe said in his hoarse, shapeless voice, "what makes you all think that? Me, I bet money it was some drunken niggers."

"I bet it was, too," Foley Raley said. He had gathered with others of the co-op.

"You shut up, you son of a bitch," Fenner Ridgel said.

"You wouldn't mean me, Fenner?" the sheriff asked, in an attempt to give some humor to the gathering.

"Well, since you ask," the big man said, hitching his belt.

"Be still, Fenner," Kane said. It was the first time he had spoken since the law had arrived. "Go home, please."

"If it'll please you, Fawther." He stalked away, swinging his incredibly big arms and fists.

"I heard an outboard motor this morning," Cornish

said. "I saw the boat leave the wharf here twelve or fifteen minutes before the explosion." He told them the all but useless story. In the little silence that followed, Saunders cleared his throat, thrust out his under lip to indicate faint, skeptical humor, and smirked proudly at the Chesapeake. "That's pretty flimsy evidence, Father," he said. "However, we'll investigate. I can't imagine a big, million-dollar corporation in Baltimore being dishonest. And why would they be concerned over your, ah, little enterprise here, particularly when it was about to fail?"

Cornish's face, dirty pale at the moment, became even more drawn, and there was a kind of harassed desperation on it. "The idea was spreading . . ." He paused; the words seemed feeble, even to himself. "You seem to know a good deal about our affairs."

The Assistant State's Attorney colored. "That, of course, is part of my concern," he said evenly.

"I'm not at all sure of that," Cornish said.

Corporal Small came back to the little group before any more could be said. "I been going through the wreckage," he said, not looking at any of them. "Not much to be seen there. That tank's torn all apart."

"I can see all of you are going to be big helps," Cornish said. The veneer which the advertising business and the Jesuits had given him was gone for the moment. He was angry and didn't mind if anyone knew it. For various reasons, all the others were embarrassed. All but Kane. They looked away from the angry priest.

"I think," Kane finally said, "that we can let it drop." Cornish turned to him almost fiercely. "On one condition," Kane went on, as relief showed in the faces of those supposedly concerned with the law. "That this unfortunate event be termed an accident—which I believe it to have been—and that the colored people not be blamed for it, by implication or otherwise."

Bucky Briscoe didn't know what some of the words meant that the priest used, but he was nodding with the others in relief and agreement before Kane had finished speaking. Cornish, his face darkly flushed but silent under his superior's implied command, listened to the half-sentences, the misty assurances with which Saunders, the sheriff, and the corporal eased away. When they had gone, Kane took the younger priest's arm and walked with him toward the shore, where the remaining whites and Negroes could not hear them.

"I don't think you should have done that, Father," Cornish said.

"I thought it best," Kane said. He was humble but could not look at his colleague. "I'm not at all sure it wasn't an accident. If it was not an accident there would be a great deal of difficulty in establishing the guilt of people in, say, Baltimore or Washington. But once the forces of law and order had said it was not an accident, they would naturally want to achieve a successful solution to it. Failing to establish the guilt of white people in Baltimore, they might resort to establishing the guilt of colored people in Ridge."

Cornish didn't speak. His set face looked out over the waters of the creek.

"If they succeeded in establishing the guilt of any of the local colored people," Kane went on, "it would set what we're trying to do back perhaps another generation. What small success we've had here is due to the whites being convinced more or less that the colored people mean no harm and merely want to support themselves."

He paused again for Cornish to answer. But the younger priest did not speak or look at him.

9

GEORGE CARROLL BLAIR was in one of his fits
of depression. As he grew older they became more frequent and he sensed, without allowing himself to actually
think it, that that was not a good thing. For like many
other people he enjoyed unconsciously the self-pity
which accompanied the depression. Often there seemed
no apparent reason for the fits; but for his current one
there were several obvious reasons. The letter from the
Great American Grocery Company was the principal
reason this time.

They had written that they were not going to renew
their lease on the large store for which they paid George
Blair's mother a hundred dollars a month. They considered, they went on, that so-called co-operatives were
a foreign idea, un-American and subversive. Since it had
been brought to their attention that Mr. Blair was affili-
ated with such a movement they did not feel that they
could do business with him or Mrs. Virginia Blair, his
client.

The days succeeding the coming of this letter had
been difficult ones for Blair. There had been the matter
of explanations to his almost deaf mother, and then the
correspondence with the grocery people. He had written
and told them that he considered the co-operative at
Ridge merely the whim of a priest, and that now that

he knew the Great American Grocery Company was opposed to it, he would certainly have no more to do with it.

Blair had never had to write anything like that before and he did not like the feeling it left in him. He had done it, he told himself, because the store was his mother's principal source of income. The grocery people had taken their time about renewing the lease and old Virginia Blair, in her loud, deaf person's voice, had complained of it daily to her son.

And now, for the past week, Blair had been pressed to avoid Father Cornish who, Blair felt, stupidly was starting his co-op again after a failure that would have taught most people a lesson. The phone rang in his office this September morning and he called his wife in to answer it. She covered the mouthpiece with her hand and said it was Father Cornish for him.

"Tell him I'm not in, that you don't know where I am or when I'll be back. Tell him anything. He's got a colossal gall." He pouted slightly to show he was not entirely serious.

"He's not here right now, Father," Martha Blair said. "Yes, Father, I'm sure that'll be all right." She hung up.

"What'll be all right?" her husband said.

"For him to be up in an hour," she said. "I'm a little tired of that," she went on as he tried to talk. "I've had to lie to that poor man almost every day this week. He's going to come up in an hour and take a chance on finding you in."

"You certainly are a help, Martha," her husband said, almost mournfully. It was a little funny, he told himself.

"You've got to face him sometime," she said.

"Maybe you'd like me to draw up his damned papers again and us really lose that rental."

"The grocery isn't moving out. Not when they have to move showcases and refrigerating units and such. And it's the only big store in town that's available right now."

"Oh, yes, they'd move. They're afraid of this damned co-op business spreading. I don't blame them. Not a bit. I'm going to the races."

"You can't," Martha said. "You might as well stay here and help get the paper out. They're not running at any of the Maryland tracks."

"Yes, they are. They're at the half-mile track at Upper Marlboro." He rose and shrugged into his coat. "Tell Father Cornish I died or something."

"I'll tell him the truth," she said, without rancor. She never became excited and she loved her husband. There were simply some things she felt she had to do at times. They had not raised their voices. Martha went back into the pressroom and Blair went outside and around the house to where his mother sat in the low-ceilinged living room with its cloisonné vases, its antimacassar, its fore-edge paintings on her son's books. The yews outside the house made that room dim by day, and in it she sat, an old woman, pleasant, slightly dulled, her skin a wrinkled ivory, her hands colorless on her black dress of watered silk, her hair colorless, too, rather than gray, in an odd, thick roll about her head. She was in her eighties and said that she remembered Sidney Lanier stopping at this house to ask for water as he walked home from the prison camp at Point Lookout after the war. He had stopped to beg food and water, a thin man with a heavy, dark beard and pleasant, tired voice. Or did she remember him? It was close to the end now.

Her son stood before her. She had become used to seeing people suddenly. She never heard them coming, and now that she was becoming ever more given to long periods of aimless, even imageless introspection, she rarely even saw them coming. They were suddenly there before her or shouting in her ear; she had become effortlessly reconciled to it.

"How are you, mother?" he said. He shouted less loudly than most others, as he had discovered unconsciously that pitch which she heard best.

"All right, son." She nodded gravely, unsuspicious. "Have you been working?"

"I have . . . and I'm feeling a little sort of stale. Stale," he repeated. It was one of the key words. "I thought of going up to the half-mile track at Upper Marlboro."

She nodded, her face without expression. "All right. I trust you have the money."

"Well, no, I haven't, mother. I've been paying some bills. I thought you might let me have fifty dollars or so."

She shook her head with a kind of slow vigor. "No, George. You have caused me considerable perturbation about the store." She turned her head partly away as he sat on a chair close to her and leaned toward her. He had even been known to kneel, at the age of fifty, to gain something from her. Today, he could not bring himself to do so; but, unconsciously, his mouth went into a kind of pout.

"Now, mother, you wouldn't want me to go ramping around, unable to do any work, all for want of a little recreation?"

"George, you go to the races too often. And besides you don't win as you used to."

"Why, it goes in cycles, like everything else, mother. You ought to know that."

"Oh, George, how you go on! Why don't you edit your newspaper and tend to your practice?"

"I do, mother. You know that I do. A man's got to get away from his work sometime."

She was silent, looking away from him as though she had not heard him. It had suddenly occurred to her that God was at once mighty and subtle. Blair could hardly know that she had just thought this; she hardly knew it herself.

"Mother. You're not listening."

"Yes, I am," she said, absently.

"It's getting late," he said. "If I'm going to go, I have to leave now." He pressed her like a child.

She had never liked to see him this way. It always stirred her, so that her dislike of his put-on childishness remained entirely intellectual. She knew, without quite knowing why, that it was not a good thing. To stop him now, she would give in, as she almost always had given in to him. "All right, George. Bring me my check book."

Leaving the house a few minutes later, Blair saw but could not avoid meeting Father James Cornish. The priest was getting out of his car and was advancing on Blair with the rather too-hearty, spreading, athlete's smile on his now tired face. The lawyer decided he didn't like him.

"Well, George, you're a hard man to catch. I've been after you for days. How are you?"

"Why, I'm all right, Father. Just been kind of busy,

that's all. I'm on my way to Baltimore right now. Got to look up some records there."

"I see. I'd hoped to get a chance to talk to you about the new co-op we expect to start."

Blair looked away. "I don't think I'm going to be able to help you, Father. I'm going to be pretty busy."

Blair saw that this priest could conceal nothing with his face and disappointment least of all; he felt a proper scorn, was even moved to bluntness. "You ought to be able to get some other lawyer in town, Father, although a lot of people will think that kind of thing is communistic."

Blair noticed, too, that this priest flushed easily. "Why, George, it's one of the things recommended by the papal encyclicals. They—"

"Oh, the Pope and I have disagreed before," Blair said. He said it with a kind of loftiness that was only, and was intended to be only, half-funny. "Can't see eye to eye with him on a lot of things."

"Well—" Father Cornish said, a sickly grin on his face.

"I've really got to go, Father. Be glad to talk some other time. Martha'll be glad to see you." He had been getting in the car as he spoke. He felt powerful, excited, and assured as he always did on his way to the track. If the priest spoke as Blair started the car and drove off, he did not hear him. He left the priest there, frankly biting his lip.

David Camalier stood on a two-horse harrow and drove it over a field to be sown in winter wheat. He was a straightly built, spare man of seventy years. His eyes were frank and clear above a slightly aquiline nose. Sweat showed in darker patches on his clean, white

shirt, and the shirt and its color were a badge he unconsciously wore to indicate that he no longer *had* to work
with his hands. Occasionally he did, though, to help his
son, Ned—so David thought—who ran the farm, or to
please his daughter, who, he liked also to think, talked
about how sturdy papa was for his age.

Dust drifted in a long, low tangent from the harrow
and made a tenuous band against the September sky.
Late wheat was in the westward fields toward the river;
tobacco on three other sides, the leaves, the rows in precise geometric pattern. Nothing, no orchard or formal
garden, is so precise as growing tobacco plants. Their
green rich and light, their spacing exact and immutable,
cared for more lovingly than children by the sharecrop-
per; delicate, easy prey of worm and fireweed and blue-
mold; to be nurtured carefully, even in death; tyrannical
as any other invalid—these plants were the rulers of that
County. They were a weed which sometimes sold for
forty-five cents a pound and men had died for them a
long time ago and for them children would continue to
starve.

David Camalier turned his horses and headed toward
the other end of the field. Above the tobacco there, his
white house showed in a scattering of second-growth
oak and beech. The soil was light, dry, rich and shaly.
The horses, two percherons, made easy going of it. They
even trotted a little. The tangent of dust accompanied
them now, blown northwest as they trotted north.

Ned stood waiting, a man in his middle thirties, lacking his father's fineness of feature. The son could do
nothing but stand watchfully by when his father decided to work around the farm. All of David's children
loved him and felt that he should no longer do any

rough work, now that he had been a County commissioner, now that he was old and his body had grown fine and seemingly fragile.

Through the tunnel of dust that went a little to his right David saw another figure standing with Ned. When he stopped the harrow at the end of the field the dust blew slowly away and he saw Laurence Kane standing there. David wiped his hands on his shirt as he came to the priest.

"This is very nice, Father. We see you too seldom."

"I don't want to wear out my welcome. I came in to see Rose. I didn't expect to find you home. You're looking well, Mr. David."

"Feeling fine. Doctor tells me I have low blood pressure. Don't know why I should. Sorry Rose isn't home."

"It wasn't important." Kane and the old man walked slowly toward the house. Ned picked up the reins; as he drove off on the harrow, even his stance showed relief.

"That was a right bad accident down your way," David said.

"Violence is always terrible where human beings are concerned. We did manage to hear his confession. Will Rose be back soon?"

"This afternoon, likely. She went up to Washington yesterday for some shopping. School opens soon and she won't be able to go up so often. Guess she'll be teaching all her life. Too bad she's not better-looking."

"Oh, she's a fine girl," Kane said with the vagueness that continued weariness often caused in him.

"Was some talk of it not being an accident down there," David said. "Some thought the darkies did it."

In the accustomed tenseness that such references brought to him, in the weariness that repeated explanation and defense created in his mind, Kane could still smile a little inwardly. David Camalier was the only man in the County that Kane knew to call the Negroes 'darkies.' It was the mark of a generation that had somehow been kindlier than his own, Kane felt. The inward smile passed, too. Kane tried to keep the tiredness out of his voice. "I really don't think it was the Negroes, Mr. Dave. They're apt to be blamed for almost everything. It's really more difficult than people realize to at once deliberately and safely explode a gas tank."

They had reached the porch and sat on the comfortable chairs there, the older man less heavily than Kane. In shadow now, the air was cool. "Guess you're right, Father. They're apt to blame the darkies for almost anything. But they could be worse off than around here. Look how they're treated farther south."

When Kane made no answer, David said, "Why, we haven't had a lynching in St. Mary's County in twenty years or more."

"Please God we never do have another," Kane said.

"Course, they've had them in Charles County and on the Eastern Shore since then," David said. "It's too bad."

"And LaPlata, the county seat of Charles, is thirty-five miles from the Capitol of the United States."

David moistened his lips. "Well, it'll never happen in these parts again, Father. You worry too much about such things. How about a highball or a julep?"

"All right. I'd like one." Here at David's or in community was the only place Kane felt comfortable taking a drink. The reason was obscure, even to Kane himself; probably it was because so many took scandal—willingly or easily—at a priest's drinking whiskey. It was also because he could drink with enjoyment only Scotch, and the great drinks in the County were rye and bourbon in varying stages of maturity.

They sat in the coolness of the slate-roofed porch. "It's gotten," David said, smiling, "that the only time you come here is when you want money from me."

"N-no," Kane said. "It's simply that I'm pretty busy. The last time you were at the races."

"So I was. I couldn't pick a winner that day, so I started betting them to place and show and did all right."

"I came this time," Kane said, "to see if you'd like to do a little lecturing on farming."

"I thought the County agent did that? Not that they'll listen to him. Or me, either."

"It's at the Institute," Kane went on, with a kind of quiet haste. "Marks, the County agent, is a good man, but he can't come to the Institute too often. People down there don't pay much attention to him, anyhow, but if they knew he was coming to the Institute too often, they'd resent it on general principles."

David nodded almost imperceptibly. He did not look at Kane and his face was without expression.

"You know about all a man can know about farming in St. Mary's County," Kane went on. "And your name is the best name in the County."

"It wasn't good enough to keep Dabson Morgan from beating me in the election for commissioner," David said.

"Even so, it would mean a lot if you came down and talked to them at the Institute." When David, looking out over his land, did not speak, Kane said, "Just once or twice a month, even."

"Well," the old man said and paused. "I'd have to kind of think it over."

The silence was broken by Rose Camalier driving up

117

in her coupe. A tall, angular girl, she got out hastily when she saw Kane. She wore a blouse and skirt, brightly colored. The hard sun on her, hatless, made her seem more shy than she was. She came toward the priest across shadow, too, and in it her face seemed to take quickly on kindness and frankness.

"You've got no more grease on you than'd fry an egg," she told Kane after their greetings. "You'll dry up and blow away some day just like papa."

She sat with her father and the priest, drinking whiskey because she liked somewhat the taste, not because it was convention or because of effect. Homeliness had always given her a greater freedom than most other women, so that her casualness was without affectation and was never misunderstood.

"You know, Father," Rose said, "I asked the district supervisor the other day if he minded our giving the children a little about co-ops in with their civics, kind of." She paused to drink while Kane watched her, his head to one side. "He said he wouldn't mind if we didn't make too much fuss about it and to stop it if we had any objections from parents."

"That's interesting, Rose," Kane said. He seemed to want to say more.

"Of course," Rose said, "we can go ahead but if anyone at the bank or any storekeeper so much as sneezes, we've got to duck."

In the silence, they had a sudden and curious knowledge that none of them were so free as they naturally assumed they were, and there was in them, except perhaps David, a kind of resentment.

Kane said, "I've been trying to persuade your father to give a talk now and then at the Institute."

"I don't see why he shouldn't," Rose said.

"I have no real objection," David said. The following silence was quick and almost as though charged.

Kane rose. "I have to go. I've said no office today and there's benediction tonight."

They said goodbye and Rose walked to the car with him. Her homely face, with its own dignity, seemed more grave than usual and colorless under its tan. Looking at her as he sat in the car, Kane felt for her some emotion that was like sorrow but was not. He remembered that she had been a brilliant student at Trinity College in Washington and that she had been offered fellowships at other schools. And he thought of Wathen McKay, wanted by Baltimore hospitals. Why did they stay here? Kane wondered. There was a parallel or a paradox but his tired mind could not pursue and grasp it, although or because he was part of the comparison.

"I'll talk to papa, Father," Rose said. "It's just the idea of speaking at a Negro school. And he's so kind to them personally. Kinder than we are. Anyhow, more natural. I have to make myself be good to them. I have an esthetic dislike for them. It's terrible," she said, quietly, almost brokenly, looking away from the priest.

Kane pressed her hand resting on the door. "You're a fine person, Rose. God bless you." She did not look at him, and quickly he let the clutch in and drove away, dreading, like Bartlett, any emotion.

Father Cornish was in his study when Kane got to the rectory. Kane had been greatly concerned for the younger priest since the accident. He was relieved now to find him looking almost happy though still worn, and with some of his old zeal returned.

"Well, Laurence," Cornish greeted his superior, "it looks as though I may have a manager for the new co-op. Father Bartlett has recommended someone. Of course, coming from Bartlett, it makes me hesitate. He's such a radical. I really wouldn't be surprised to see him leave the Order some day."

"Whom is he recommending?"

"Someone named John Cosgrave. A graduate of Georgetown."

Kane had a quick sense of foreboding, sharp enough almost to create the sense of shock. "I've met him, I think—" He glanced at the note Cornish handed him. It said nothing about Cosgrave's having gone also to Harvard. Kane thought of telling Cornish that Cosgrave had gone to Harvard; it would effectively prevent Cornish's taking him as a manager.

"Say," Cornish said, his face lighting up, "that would be the Cosgrave that ran second in the half-mile in the Intercollegiates. Why, we could start a track team at the high school, too. And he could coach it."

Kane looked at his colleague and could not speak. Zeal, he thought, turning away with an odd, almost ducking motion of his head. Their function as an Order, Ignatius of Loyola had defined four centuries ago: ". . . to glorify the name of Jesus by its learning, by its zeal, and above all by its holiness."

Zeal was one thing they had, anyhow, he thought. And God knows, there is little enough of it! He was very tired, he realized; tiredness could make anyone morbid. He was too imaginative for the job. He must try to finish his office before supper.

10

WATHEN McKAY'S waiting room was almost always crowded. Although they were among the first there this evening, Mrs. Saunders and Jane waited until all the others had gone. When McKay finally opened for them the door leading to his office, Mrs. Saunders rose and with a slight gesture of admonishment, indicated to Jane that she should remain in the waiting room. McKay looked at Mrs. Saunders curiously and not pleasantly as she moved into the office; he closed the door behind her reluctantly.

"Look, Mrs. Saunders," he said, "I don't care to go through this business again. I have to return to the hospital tonight and besides I'm tired. Jane is the patient, not you." He paused, as though there might be some doubt about this. "And sooner or later, if she is to be treated properly, she must be examined."

Mrs. Saunders sat down with rigid bearing but downcast eye in a sort of embarrassed determination. "I understand that perfectly, doctor. I—"

"I wonder if you do?" McKay said.

Mrs. Saunders stared at him with rigid mouth. "I don't have to take your abuse, doctor. There are plenty of other good physicians in Washington and Baltimore."

"I wouldn't mind your going to one," McKay said quietly. "If you pick out a psychiatrist, as you may have to, you might have him check Jane's background and upbringing pretty thoroughly."

Mrs. Saunders' once pretty face colored and the thin mouth tightened. "You take advantage of the fact that we are not anxious to make our misfortune known."

McKay literally bit his tongue to keep from saying that it was pretty well known, anyhow. After he had controlled himself, he turned back to Mrs. Saunders and said, "Well, are you going to let me examine Jane or not."

Mrs. Saunders did not answer immediately. Signs of struggle showed in her face. "Yes, you may examine Jane, but only if I am in the room."

McKay shrugged wearily.

Mrs. Saunders began to cry dryly and almost silently. McKay watched her with only a hint of pity in him. "We've always brought her up so carefully," Mrs. Saunders said. "And this kind of thing may come as a shock to her. Why, for years I even made her take her baths wearing a nightgown." She sniffed and wept tears.

"Jesus Christ," McKay said softly. "I wouldn't doubt it. Where did you get that idea from?"

"It's what I had to do when I was at convent school," Mrs. Saunders said. The tears had relaxed the tension in her and she was belligerently defensive again.

"You might be interested in knowing that the good convent schools no longer go in for such Jansenistic practices," McKay said.

"I don't know what you mean?" Mrs. Saunders said, because there was nothing else she could say.

"Well, I'm not going to explain it to you. Look it up in the Catholic Encyclopedia. Finding Jansenism in there may convince you better than I can that it is a legitimate subject for discussion. I'm sure your husband has a copy of the Catholic Encyclopedia in his library." Even if he's never opened it, McKay finished to himself.

"I'll do that, doctor," Mrs. Saunders said, almost humbly.

McKay stared at her without sympathy for a moment before speaking again. "I think I can dispense with the mental examination right now, Mrs. Saunders, but I would like to check her physically."

Mrs. Saunders rose and with obvious effort inclined her head once. "As you wish, doctor," she said. "I will retire." She stood aside as McKay opened the door. Through the doorway, he could see Jane staring at them. It seemed to him then that he had never seen such a strangely beautiful face. Pity and something like fear showed through the definite mark of wantonness, but the face did not look older than its seventeen years.

"Come in, Jane," McKay said quietly.

She came toward him, at once uncertain and eager, and he felt the heavy change in himself and cursed inwardly. When Jane was in the room, Mrs. Saunders, without looking at her daughter, turned to leave. McKay touched her shoulder. "You can stay, Mrs. Saunders," he said.

The cabin James Washington owned was just off the Institute land and clearly visible from the Institute's steps. James had gotten a job in Anne Arundel County after attending the funeral Kane had taken him to. His cabin was now occupied by his younger brother, Willie, and by Kane's youngest acolyte, Kezer, their nephew. Kane had been busy in Baltimore and with charters for his credit unions, and did not know that for ten days, a colored girl named Elsie Greene had been living with Willie in James's cabin. She had been living previously with Peter Jurdan, an older Negro, who had been employed about the Saunders farm at three dollars a week. On this and what food he could pick up from the farm, she and Peter had kept alive. With the beginning of fall, Mr. Saunders had dismissed Peter. Elsie, out of the sheer necessity of hunger, had gone to live with Willie Washington, who had a crabbing skiff and would thus be making money up until November.

Willie and Elsie were sitting on the cot that stood in one corner of the single-roomed house, staring dully at the stove. Both of them were hungry. The door opened without a preliminary knock and Peter Jurdan came in. He stared for a moment at the two sitting on the cot and they stared dully back.

"Ah sees you two are pretty lovey-dovey, all right," Peter said.

Elsie shook her head indifferently. "Been too hungry," she said.

"Then what was yoah idea in leaving me to come over here?"

"Ah was even hungrier over there."

Peter looked at her uncertainly. He himself was so weak from lack of food that anger was in him only as a kind of shadow of itself.

"Why don't you go away?" Willie said. "This girl don't want to have nothing more to do with you."

Peter stared at them alternately. Anger was trapped between its inception in his mind and its fulfillment in his body. A gap of physical weakness lay between and anger could not get through. "Ah ain't feeling very good," he said, "or Ah'd do something about this."

"What could you do?" Willie said, dully.

Peter stared at them in his futile anger. "Ah got a gun. When Ah gets shells Ah might use it."

"Ah got a gun, too," Willie said. "And Ah ain't got shells yet, neither. So why don't you run along?"

Peter's stare broke and he looked around the room. Although virtually every object in it was visible, he could see no food. There was some grease that had cooled in a frying pan, and Peter stared at it with interest. His anger went as soon as he saw the grease. He was still staring at it when the door opened and Kezer came in from school.

He was a small, bright boy of eight and like all Negroes and many children he had what amounted to an instinct for the recognition of evil. It was in the room now and the boy stood silently inside the door, trembling.

"What you want, Kezer?" Willie said.

"Like something to eat," the boy said, grinning faintly.

"Guess we all would," Elsie said, almost to herself.

"Where this boy come from?" Peter said.

"Come fum Virginia," Willie said. "His people there right poor. What's it to you, anyways?"

"He sure come to a good place if his people right poor in Virginia," Peter said. He managed a sort of chuckle.

This idea had never occurred to Willie. Now that it had been called to his attention he resented it and resented even more Peter's calling it to mind. "Ah certainly wish you'd go," Willie said. "You just generally a nuisance."

Peter opened the door and, chuckling purposely, went out into the early evening.

"Ain't nothing to eat?" Kezer asked, almost brightly.

The other two stared at him dully. There was food, not much, and hidden under the bed. For the first time, Willie resented the food the child ate. When the grown-ups did not answer him, the boy went to a corner and sat down in it, almost cheerfully, to wait.

11

DRIVING south on Route No. 3 out of Baltimore, crossing the rolling country that lies between Washington and Annapolis, John Cosgrave felt happier than at any time since he had left his home in Brooklyn. The last two or three days there had been more difficult than the past year's days had prepared him for them to be. He had sensed vaguely during his last few months at Georgetown, the year at Harvard, the split that had begun to come between himself and most of his friends and his family. Yet part of him had prepared itself quietly for that time when the break should be complete. A man's spirit could be prepared for that time, he realized suddenly, but not his body. The thought shocked him. Like many young men, he had a tendency to romanticize his body, so that although he knew much about what made him a good runner he knew less about what made him an animal as well as a man; and he was only beginning to know of the body's many subtle treacheries.

It seemed to him that his stout mother's tears, his father's silent disgust, the mocking by his brothers and sisters were natural—even expected. Sometime, somehow, I must have left them. But not her I love! He was twenty-four and he thought romantically. He would think like that occasionally—in bursts of bad verse—for some time to come. And still it might be accomplished that part of him would not die.

So he did not think consciously of his family although they had left him fatigued and worried. He thought principally of Mary Larkin. She had seemed a little amused under her outward disappointment that he was going away to take a job that was, to herself and her friends, so strange. Cosgrave thought sullenly of what her family had probably said. He found that he was angry at her family with its high place in Irish Catholic, religio-political circles. This anger was new to him. At Georgetown such connections were well thought of by almost all the students and priests, who were even somewhat in awe of such people. Cosgrave remembered now the slight sense of shock when remarks of other undergraduates had implied that they thought him a pretty clever fellow to be connected in any way with the Larkins. He had gone with Mary Larkin because he liked her face and thought it beautiful, because she had seemed to have, like himself, an interest in verse. It had truly not been in his mind that her family had money and influence. The anger had been slow in him that at school they thought his interest was because of those things.

It was, too, he saw—again suddenly—a commentary on their curious attitude toward sex, on why so many of those undergraduates who patronized the Negro whorehouses would scarcely think of touching the daughter of a Tammany chieftain.

Cosgrave broke his line of thought. He was on ground now of which he was still unsure. Cromwell had left indelibly his mark on Ireland, and the American Catholic Church was principally Irish in its tradition. So that Cosgrave could be troubled in Maryland in September, driving, between tobacco fields, into a madness only Laurence Kane could have foreseen and he not clearly.

Cosgrave finally noticed the tobacco. He didn't know what these plants were, and stopped the car to look at the patterned leaves, the pink and white blossoms rising over a few of the larger ones. There was something almost architectural about these plants, something planned and quietly sure. It seemed that a power emanated from them, a thing only partly due to their orderly arrangement as plants and in rows.

A man in faded denim watched Cosgrave from a nearby snake fence. He seemed confident and assured in spite of his farmer's clothes. "What kind of plants are these?" Cosgrave said.

The man spat before saying, "Tobacco. Where you from?"

"New York." He laughed a little in embarrassment.

The man spat again and looked pleased with himself.

"Nothing but tobacco?" Cosgrave said. "Don't you raise anything for yourself?"

The man looked at Cosgrave. "Why should I waste a acre or a half-acre on raising vegetables when tobacco's apt to average twenty, twenty-five cents a pound?" He spat again and slid off the fence, turning toward his house, a handsome one but needing paint.

"What County is this?"

"Charles," the man said without facing Cosgrave.

Driving south again, Cosgrave felt happier, for no reason apparent to him. It even seemed to him that he should not be happy. The sun was warm now at midday, the frequent tobacco fields gave assurance, an impression of richness to the country. Pumpkins were bright through the fading corn. Just south of Mechanicsville he missed the Three Notch Road that would have saved him miles on the way to Ridge, and took the main road, No. 5. Calverton pleased him as he drove through it. He had not expected to find a town with a square in this country. Most of the houses were ugly but leaves had begun to fall and as he made the turn into town he could see girls playing on the grounds of the little convent school. The wind off the river was still soft and people walking seemed kindly. He was glad that he had come. As he swung out of town past Clement's Drug Store he felt fine and was beginning to drive fast.

The land changed perceptibly below Calverton. The woods were thicker, in places were almost forest. The town of Great Mills was a single line of unexpected ugliness on either side of the road and quickly past. St. Mary's City on its half-moon of a bay, had a kind of orderly desertion to it. There was no one near the girls' seminary on its rise. Cosgrave stopped his car to look at the statue of Tolerance at the roadfork. It was romantically done, the amorphous folds of a stone garment concealing carefully the lower half of Tolerance's apparently male figure.

Looking at the word 'Tolerance' in stone, Cosgrave honestly felt that he might help bring tolerance to this place. It could even be said that he felt inspired. A little farther south, he remembered hearing, was another statue, to the Jesuit martyr, Andrew White. But that statue, he found, was set back from the road, and Cosgrave decided to go on to Ridge where he felt they might be expecting him by now.

The holly trees that grew in a double row before the rectory at Ridge were another thing to please him.

There was no one in the square, ugly rectory but Father Cornish. He hurried down to greet the young man, whom he had never seen. In his shirtsleeves, lacking collar or clerical vest, the priest seemed powerful and assured.

"John Cosgrave," he said. "How are you?" just as though he were greeting an old friend. "Right on time. It's good to see you."

Cosgrave wondered what it was he had been on time for, but said, "Thanks, Father. I'm glad to be here."

"Bring your bags up. You're going to live here with Father Kane and myself. Be a kind of lay Jesuit." He chuckled aloud.

"I hope you can stand having me here," Cosgrave said.

"Oh, we Jesuits are used to working with laymen. And there's plenty of work to be done. We'll have to be discussing things all the time. And anyway you mightn't be too happy boarding out around here. Most of the houses aren't endowed with what they call conveniences." He laughed, showing Cosgrave into a room upstairs, plainly furnished with an iron bed, a chair, and a chest of drawers. "We live simply you know," the priest said. "None of the undergraduate luxuries one is accustomed to at Georgetown."

"Oh, I wasn't expecting them."

Cornish continued to grin, but now without mirth. It occurred to Cosgrave that the priest might have misunderstood him.

"Just drop your bags and we can go into my study for a talk. That's quite an expensive car you have for the manager of a co-op. We won't have supper for a while."

"Is Father Kane around?"

"Oh, Laurence—I never know where he is. You'll get

131

used to that. He's almost never over here. Right now, he's probably over at the Institute or visiting somewhere in his parish. He'll be in for supper, probably, though. He knows you were due today. That's about the one meal we can rely on his being here for. I think he's like Elijah, fed by ravens," he finished in an inspired burst.

Cosgrave thought that this priest was all right, that he could work with him. He was disappointed that apparently he would not see more of Kane, but this priest seemed a good man. The 'study' was a good-sized room whose windows looked out on St. Jerome's Creek and the bay. There were several hundred books in the room, some of them quite old and Cosgrave remembered, with the feeling of strangeness the thought gave most people, that a Jesuit, when transferred, could not take his books with him but must leave them behind.

"Sit down," Cornish said. "Smoke? No, that's right, you ran, didn't you? Throwback to that, I suppose. We all expected you to win the eight-eighty at the National Collegiates. The old Georgetown track tradition and so on. It was something of a disappointment, although I guess the competition was terrific. I suppose you were a bit stale?"

"Oh, I don't know. I don't think about it much any more."

The priest apparently resented something without knowing quite what it was. "Some said you quit in the stretch," he said. He had not intended to say it. "Of course, I don't believe that. The Irish never quit." He chuckled quietly.

Cosgrave's features were suddenly unreadable, nearly masklike. "It's unimportant," he said quietly.

His grin almost fixed, Father Cornish changed the subject without even knowing that he did. "Well, anyway, it's good to have you with us. Someone that's intelligent. Your predecessor, the Lord rest him, wasn't exactly the brightest person in the world. And being a native he was not particularly sympathetic to the Negroes. And we have to work with the Negroes to some extent, although of course they are all in Father Kane's parish. That is, we're going to work more with them. Of course, we all have our own antipathies. Mine is Jews." He laughed. "That shocks some of my colleagues, but they haven't had to work near Jews as I've had to, in the advertising business and even here. Grasping—why, there's no word for it. Just the other day I got a letter from one of the local storekeepers, a Jew, asking me to come in and see him about the bill for the rectory groceries. Imagine? It's a monthly bill and it was only a couple of weeks overdue. I was waiting for some money from people in Baltimore. Well, I went down and I told him off. His name is Berger and I made him itemize and read out every article on the bill. And the more he read the shakier his voice got because he knew what was coming. When he was through, I paid him in cash, made him sign a receipt, and then told him he was getting no more business from us. Why, I'd rather deal in the colored store up the road. It's the only way to teach a Jew a lesson—in the pocketbook."

The young man's face was now quite immobile. Father Cornish couldn't understand the few words Cosgrave said. For some reason not clear to himself, the priest again changed the subject. "But there's none of them in the co-op, thank Heaven. And about that, your principal concern for the next few weeks ought to be getting to know the people, especially those in the co-op.

I'll take you around some myself. I'm glad you have a car, though. You may have to run up to Baltimore or Washington now and then. And there's no other means of transportation around here. Not even the bus runs below Calverton. We'll supply gas for the car out of the co-op pump. And you'll get your board and room here. Outside of that I don't know what we can pay you, maybe five dollars a week, maybe eight, we'll just have to see what the co-op can afford."

"I didn't come down to make money," Cosgrave said.

"I know, I know. We'll be lucky to keep going, even. It'll be years before we can pay you anything worth while. I hope you aren't thinking of marrying?" He laughed, almost silently, his fluent eyebrows raised.

"I have a girl, but I'm not worrying. Maybe I can just help you people get started. My girl will wait a year or two."

"Of course, there are some nice girls down here, too. In Calverton. And at Medley's Neck the Camalier girl. Then there's Jane Saunders. She's nearer here, around St. Mary's City. I hear she's not going back to school this fall. She's a very pretty girl. And you'll like her family, too. Her father's is quite a success story. A man making his fortune before he's fifty and then retiring to this fine, old country to live! He has a model farm. Perfect. Biggest barn in the entire County. We'll go there soon, tomorrow perhaps. I'd take you there today but it's getting late."

"Don't worry about companionship," the young man said in his slow voice. "I'll be pretty busy with the work, I guess."

Someone began to ring a dinner bell downstairs. The priest rose. "That's supper," he said. "We eat early here, around five-thirty. I'll see you downstairs in a minute. But that's the way I like to hear you talk, though. The old Georgetown fight. We'll be ascetics if we have to be to put this thing across."

Cornish did not notice the slow, almost rapt smile his words had produced on the young man. Although he did not know it, the priest had finally said the right thing.

After the first autumn rains the road to Fenner Ridgel's house looked more impassable than it was, so that Cosgrave left his car a hundred yards from the house and walked toward it. A covey of quail burst upward out of the wet grass. He watched them sail across one arm of the creek and settle in heavy brush on the other side. It was a good country, he felt again, where holly and tobacco grew and cedars were near every wire fence.

Because he was walking and not driving, he surprised Fenner, sitting on a crab-car, whittling slowly and savagely. Cosgrave smiled at the big man's preoccupation; he could not know that Fenner was thinking of his enemies. Fenner watched Cosgrave come closer and greeted him unintelligibly.

"Cosgrave's my name. Father Cornish asked me to stop in and see you."

Fenner stood up to shake hands. He looked down at the young man. "Pleased to meet you. Sit down."

"You've got a nice location here."

" 'Tain't for sale."

Cosgrave laughed and some of Fenner's anger went toward him. "I'm not thinking of buying. I've just come down here to work with you people on the new co-op."

"You're certainly keerless with your time, then," Fenner said. "Seems like a feller like you would have better work to do."

"Why, that's good work, isn't it? You wouldn't be in the co-op if you didn't think so?"

"Don't know about that," Fenner said. He looked at where his knife was cutting savagely into the wood. "Don't know that I'm in it. Didn't like the way it was run last." He talked lower, mumbling his words not unlike a sullen child. It occurred to Cosgrave that he himself could move Fenner to violence or its opposite, as he willed. It was a new thought for Cosgrave and he could not decide whether it pleased him.

"I guess there were some mistakes made," Cosgrave said. "But we've learned by that. I've studied a little about such things and that's why Father Cornish brought me down here."

Fenner kept looking at his whittling. "Don't see how we could pay a city feller enough to stay down here."

"Don't worry about that. I'm not. The main thing is to get the co-op started again, which we've practically done."

"I know about that. But it won't last. People'll be agin it. Take that no good lawyer cousin of mine in Calverton, George Blair. First he was with us, then he was agin us. Wouldn't even fix up our papers for us."

"I haven't met Mr. Blair but I've heard a lot about him."

"You'll hear a lot but that's about all. Don't know how he manages to hang on in politics or nothing. Started out being an important man. Now he's nothing but a horse-player."

Cosgrave laughed. "We have to expect opposition.

136

Father Cornish tells me Mr. Foley Raley left the co-op because when he went to the bank to get money to buy a new boat they wouldn't let him have it and later they gave him to understand that it was because he was in the co-op."

"Mr. Raley! Mr. Raley! Foley Raley! That son of a bitch! If I stay in the co-op it'll be because he's out of it." He shook his big fist overhead like a brand.

Cosgrave forced a smile. The sudden violence was a surprise. "I just used him as an example of the opposition we can expect from various sources."

"That's all he's good for, a bad example. I hate him."

"Well, why?"

Fenner looked up angrily, and Cosgrave realized he shouldn't have asked the question. Apparently Fenner was satisfied with the innocence of Cosgrave's intention, for he looked down again. "Just do," he said, barely audible.

Cosgrave didn't speak, looking for the source of his own confusion. In the silence he heard a boat being sculled nearby, and turned to see a Negro ground his skiff on the brown sand and walk toward them. The gray, diffused light showed clearly the details of the Negro's face, ageless and scarred. He wore the ragged, faded clothes which seemed almost their uniform in this country.

Coming up to them, the Negro spoke to Fenner Ridgel, disregarding Cosgrave with care, with what might have been even fear. Cosgrave couldn't understand their greetings. It was as though the greetings had something of shame in them, as though both men, illiterate, still realized that in a friendly greeting they spoke against a long convention, against the night.

"What you want, Loker, money?"

"Dat's right, Mr. Fenner." The Negro spoke hoarsely.

"How much?"

" 'Bout two-bits."

"By God, Loker, there ain't many two-bits around."

"No suh."

Fenner reached elaborately into his pocket and gave the man a quarter.

"Thank you, Mr. Fenner. Bring it back next time I get rid some crabs."

Fenner didn't speak. They watched the Negro push his skiff off and scull away.

"Probably wants a drink," Cosgrave said. "He's got a mean face."

"That man's hungry," Fenner said. "He got cut bad in the face when he was a boy."

Cosgrave grew dull red. "I'm sorry. I don't know why I said that."

"That's all right. God knows, there's enough drunken niggers around."

Cosgrave felt stupid. His pleasure in the new country, his sense of doing something good, were gone. He stood there, feeling sorry for himself, hardly realizing that minutes had passed without either of them speaking.

"Young man," Fenner said, as though after thought, "I want to ask you something. You seem like a smart, young feller, went to college and so on."

Cosgrave turned to him. Fenner looked rather strange, his eyes a little wild, almost as though in fear. "You look at me," Fenner said, "and tell me. You think I got any nigger blood in me?"

"No. You're lighter than I am."

"You sure of that?"

"Yes, sure."

Fenner let out his breath. "I git to worrying about it at times, specially when my wife's away. Don't know why. Just that there's some light-colored niggers floating around and some of us got to take care of them 'cause we're related. You take that Loker Abell just was here. Works on John Mattingly's boat when he's needed—him and John are first cousins. John feels that on his conscience and he keeps Loker on, good times, and sometimes bad. Me, I'm not sure of nothing though my papa and mamma were right white. But I never know when I *might* be treating a cousin bad, so I treat them all—the niggers—good when I can."

Cosgrave felt confused. Father Cornish had told him Fenner could neither read nor write. Fenner noticed, perhaps misunderstood, the younger man's silence, and stood up. "Well, young man, I got work to do. You tell Father Cornish I'll try that co-op business once more. Specially now that Foley Raley's out. And you come around again some time. Anyone around here start picking on niggers, you tell me and I'll twist their mouths round the back of their heads." He shook the fist again.

"Next week," Cosgrave said in a kind of gasp. "Start bringing in the fish to the co-op next week."

Cosgrave walked toward the car feeling as though something quite different from what he had just seen and heard had happened to him. He felt at once pleased and uneasy. Watching a teammate in a close race was a similar experience, but less debilitating.

The light, stronger now in the west, made his dark, lean figure, outlined against it, seem shambling and uncertain to the big man near the creek watching him go.

139

Early in October the first bad storm came, and not until then would a stranger know that summer had gone from that country. With Father Cornish, Cosgrave drove up to Calverton in the rain. Although in sun the country had pleased Cosgrave, he felt now as if it had been made for storm. It lay between waters, and the cedars, leaning now westward against their natural bent from the wind that crossed the Potomac, still moved easily and surely.

"Calverton we avoid," the priest said, heartily, "except when it's necessary to go there."

"Is it so unpleasant?"

"No. It's just that it's the County seat and pretentious. A sort of necessary evil." The priest had grown avuncular, even a little patronizing with the young man. It was a kind of defense, unrealized by either of them.

In Calverton the square was almost deserted in the rain as they turned and drove west to where the courthouse stood above St. Clement's Bay and the ice plant. Gregory Fenwick, the tall, thin assistant clerk of the court, registered Cosgrave as a citizen of Maryland. After doing so, Fenwick stood behind the long table, respectful, sincere, and disapproving.

"John, here," Father Cornish said to the clerk, "is going to be the new manager of our co-op."

"So I understand."

"He's a Georgetown man," the priest said. "A Hoya like you and me." Father Cornish grinned pridefully at Cosgrave, as if the young man were a prize animal in a show.

Confusion showed on the lean face of the clerk. He considered that co-operatives were what he called communistic and he believed the priest to be involved in one solely through ignorance. "Is that right?" the clerk murmured. If it were so, he thought quickly, he must write to the Alumni Association and ask if they knew what the university was doing. He was angry but it did not show other than in his gravity; for the Church and its priests he had respect if seldom understanding. He bowed this priest out of the office with the grave courtesy which came naturally to him.

"He seemed to know all about me," Cosgrave said, outside.

"News travels fast in this kind of a community. You see, here the County rather than the town is the unit. And everyone is related, all over the County. You can't say a bad word about a man but what his cousin is in the room with you."

"It ought to make for the semblance of charity, anyhow," Cosgrave said, smiling.

"How's that?" the priest said, turning a blank face to him. But Cosgrave had started through the rain toward the car. The only parking space was near Raley's Bar and the priest stopped the car there. "I have some things to pick up at the drugstore," he said. "And it's a bit chilly. Maybe we could have some coffee there or in the restaurant."

"All right. If you don't mind, though, I'd like to have a drink first. I'll be right with you."

"Certainly," the priest said, somewhat alarmed. "Go right ahead. I'd join you but I'm in uniform, as it were."

The bar in Raley's was plain and there was nothing on the floor but the spittoons. Slot machines stood next the wall opposite the bar. Four men were playing pitch at one of the three round tables near the far end of the bar. A somewhat naked girl above them asked win-

141

somely in lithographed print why they didn't try Bailey's Bourbon: it was mellow and smooth. Three more men watched the game. All seven of them looked up as Cosgrave entered and all but one stopped talking. Jimmy Gordon threw his hand down and got up to serve the customer.

"Yes suh, what can I do for you?" He knew exactly who Cosgrave was in his relation to the County, and his voice was round, full, and almost soft with a fond, false heartiness. For wasn't Cosgrave an outlander and working with Laurence Kane and therefore, *q.e.d.*, a nigger-loving bastard?

"Scotch and soda."

"By God," Gordon said, turning toward the ranked bottles, "there ain't many people orders that down here, except summers. Have to open a bottle for you."

"There's one open at the other end."

Gordon looked at it sullenly and elaborately before picking it up. He poured Cosgrave a drink, slopping it over onto the bar.

"Pretty wet out," Cosgrave said.

"Yeah, it looks like rain, all right."

Someone at the table laughed. John Raley, containing his own laughter, said, "You hush there. We'll be getting a bad name with the clergy." He rose, a smile of welcome on his round, bland face, and came along the outside of the bar. "My name's Raley," he said. "Yours is Cosgrave, isn't it? Heard you were down this way. Glad to see you. I'm a college man myself, even if I do run a bar. Good old William and Mary."

"Have a drink," Cosgrave said after shaking hands.

"Don't mind if I do. Seagram's and a little water, Jimmy."

"Nice country down here," Cosgrave said.

"Right nice. All of us like it. Hasn't changed much and isn't likely to. You working with Father Kane, aren't you?"

"No, Father Cornish."

"That right? We heard it was Father Kane. No matter, though. Glad to have you down here."

"Thanks. You've got a nice bar here."

"It isn't much but it gives us half a living. Now if we could run a little whorehouse in the rear, we'd really make some money."

At the table, they laughed dutifully, without mirth. "But my aunt," Raley went on, "she owns the building. She wouldn't like it."

"Too much amateur competition," Jimmy Gordon said. "What with nigger wenches and so on." Again the dutiful laughter.

Cosgrave smiled, also dutifully. He finished his drink and slid the glass down the bar as a compromise with a sudden impulse to violence. "I have to get along, Raley. Father Cornish is waiting for me. See you soon."

"Sorry you have to rush off," Raley said. "Just going to buy you a drink. Drop in again."

"I'll do that." The rain felt good as he closed the door behind him. It was a good bar, he thought. He could come there once in a while. Not that he'd ever feel lonely with so much to do.

In Clement's Drug Store, Father Cornish was talking to a well-dressed and preoccupied man. "Here he is now," Father Cornish said as Cosgrave entered. "Come, John, meet Mr. Blair."

"I'm very glad to know you, indeed," George Carroll Blair said, bowing slightly. "Welcome to St. Mary's

143

County." His face creased into a smile that was almost skeletal. Cosgrave saw how thin the man was and was surprised at the feeling of pity and scorn that came up in himself.

"Thank you," Cosgrave said. "It's nice to see you."

"We are very glad to have you here," George Blair went on, rather gravely. "I hope you'll feel free to call on Mrs. Blair and myself at any time. And use my library. My relatives were associated with Georgetown University for generations and I feel intimately connected with the university although I never attended it. I went to the University of Virginia."

"Thank you. I'll certainly be in."

"John is to manage our new co-op," Father Cornish said. "You see, we will not be dismayed." He grinned faintly.

In return, George Blair smiled fondly. His lower lip came in and he looked more like a death's head than before, a smirking skeleton. "I wish the young man luck. You certainly have a task on your hands, Mr. Cosgrave. This County hasn't changed in generations and it isn't likely to change. Why, it and its neighbors are the only counties in the whole United States where they still sell tobacco in hogsheads instead of on the loose-leaf market. If you think that you can change St. Mary's County, you're mightily mistaken. Not that I want to discourage you or anything like that." He looked at Cosgrave with an air of affected innocence.

In the back of the drugstore a juke-box began to play. Boys and girls in their middle teens left their Coca-Colas on the tables and began to dance with furious limbs and solemn faces. Cosgrave watched them over Father Cornish's shoulder and did not answer George Blair.

Blair laughed. "That bothered him, Father. Don't take me seriously, young man. No one does, any more. By the Lord, I couldn't even swing the last election to Mr. Dave Camalier."

"It was amazing that Mr. Dave lost," Father Cornish said. "He's a practicing Catholic and this is a Catholic community. And we all know neither Dabson Morgan nor his wife even go to Mass."

"They don't know that down-county," Blair said. "Just as Waterloo was won on the playing fields of Eton, so Dab Morgan won the election in the grave-yards of St. Mary's County. Every time there was a fu-neral down-county, Dabson would show up and be hanging over the grave with a pair of rosary beads in his hands a yard long. I expect he'll be hanging over mine, though he knows I hate him. You priests down there should have told the down-county people about what a faker Dabson is."

Cornish nodded slowly. "We try to stay out of poli-tics," he said, heavily. "But something should have been done."

"Go on," Blair said, with one of his knowing and ter-rible smiles. "Dabson promised you priests he'd try to get state support for your school buses."

"Not entirely," Cornish said. "And you sound pretty much like an anti-cleric to me, George."

Blair laughed like a little boy, but silently. "I always have been. The Church would be fine if it didn't have any priests. But to get back to Dabson Morgan. He ought to take better care of his wife. By God, what's the use of being a success in politics if your wife's run-ning around with someone else."

"You oughtn't to say that," Father Cornish said with

a kind of brisk sorrowfulness. "Talk like that is uncharitable."

"I'm just an old reprobate, anyway," Blair said. "Now, I've got to get along. Glad to have seen you, Mr. Cosgrave. Don't forget to drop in and see us at the paper. Maybe you could write us an editorial or something, sometime. Goodbye." Cosgrave could see the death's-head grin fade with the same speed that the head turned away from him.

"You, you mustn't take George Blair seriously," Father Cornish said as the door closed behind the lawyer. "No one down here does. At least, not any more."

Cosgrave was surprised to see the priest's face deadly serious. "I don't think I do take him seriously."

"What do you think of him?"

"I don't know." His opinion had changed more than once while they talked.

"I had some coffee with him. Do you want any?"

"I don't think so."

"Good. Then let's get along. We have several more calls to make."

It was a Friday and school was out. They had to pick their way through youngsters from the high school up the road and from the convent school, St. Basil's. The young girls looked at Cosgrave. Everyone had looked at him but he had noticed only the girls. He turned to the mirror behind the soda fountain, mildly disturbed by their glances. His face seemed more handsome than he had remembered it. He had never thought of himself that way. Away from the city, from the many subtle antagonisms that he had grown into, from footracing . . . a change had come to his face. It was less strained, even kindlier—as kindly as a young face may

146

be. And some trick of the wet air had accentuated the change.

Passing the Medley's Neck Road as they drove south, the priest said, "We won't bother going in to see the Camaliers. The Saunders are expecting us to tea."

Cosgrave didn't speak. They drove on past Great Mills and into the lower County, where, the Chesapeake and the estuary of the Potomac invisible on either hand, the sense of waters was still strong on the rolling fields, the sudden forests of the place. They turned off on a dirt road that ran between two wire fences and, beyond a belt of trees, came to a new, white house on a rise overlooking the Potomac. There had been some attempt to copy the old houses, but the proportion was not there, the gables looked plastered on. No sundial was in the formal garden, but an iron milkmaid, a slightly distasteful smile—as though she disliked cows—on her face.

Getting out of the car on the circular drive, Cosgrave could see the Potomac below him, echelons of white-caps moving toward him across the brownish water, Virginia a darker smudge in the rain, five miles away and a foreign land. The wind had shifted to the southwest while they drove and now blew the rain in Cosgrave's face; through it, all down the long slope, he could see cedars blowing toward him. There were two tobacco barns on the slope and farther off, one for cattle. He turned to the house, following the priest. The rain coming across the river had made him quieter. The door that gave onto the terrace was open for him under the wide overhang of the roof, and Father Cornish and a heavy-set man were just inside it, watching him come through the rain. A fire burned behind them in a rich, dark room.

The big man's voice was hearty in welcome and his wife, a tall handsome woman, somewhat unassured, came across the room and greeted Cosgrave fulsomely. It was a fine, long room they were in, overfurnished with antiques.

"Things are rather confused," Mrs. Saunders said, clasping her hands and smiling delightfully in her best woman's magazine manner. "It's the cook's half-day off, and right after *she* left, the upstairs maid was taken ill and we had to pack her off to the doctor's in the truck. We couldn't take a chance on her being ill in one of the cars. They pick the most *inconvenient* times. Tea will be a *little* late. I hope you won't mind?"

"My tea won't be late," her husband said in his hearty voice. He moved toward an elaborately arranged tray of bottles and glasses. "No sir. What'll you have, Father, and you, Mr. Cosgrave?"

"I think I'll wait for tea," Father Cornish said.

"Scotch," Cosgrave said.

"That's right, Mr. Cosgrave, a man's drink. None of this bourbon and rye they use down here. Got to have their drinks sweet like a child's. Straight?"

"Soda, if you have it. If not, water."

"I hear you're from New York," Mr. Saunders said. "We're from close to there ourselves, Newark, New Jersey. But we don't go back much. This is the place. Nothing like it, finest country in the world. My wife's originally from it."

"It's pretty nice, all right."

"There, tell me if it's not strong enough."

"Just right."

148

"Father Cornish tells me you're engaged in the same sort of foolishness he is. You know what happened to your predecessor?" Mr. Saunders laughed.

Cosgrave smiled politely. He saw that Father Cornish and Mrs. Saunders were engaged in a fond, laughing conversation; he could not hear them. "I'll be careful," Cosgrave said, "and try to avoid accidents."

Mr. Saunders smoked a cigar thoughtfully for several moments before saying, "You're a pretty serious young man. Where'd you go to college?"

"Georgetown—and Harvard."

"That's it, then," Mr. Saunders said. "That's it, all right." He drank. "Harvard made you too serious. Now, you never find anyone from a Catholic college that's too serious. Georgetown's a good school all right, but I like Notre Dame. Naturally, of course. I went there. I was a personal friend of Knute Rockne's. There was a guy. When he died, they broke the mold."

"He must have been a good coach, all right."

"Good? Say, that guy was the best. But he was more'n that. Kind, tolerant—we learned things like that from just being near him."

"So I heard. He treated the Negroes on the team well, too, didn't he?"

"Niggers? Why, we never had no niggers out there. Where'd you hear that?"

"I can't just remember. Someplace around."

"Hell no, they never let no niggers into Notre Dame. I suppose if some of them out there that are like this screwball, Father Kane"—dropping his voice—"had their way, they'd be letting niggers in. But thank God the smarter priests know enough to keep them out." He grew light again, merry, the good host. "Why, you

149

don't go for that kind of stuff, I hope? By God, you'll have a hell of a tough time of it in this neck of the woods, if you do." He laughed. "Have another drink."

"I wonder where Jane is?" Mrs. Saunders' rising voice interrupted. "I'm relying on her to help me today, with the servants gone."

"Haven't seen her since lunch," Mr. Saunders said. "I never know where she is. She comes and goes."

"I understand she's not going back to school this fall," Father Cornish said.

"No." Mrs. Saunders' voice flattened. "Dr. McKay thought it best for her not to. She was to enter Trinity College, too. And she's only seventeen."

"Nerves," Mr. Saunders said broadly. "He says she has nerves. Damned if I know."

"Dr. McKay is something of a psychoanalyst, too." Mrs. Saunders' voice rose into high thoughtfulness. She nodded to let them know that she was implying more than she said. There was a moment of silence. Cosgrave looked out at the steady rain, the river beyond it now almost invisible as the light failed.

"Well, Helen, you might get Father some of that tea you're talking about," Mr. Saunders said.

As Mrs. Saunders rose there was the sound of a door closing and a girl in a raincoat came into the room through the kitchen.

"At last you're here, Jane," Mrs. Saunders said. "You come and go like the wind. Gone with the wind." She smiled at her guests, turning her head to do so.

"Where you been, Jane?" her father said. "Here, Father Cornish and this young man been waiting on you."

"How are you, Jane?" Father Cornish said, advancing

to meet her. "Haven't seen you in a long time." Close to her he smelled a scent which seemed familiar but which he could not place. Her answers to all of them were murmured, enough to be indistinct.

She was conscious principally of himself, Cosgrave saw. It was difficult to see her face clearly under the heavy, rubber, storm hat, even when she turned to acknowledge his introduction. She turned then to face her mother and so that her side was to Cosgrave, slipping the coat off her left shoulder, the nearest to Cosgrave. She held the slight strain of the position a moment, the breast, under the white of her dress, pressed out firmly and sharply. Then the coat slipped off and she was in white, the fair hair barely to her shoulder.

"Now, Jane, if you'd go in and start the tea, I won't have to leave Father Cornish."

"All right." She seemed a little breathless.

"Can Jane manage it alone?" Father Cornish laughed. "There are so few girls today in her walk of life who can do even such simple household tasks."

"Jane'll manage," her father said, heartily.

"Why—" Mrs. Saunders said at the same time.

"Maybe I can help," Cosgrave said. He had not intended to speak. He had even moved slightly toward the kitchen. "You people probably want to talk to Father Cornish."

"Why, it's not necessary," Mrs. Saunders said, with a half-hearted concern. She saw he was partly across the room.

It seemed to Cosgrave that he moved strangely, conscious and ashamed and unsure of his own intention. The girl had not spoken but gone before him into the kitchen. Cosgrave felt that tension of some sort passed from him when they were alone in the large, white room. It was just dark enough to light the globe overhead in the ceiling, but the girl didn't touch the switch. Cosgrave watched her, outlined against a window as she filled a kettle. She's terribly good-looking, he thought, and began to remember uneasily Mary Larkin in New York.

"Is there anything I can do?" he said. "Now that I'm here." His voice even sounded cracked a little, like a boy's, his last words an admission of guilt.

"You could carry a tray out to them, if you would."

He was near her as she put thin cups on a silver tray. She would not look at him, he saw, and yet each thing that she did seemed assured, even to the way that the scent she wore blended with her body-musk. She brushed him once as she turned but he knew it was accidental.

"Do you think you'll like it down here?" she said.

"I think so. It's a fine country."

"It is, all right. I was walking down to the river and back just before I came in."

"I'd like to have been with you. I haven't had much chance for walking yet. We've been driving over most of the County, it seems, seeing people."

"Did you like them?"

He was slightly surprised. "Most of them."

"You can take that out if you want to . . . and then come back."

He pushed through the swinging door with the tray and laid it on a table near Mrs. Saunders. "How is Jane making out?" Mrs. Saunders said.

"All right, I guess."

Father Cornish was grinning uncertainly, glad that

Cosgrave was making himself at home. He had been somewhat afraid of the boy's diffidence, he told himself. Down here, people were hearty. Right now, Mr. Saunders was laughing heartily at one of his own jokes.

Going into the kitchen again, Cosgrave saw that there was still no light there but that of the day's end. The girl had arranged cakes on a plate and was standing, perhaps pensively, watching the kettle. The gray light touched her cheekbones, darkened the delicate hollow in one cheek. The mouth, which he knew was full, seemed chiseled and more delicate. He went over to her without haste and put an arm around her. She didn't move or turn. There was, behind him, a whole convention of bright, meaningless things to say, but he could not think of any of them now.

He hesitated, until her hand touched his own. She was going to put it away, he was sure. Her fingers closed lightly on the hand. He turned and kissed her. The hand had been raising his own, had dropped it as he kissed her. She seemed assured again, even though his kiss apparently moved her more than his own experience told him it should. Her breasts against him were unbelievable, having the bright, hard, fruit-like quality of those imagined. Something that had the quality of pain, but was its opposite, spread in him. They heard Mrs. Saunders moving in the other room and they broke apart.

"You're very lovely," he said. His own graveness surprised him. It seemed to him that gravity had informed unduly this little thing of an embrace and kiss. It occurred to him that they had not smiled nor spoken.

"My Lord," Mrs. Saunders said as she came into the room; "I don't see how you children can see in this place." Her voice was trying to be pleasant.

The light blinded Cosgrave for a second. Then he saw Jane, still grave, watching the kettle, which had begun to boil. She looked virginal despite his memory of her breasts. He noticed dully and resentfully that Mrs. Saunders seemed disturbed out of proportion to the incident. He turned to the window. Looking for the now invisible rain, he started hearing it once more.

12

MELISSA MADDOX made them pancakes of water-ground meal and served them with country old ham the first cold morning. It was a Saturday, always a busy day for the priests, but only Cosgrave ate well. Like most priests, they rarely had an appetite in the morning. Cornish ate a pancake or two but Kane sat there, more pre-occupied than usual, even his coffee growing cold. Cornish urged him to eat but he didn't seem to hear and Cosgrave wondered how it must be at the Negro convent, where the nuns would be diffident about pressing food on Kane.

"I wonder when they'll be here?" Kane said. He had not heard his colleague speak to him. His voice was quick, low, somewhat husky.

"Soon," Cornish said. "They'll be on time. Their letters were very businesslike. Especially Miss Wellman's. Of course, she's Mrs. Marston in private life. Her husband will accompany her."

"You know something about them, John, don't you?" Kane said.

"Not personally. Except that they're probably liberals. The personnel is, of almost all those foundations interested in social work of any sort."

"You're sure of that?" Cornish said slowly. He had become very serious.

"Reasonably so."

Cornish strummed on the table and pouted judiciously. "You know, if I'd known that, I'd never have applied to them for more money. They sent me four hundred dollars for the first co-op without investigation, but now that I want money for an oyster-shucking house, they send people to investigate. And it's only a matter of seven hundred and fifty dollars."

"They probably just want the trip," Cosgrave said.

"No, John," Father Cornish said. "That's cynical. In this business we must be anything but that."

Kane saw John Cosgrave's mouth narrow, and rose to interrupt any possible reply. "I've got to get over to the Institute. The County agent is going to talk to the farming class this morning. I wish you luck."

"We'll probably be over there before the morning's out," Cornish said. "They said something about wanting to see the Institute if they had the time."

"Oh, sure," Kane said. "Maybe I can get some money out of them." It was hard to tell whether or not he was serious. "I hope our neighbors to the south behave. I've been expecting trouble." He was gone and to Cosgrave it was as though some quality like that of light had left the room.

Cornish said, "Laurence is a great man," rather absently.

"What did he mean?"

"Some colored people who live just off the Institute's land have been having domestic trouble."

Cosgrave looked at him but the priest was staring at the table. Melissa came in, as shapeless and ugly as an old boot. For some reason obscure to both of them, she had amused and pleased Cosgrave since he had come to the rectory. "You're getting better-looking all the time, Melissa," he said.

"Go 'way, young man. I wasn't that, even when I was your age."

Cosgrave laughed. The priest continued to stare almost grimly at the table. Melissa piled plates and started toward the kitchen door. Opening it with her foot, she said in her high voice, "You better get over to your shop, young man. My man, Havenner'll be needing gas this morning."

"I'll run," Cosgrave said.

"Just drive your car," she said, the door closing behind her.

"I hope things are in good order at the co-op," the priest said. "They'll be over there with me this morning, of course."

"I swept it yesterday. Everything's in shape." Cosgrave rose and shrugged into a leather jacket.

"I don't suppose," the priest said thoughtfully, "that we could get some late fall flowers, like dahlias or something, for the counter? Do you think that might impress them that it was—well, kind of different?"

"No," Cosgrave said from the door, and closed it.

Father Cornish blinked. Now, what could the boy have meant by being so abrupt? He was a very odd young man, indeed. But efficient. And the fishermen didn't dislike him. The priest rose, brushing the crumbs from his new, silk, clerical vest, given to him, like most of the things a Jesuit possesses. He was going to show the visitors that however isolated they might be here, they did not become slovenly. It was why he had put on the new vest. Like the British dressing for dinner in the jungle, he thought gravely.

Havenner Maddox was waiting with his boat tied to the wharf by the co-op when Cosgrave got there. Havenner was a slight, weathered, patient man. Loker Abell was with him, his somewhat negroid, lined face giving as usual the impression of a sardonicism that was permanent. John Mattingly had found it difficult to work steadily after his son's death and had laid up his boat. Loker had been working with Havenner Maddox on and off.

"Sorry I'm late," Cosgrave called across the wharf.

Havenner waved the apology off. He watched Cosgrave open the co-op's door and take the key to the gas pump off the wall. Havenner was vaguely pleased that anyone as well-spoken as Cosgrave should be working in the co-op. It made it, for Havenner, the right thing to belong to.

"How many?"

"'Bout five." Their tanks would hold up to forty gallons but they rarely took more than five.

"Nice morning, Loker, isn't it?" Cosgrave said to the quadroon. His pleasantness to Loker, as to all the Negroes, was a little forced. Loker knew it, but Cosgrave himself did not.

"Be a pretty evenin', too," Loker said. He was a relatively simple man, but his saturnine face made him appear deep and even sinister, annoying some white people. And yet, merely hunger and the thin scar had given the face its quality; he had less malice than most men.

"You'll be taking the poles down soon, won't you?" Cosgrave said.

"That's right," Havenner said. "The rock fish'll go to the bottom and the others go south soon. Ain't much use keeping the traps up then. You're getting to know this business."

"That's what I'm here for."

"It's a puzzle to we," Havenner said indistinctly.

Cosgrave didn't press the fisherman; he himself was reaching a time when he continually doubted his own intention. He thought, irritably, that it was a week since he had heard from Mary Larkin, and suddenly, strong enough to dismay him, a lust for Jane Saunders came to him.

"Anything else?" he said.

"I guess not," Havenner said. "We'll go trolling for rock some morning if you'd like, after the traps are down."

"Like to." Cosgrave wondered what Loker Abell would do after the fishing season. Go oystering probably, with Havenner. But someone said oysters were at twenty-five cents a bushel and that was hardly enough to give an oysterman a living. Cosgrave went along the wharf to cast off, but Loker had been holding the boat fast with a loose end of rope. He let it slip and the boat drifted off as Havenner turned the flywheel by hand.

"Ought to get yourself a little womanly companionship here," Loker said. "Must get right lonely at times."

Cosgrave smiled conventionally. The motor caught and the boat circled inshore and then headed out toward the Chesapeake. A haze lay on all of the big bay that could be seen, thickening with distance. Nostalgia for nothing he could easily identify came to Cosgrave, was confused with the annoyance over Mary's not writing, with the sudden, dying lust for Jane. With quick, mor-

159

bid clarity he could see them laughing at him in New York, could see the patronizing quirk of his economics professor at Georgetown. "Christ," he said aimlessly. He did not realize it was a way of prayer new to himself: offered as casually as a curse and out of what he could hardly know was already despair. He forgot about the visitors coming and lay down, tired, on the coils of new rope next the counter.

He drowsed, waking suddenly at the sound of a car approaching. It was not Father Cornish, but Jane. He could see her in a convertible with the top down. She was in white again although the day remained cool despite the strong sun. A pulse beat in his belly and a new confusion disturbed him: Mary Larkin was more beautiful than Jane but physical desire for Mary had been a thing vague, unspecific, and to be indefinitely postponed. There had been girls whom to look at was to want, to touch was to be on fire. But you were not in love with such girls . . . nor ever wanted to be.

So Jane, whom he had seen only once, puzzled him. She was good-looking—although he did not love her as he once thought he loved every good-looking girl he knew more than casually—and she came from a good, well-to-do family. She was someone to be kissed but not touched (the Georgetown classifications were unconscious but exact), and to be treated with a casual, slightly deferential, slightly humorous respect: a true convention.

So his lust was very disturbing to him.

He stood in the doorway of the co-op and did not go out to meet her. "And how are you today, Mr. Cosgrave?" she said as she came across the muddy ground. Her breathlessness, her bright young casualness and affectation of gaiety fooled only part of him. She was mocking him, another part knew, she was even mocking herself.

"I'm doing all right," he said. "Seems odd to see you in this place. I think of it as sort of having a sign—for men only."

She laughed. "I used to come over here." She stopped suddenly. "Dad wanted some hooks and didn't want to go up to Calverton. So he sent me over here. We're taking the boat out on the river after rock-fish. We'd like to have you if you could come along."

"I'd like to but this is pretty much an all-day job at this time of year. And we're expecting visitors."

There must be something bright and twitting to say. Almost all the girls he knew in Washington and New York could have said it; this one didn't even know the right answers. She was looking out over the creek toward the bay. Her skin was smooth and clear and he thought of how it would feel to the touch. Neither of them spoke and she did not look at him.

"You're very lovely," he said. He told himself that he was sorry for her. His remark seemed to amuse her secretly. "How about the fish-hooks?" she said.

"I'd forgot."

Going to get them in the co-op he felt an obscure pleasure. He tried to tell himself that she amused him, but he knew that wasn't the truth.

"They look pretty big," she said. He had not known she had followed him into the store.

"It's what the natives use. Rock have a big mouth."

"I guess six will be enough."

"Spoons would be better," he said. "That's what they use mostly around here for trolling."

"Dad likes to fish as they do in Florida, with strip-bait."

He turned from her, dropping the hooks slowly into a paper bag and noticing that his hands trembled slightly. He made a weak effort to convince himself that he should feel some sort of shame, and he thought of Mary Larkin: he had the romantic idea that the thought of her should fortify himself in a time like this. He thought that outside he would be all right and that he should go outside; he put his arms around Jane quietly and was kissing her. The breasts seemed like something sought after for a long time, so long that you didn't believe in them. He thought, too, that he'd better not see her any more: avoiding the occasion of sin, the theologians called it.

"Do you treat all your lady customers this way?"

"We don't have any. You're the first." He felt childish. He had managed to get as far as the doorway; it was as though his body were a drunk's, hard to handle. He would not see her any more. She was an occasion of sin and besides there was Mary to think of; he was practically engaged to her.

Father Cornish's car, followed by a large, expensive coupe, was coming over the ruts. That would help, Cosgrave thought. He walked with Jane to her car. He felt easier. He would be cooler, he thought, slightly formal, even.

"Goodbye."

"Goodbye. I hope it's what your father wanted."

"They'll do, I'm sure." She started the car and he came suddenly closer to it. "If you aren't going to be busy tonight," he said. "Perhaps we could go someplace."

"There's not many places to go, down here. But if you like, you can call, about eight."

He didn't speak as she drove away. He felt chagrined and stupid. The other cars came up. There were two men and a woman in the big car with the New York plates. Father Cornish was already out of his car, waiting for the others to alight, his wide grin fixed and ready, the heavy eyebrows arched.

"And this is it," Father Cornish said, one arm spread, as he led the visitors toward the co-op. The lady's head and one of the men's began to nod gravely.

"What a lovely setting!" the lady said.

"Ah," the priest said, "we chose it so. No need to have our little enterprise ugly simply because it's a commercial one. I was in the advertising business myself for a while."

The lady was looking at Cosgrave rather fixedly. She was in her early thirties, the men somewhat older. "And this is our manager," Father Cornish said, "Mr. Cosgrave, John Cosgrave. We're fortunate in having a university graduate for the position. Mrs. Marston, Mr. Marston, and Mr. Bowley, John."

They all nodded and Cosgrave noticed how well dressed they were and became conscious of his workshirt, leather jacket and lack of tie. "What a delightful place to work in!" Mrs. Marston said. "The view alone is priceless."

"Yes, it's nice," Cosgrave said.

"What university, Mr. Cosgrave?" Mr. Bowley said. He had a narrow, bony face, handsome in an inbred, delicate way. He wore on it the shadow of a severe contempt for the world. At times, it could be seen, Mr. Bowley thought of himself as something of an ascetic.

"Harvard—and Georgetown," Cosgrave said.

Mr. Bowley nodded, puzzled and therefore displeased. Father Cornish turned to Cosgrave almost as though struck. "I didn't know you'd gone to Harvard, John," he said in a flat, surprised voice. He caught himself too late and flushed. Both he and Cosgrave were startled to find that there was nothing to say.

"Ah, what volume of business?" Mr. Marston said in the brief, uneasy silence. He was holding, almost invisible in one hand, a small pad of paper and was prepared to write on it.

"Well," Father Cornish said and looked at Cosgrave.

"That's hardly a question we could answer properly now," Cosgrave said. "We've only functioned for a few weeks under our new incorporation. We've been sending about twenty-five hundred pounds of mixed fish a week to Baltimore. But the amount varies greatly. Last week there was twenty-seven hundred pounds, this week only about nineteen hundred. And it will probably decline steadily as the weather grows colder."

Mr. Marston wrote calmly. Mrs. Marston continued to look at Cosgrave. She was pretty except for the rather too firmly set mouth. "And now oysters?" Mr. Marston asked.

"Yes, they're bringing in some oysters already although the price is very low. And there'll be some late fall party-boat, that is pleasure, fishing for rock. We'll sell a little equipment and gasoline to the party-boats."

"Rock?" Mr. Bowley said.

"Striped-bass, they're called farther north."

"And the oysters?" Mr. Marston said.

"The price now is twenty-five cents a bushel—hardly enough to operate on. That's why we thought if we could open an oyster-shucking shed here we might be able to pay the local oystermen more than that."

"But why is the price so low?" Mr. Bowley's quiet, refined voice expressed annoyance.

"There are many factors," Father Cornish said, clearing his throat. Mrs. Marston stopped watching Cosgrave long enough to nod understandingly.

"So far as can be determined," Cosgrave said, "the main reason lies in the practice of certain wholesalers. Most oysters are sold to the consumer already shucked, that is, out of the shell. Wholesalers are required by law to wash the shucked oysters in fresh water to rid them of particles of shell. What the law overlooked is that if oysters are left long enough in fresh water and churned around in it by a blower or air-hose, they swell in size and it takes fewer to make a gallon. The wholesalers have taken advantage of this."

"But just how does that lower the price of oysters?" Mr. Marston said, almost petulant.

"What the wholesalers overlooked is that this process not only increases the size of the individual oyster but also makes it virtually tasteless. To put it briefly, people have stopped buying shucked oysters in the quantity they used to, because they are frequently tasteless."

"And so the price of oysters is down," Mr. Marston said, nodding and scribbling.

"Very interesting," Mrs. Marston said.

"Still," Mr. Bowley said, "I feel that this co-op and all similar enterprises should persevere. Even if the men have to go hungry to keep it functioning at that price for oysters. It is only by practicing a new asceticism that the revolution will be accomplished. Asceticism with a purpose." This last, of course, was for the priest's benefit. Mr. and Mrs. Marston both nodded, were nodding even before Mr. Bowley finished. Father Cornish grinned palely.

They inspected the store: the rope coils, the hooks, the kerosene drums, and anchors; the privy over the water (they thought it rather cute) and the ash oars, new and white, standing in a corner.

"You've pretty well eliminated all signs of the—ah—accident, Father," Mr. Marston said.

The priest nodded while trying to think of something to say, and in the silence Cosgrave saw that they were all looking at him. Mrs. Marston said, smiling, her mouth slightly pursed to show her deep appreciation of something, "I would imagine it would prey on you, Mr. Cosgrave?"

"No. I never think of it." He had not intended to boast; it was simply a spontaneous statement. There were, indeed, a number of things of which he was afraid: death was not one of them; mortal sin was. He saw that the others, even Cornish, had misunderstood him. Mr. Bowley even looked a little scornful and thoroughly unbelieving: after all there was a limit to asceticism.

They left Cosgrave and the co-op, then, the men saying cursory goodbyes, Mrs. Marston somewhat more warm; he was to be sure and call her when he next came to New York, and tell her about the co-op and how it was making out.

Cosgrave watched them go. Cornish drove off slowly ahead of them. Mr. Marston got in the car on the far side to drive. Mr. Bowley helped Mrs. Marston into the car on the side nearest the store. It was difficult to see Cosgrave against the dim interior of the store, even if they had been mindful of him. Cosgrave was rather surprised to see the ascetic Mr. Bowley run the edge of his forefinger delicately along the crease of Mrs. Marston's buttocks where they showed briefly through the tailored skirt as she got into the car. Mrs. Marston didn't seem to mind, even looked rather dewy and pleased as she settled herself next her husband in the seat of the coupe.

Cosgrave watched them drive off. He was obscurely annoyed. Then, despite himself, he began to grin slowly. There was pity in what had happened, too, but it would be longer before he knew that. It was something, now, that he could even see it as being a little funny.

As the two cars bearing Father Cornish and the visitors drove in on the winding dirt road that led from No. 5 to the Institute and its surrounding buildings, Laurence Kane was coming out of the convent. He had just finished his lunch, and three of the Negro nuns followed him through the door onto the little porch. He stood aside, holding the door open for them, and they swept past him on the way to the church, the two younger nuns moving as a pair in front of the mother superior. They were going to clean the altar and put fresh linen on it for Sunday's Mass, and after that supervise the children who would come to have Kane hear their confessions.

Mrs. Marston stood, or rather crouched, entranced, halfway out of the car. "Negro nuns!" she breathed. She was not unlike a half-starved ornithologist in the desert or jungle, coming upon a non-extinct dodo-bird.

"Yes," Father Cornish said, smiling nervously. "Their mother-house is in Baltimore."

"Very interesting," Mr. Marston said. "Amazing."

Mr. Bowley said nothing. He was again puzzled and therefore again displeased. The mother superior, a woman by no means light in color and with a bland, intelligent face, bowed and smiled to Father Cornish at a distance. The younger nuns, not very graceful, even in their robes and wimples, looked straight ahead.

Kane, his face pleased and a little eager, was coming toward his visitors. They noticed, principally, that his Roman collar was too big for him. He greeted them quietly, even with a kind of humility: pity was quick in him, too much so, perhaps, too frequently without apparent reason.

"We'd like to see everything, Father," Mr. Bowley said. He was more impressed by Kane than he had been by the other priest.

"We've heard about you and the Institute even in New York," Mrs. Marston said.

"Yes," Mr. Marston said, smiling falsely. He was not impressed.

"Probably some of my Brooklyn relatives popping off," Kane said. "I think it would be better if we looked at the church first. It will be full of children in a little while, whereas the Institute will be comparatively free this afternoon."

"Ah, I don't know that it will be necessary for us to see the church," Mr. Marston said. He had his tiny pad and pencil out.

"Of course. As you wish. It's functional and it is the Negroes' own, they helped pay for it. I just thought you might like to see it. Some people have thought it about the nicest Negro church in the country. A rather odd distinction." He laughed. He was more nervous than usual.

"By all means, let us see it," Mr. Bowley said.

"Yes, by all means," Mrs. Marston agreed.

In the church the nuns had begun their work on the altar. The two priests genuflected as they entered and the others stood, a bit awkwardly, the men's hats in their hands.

"The beams, you'll notice, are hand-trimmed," Father Cornish said.

"We hired local labor where we could," Kane said, "and the Negroes did the beams themselves."

"Just as in the days of the guilds," Mrs. Marston said. "It's wonderful, the people building their own church."

"Not all of it. They simply weren't that skilled." Kane went before them, explaining, as he had a hundred times before, how they had managed to have fine woodwork and masonry and a good altar by keeping them all simple —all but the tabernacle with its rich gold and bronze.

"It's too bad you have no stained glass," Mrs. Marston said. The light through the translucent yellow windows was not rich but it did not seem inappropriate.

"That will come later, we hope," Kane said. "We just weren't able to afford it." He wondered if it were possible that they could be interested in giving stained glass to the church. Not very well, he concluded. He really couldn't blame them. The Institute was a more obvious charity and right now more in need of money than the church.

"The benches were made at an orphanage," Kane went on. He knew it by rote, so often had he gone over it for assorted monsignori and their lay equivalents. Most churchmen, he knew without resentment, considered him a kind of clerical clown, too intense, zealous, lacking prudence—as they put it—a bit of a goof, a gatherer of old clothes. These present visitors were uneasy, he saw, but they did not consider him unduly foolish for a priest. He was grateful.

Mr. Marston had continued to write. He saw that his wife and Mr. Bowley were being taken in by this Father Kane. But he would not be taken in, he knew. As they were preparing to leave the church, he glanced around the walls over the stations of the cross, and near a beam caught the dull reflection of the small window Kane had put in the wall of his room just above the floor so that he could make a 'visit' as he rose in the morning. Mr. Marston scribbled quickly. "Concealed peephole high in wall for spying on Negroes at rites." He smiled, felt pleased and even relaxed a little. There wasn't much he missed, he told himself again.

Father Cornish had to leave now to hear the afternoon confessions at St. Patrick's. So that Kane was alone with the visitors when they went over to the Institute. Samuel Raife, quiet, assured, even a little distinguished in his one good suit, came down the steps to meet them. He had been waiting there for some time.

"And this is our dean," Kane said. "The Dean of the Institute, Mr. Raife."

Some of the Negro's own bright gravity seemed to communicate itself to all of them, even Mr. Marston. Mr. Marston was impressed, Kane saw; it made the priest feel better to know this. After the amenities, the Negro said, "I'd like to show them the new domestic science room first, Father. Don't you think that would be best?"

Mr. Marston scribbled, "Subject to priest."

Kane glanced nervously toward a cabin to the south, just off the Institute's land.

"I th-think so, Samuel," Kane said. "It's not really

new," he explained to the others. "It's just that we've sort of refurnished it. New kitchen chairs and fresh oil-cloth on the tables and so on." He hesitated, prepared to smile, feeling tired and stupid. Something appalled them, he saw.

They went downstairs and along a slightly damp corridor. The windows of the domestic science room were high and most of the room itself below the ground. The somewhat old chairs and tables were freshly painted white. Some wooden cupboards and closets were here and there along the wall under the windows; and just off the room they could see a narrower room with two sinks and two kerosene, three-burner stoves in it.

Mrs. Marston blinked brightly and opened her mouth to speak. To her surprise no words came out. Then she tried to think of something to say, but finally closed her mouth and smiled, a bit foolishly.

Mr. Marston said slowly, "Ah, there being no gas down here, I daresay you could use electric stoves. I notice you have current."

"Yes, we have," Kane said. "But it wouldn't do to have electric stoves. At least not more than one. You see, the only chance they'd have to cook with electricity would be if they were working for some of the summer people. In their own homes they use wood. The oil stoves here might even be called an optimistic experiment." He smiled awkwardly. Kane saw that they were all, except perhaps Mr. Marston, embarrassed. He thought it might be due to his own stuttering and dullness and so tried to shift the burden of the talk to Samuel.

They went laboriously through the cold building. Mold showed on the wall of two classrooms. A door which Samuel jerked hard to open almost hit them as the upper hinge pulled out of the wood.

"I'd forgotten about that," Samuel said. "Our best wood-workers are up in Calvert County shucking oysters but I meant to get someone to do it. I guess I'll do it myself." He had not been fazed by anything, the mold or the building's chill. It was the school of which he was dean. He spoke of it quietly, even cheerfully, and of what he and Kane and the two other Negro teachers hoped to do. He was definitely optimistic and he had not noticed particularly his visitors' faces.

Mr. and Mrs. Marston and Mr. Bowley, even Kane, for the moment, found it depressing. "Very discouraging" was the way Mr. Marston put it later in his report. In that cold building, Mr. Bowley, looking at the bright face of love where it showed occasionally in outline through the back of Mrs. Marston's well- (Oh, very well!) tailored skirt, was not moved to caress it, even though the proximity of Mr. Marston and his pad and pencil almost moved him to do so.

There was a lull in speech, seemingly in time. In it, Samuel's voice grew uncertain. They went outside on the little stone porch and in the cold air Mr. Bowley sighed audibly.

Outside, it was even more discouraging. The Negro shanty Kane had been worried over was about three or four hundred feet to the south, just off the Institute's land. As they stood on the rear porch overlooking the long slope to the Potomac, a Negro man ran out of the shanty. He was followed by another Negro carrying a shotgun. The first Negro flung himself on the ground, kneeling, his arms covering his head which was touching the ground. (For all the world like the female's position in *coitus a tergo*, Mr. Bowley later thought.) The second Negro, without hesitation placed the shotgun's muzzle something less than a foot from the kneeling man and pulled the trigger. The report was very loud in the stillness. The kneeling figure moved slightly forward but did not otherwise alter its position except to relax almost imperceptibly. From the steps of the Institute the visitors could see that the wound was quite a large and serious one. The Negro with the gun stood stupidly near by, the gun, loosely held, pointing toward the ground. The bright sun showed the colors of his faded clothing.

On the porch, Mrs. Marston collapsed. Mr. Bowley and her husband held her, and Mr. Bowley, somehow—although later he forgot it—turned to look for Kane. He saw him running awkwardly toward the two Negroes. Watching Kane the visitors did not see Samuel Raife near them. The dean had not moved and was crying quietly as he, too, watched Kane running, running in the night.

And now the light failing on the river. The sky over the Nomini Cliffs was still bright, but the cliffs themselves in shadow. Overhead the sky had clouded solidly as the afternoon wore on, so that the bright patch above Virginia was like the mouth of a cave. Cosgrave walked toward the Institute, after parking his car near the church. The light to the west was before him. He wasn't quite sure why he had come. It was more than morbid curiosity, he felt, and perhaps it was.

There were no people in sight near any of the buildings except the shanty. There, Bernard Hebb, the tall, yellow man who ran the Institute's farm, stood watching several other Negroes putting the dead man into a dowdy-looking hearse while a white man stood distastefully by and watched. The body had stiffened in its kneeling position. Kane had so feared what the "law" might do to the Negroes that he had not straightened the figure out, but given conditional absolution to Peter Jurdan, already dead when the priest had reached him.

The white man and the Negroes, all but Bernard Hebb, got into the hearse and drove away just as Cosgrave passed the Institute and moved toward the shanty. Bernard Hebb saw him coming and walked a little way to meet him. They knew each other slightly. Cosgrave saw there was something at once heroic and pathetic about Mr. Hebb in his leather jacket and cheap breeches, about the lined and sorrowing face.

"Good evening, Mr. Hebb."

"Evenin'. Evenin', young man. This is a mighty bad business, ain't it?"

"I guess any killing is, Mr. Hebb. What happened? I mean what made the other fellow kill him?"

"Woman trouble. That usually the case. Or drinkin'. Too much drinkin'. Father Kane, he know about it, but he was kept away from them by them visitors coming."

"The wife of one of them, I suppose, was responsible."

"No. Girl just living with the one that did the shooting. Other man were getting three dollars a week, work for Mr. Saunders. Then he lose the job and they can't eat, so the girl she come over here to live with another man got a boat he go crabbing in."

"Jesus Christ."

Bernard Hebb looked at him sharply. "You oughtn't talk so, young man. You working for the Church and all."

"I know. I'm sorry. I'm not exactly working for the Church, but I still oughtn't to say it."

Bernard Hebb looked away, past the Institute. A strange car was coming over the bad road toward the house. "Sheriff's man coming, I guess," he said.

"What for? I'd heard the State's Attorney was here already."

"He here and gone. They coming now get that boy inside what done the killing."

"Inside? Who's with him?"

"No one. He all alone."

"Why doesn't he escape?"

"Where he go? Water on three sides of this county. Oyster police boats get anyone on river or bay. He too frightened to move. No money. No shells, even. He used last shell to kill that other boy."

The car, a cheap, black sedan, pulled up and Jimmy Gordon, the bartender in Raley's Bar, got out, carrying an automatic shotgun. Another, bigger man stayed in the car and leveled his gun at the shanty. They were both dressed in hunting clothes and were wearing tarnished deputy sheriff badges on their coats.

"Hello, Cosgrave," Gordon said. "How are your niggers doing?"

"I wouldn't know."

Bernard Hebb, without having moved, seemed to have retired. His yellow face was like stone. Gordon faced the shanty, his gun loosely hooked in his left arm. "Come out of there, you nigger son of a bitch before I fill that goddam shack full of buckshot."

"Yes, suh," a dead voice said. "I's comin'."

The rickety door opened slowly outward and Willie Washington in dirty blue shirt and patched trousers came out. His toes showed through one shoe and his eyes seemed rimmed with blood.

"Get in that car, you bastard, and if you move I'll blow the Jesus out of you."

"Yes suh." He moved, shuffling to keep his shoes on, toward the car. His hands were half-raised and his mouth was open. No one could have said how old he was.

"I thought it was customary to read a warrant?" Cosgrave said.

"By God, another goddam nigger-lover. All right, I'll read the warrant." Gordon turned to the Negro already in the back seat of the car and read the warrant in a loud, ironic voice. Then he turned to Cosgrave. "Satisfied?"

Embarrassed, Cosgrave didn't speak.

"Goddam, Pete," Gordon said to the big, white man in the car, "you'd think some people'd learn to mind their own business."

"You sure God would," Pete said, laughing.

"Well, I'll see you, old man," Gordon mimicked to Cosgrave.

"Yeah, in church."

Gordon colored slightly. As he turned the car to drive away, Cosgrave could see the St. Christopher medal nailed to the dashboard. For some reason he remembered the words, often in French, on such medals. *Regardez St. Christophe. Puis va-t'en rassuré.* Watching them go away, Cosgrave said, absently, "Nice people."

"I don't want to talk, young man," Bernard Hebb said. He walked toward his house on the other side of the Institute.

Driving back to the rectory, Cosgrave finally decided not to see Jane that night. It had been a bad day for

176

him. He told himself, romantically perhaps, that he knew lust when he saw it, and perhaps he was right. Bothered by the thought of Jane, earlier in the day he had phoned Mary Larkin long distance, thinking that would help. She had told him, principally, that she was going to the St. Vincent's Hospital dance that night, and she hoped he wouldn't mind that Jimmy Haggerty was taking her. No, he had told her, he didn't mind.

No one was at the rectory when Cosgrave reached there. Kane was in Calverton seeing about a lawyer, Cornish had had an unexpected visit from relatives in Washington and had taken them down the road toward Point Lookout for dinner. They would both be back in time for Saturday night confessions, Cosgrave knew, and wondered why he thought of that now. Melissa had laid a cold supper on the table and Cosgrave ate a little, hardly tasting it.

They had a very small chapel in the rectory and permission to keep the Host there. Every evening, after dinner, the two priests and Cosgrave made a brief 'visit' in the chapel. Cosgrave entered it alone now after his supper. It was difficult to pray. He remained there longer than usual, his face in his hands. The thin, red light from the sanctuary lamp washed over him, picking out his knuckles, the angles of his face and clothed body. It was fortunate that he could not stand aside and see himself. His self-pity and unconscious pride would have been boundless: Such a sad brave figure, he would have thought: the young man struggling against the bonds of the flesh.

He rose presently and went upstairs. The old-fashioned phone was fixed to the wood of the hallway. Turning the crank on the side of the box, and then waiting to hear her speak, he felt the tension grow in him. So that he could scarcely talk when he did hear her voice.

"Hello, how are you? This is John Cosgrave."

"I'm all right. I didn't expect to hear from you so soon before you came over."

"Yes," he said and laughed nervously. Well, say it. It was, he discovered, not easy to say. There was an awkward silence. "I don't know whether I can get over tonight or not." He had not intended it to sound so weak.

"That's too bad," she said, quietly, after a moment.

"Something's wrong with the car—carburetor, I think —and I can't get it started. And Father Kane and Father Cornish are away, so I can't borrow one of theirs."

"They'll be back soon for confessions, won't they?"

"I suppose so." He hadn't thought of that. "But they'll likely need their cars later."

"I could come over for you," she said. "You should have remembered."

He wondered if he had. "I didn't want to ask you," he said.

"Silly, I'll be over in a little while."

He noticed vaguely that they were as familiar as though they had known each other longer than they had. He hung up and sighed. Like all young men, he felt unconsciously that the sigh justified himself, signifying that his intention, at least, had been good. He dressed slowly in his bare room with its iron bed. A Georgetown pennant or two, Father Cornish had suggested, to brighten it a bit. Cosgrave had wanted nothing for it. The mood of an ancient asceticism had been on him; it had been a little while, even, before he placed Mary Larkin's picture on the plain, painted dresser.

He looked at the photograph now, the shapely mouth

178

drawn out almost to straightness—like his own when in training for racing, he noticed with sudden shock; the fine large eyes that—oh, yes—understood; the delicately tilted nose; the dark, silken hair. He felt tired again, and now dressed, hesitated dramatically. He was aware of the pose but not of the reason for it, of his own false and heroic intention.

The front doorbell rang. It was too soon for Jane, probably it was one of the parishioners. He went down and opened the door. A tall, homely girl stood there, hatless, and asked if Kane were in.

"Everyone's away," Cosgrave told her. "You may be able to find him later at the Negro church, hearing confessions. It's been a tough day down here."

"I've heard," the girl said. "You're Mr. Cosgrave, aren't you?"

"Yes. Won't you come in. I'm leaving shortly, but—"

"All right. I'm Rose Camalier. Father Kane has spoken of you."

"Nothing good, I imagine. You teach, don't you, up-county?"

"That's right. I thought we might talk about co-ops sometime."

"I'd like to. It's too bad about tonight. If I'd known—"

"I phoned but there wasn't any answer," she said.

"I guess Melissa didn't hear the phone from the kitchen. Won't you sit down? One of them ought to be home soon."

They had gone into the little parlor across from the chapel. In the granular light from the single electric bulb, Cosgrave saw how plain she was, her pleasing gravity. It was as easy to talk to her as to a man. An odd gratitude came to him that she should have come now, in this time. He felt easy, even sure.

"It's so good of someone like yourself to come down and try to help us here in the County," Rose said. "Our intelligent young people all seem to go off to the cities."

"I'm really sorry to have to go out," Cosgrave repeated. "It's a pleasure to find others down here interested in co-operatives."

"We want to talk about it in the schools," Rose said, "but we hardly know how to begin. We—"

An auto-horn sounded outside. Cosgrave started slightly. "I'm sorry to have to leave you," he said, rising. "One of them should be back soon. I—we—"

He left her there, Rose seemingly as confused as he. Outside, the southwest wind was blowing. It was softer than it had been during the day. He got into the coupe without speaking. It was warmer there and Jane's scent was a sudden delight. He was afraid to look at her in the dim light from the dashboard.

"Where do you want to go? We could go up to Calverton to a show."

"It's too far," she said. "I don't want to go to one."

"Whatever you say." He felt that somehow, saying this, he had implied more than he intended. Her face assumed an odd smile, he saw, but thought it might be the uncertain light. She was looking ahead as she drove out between the holly trees to the Three-Notch Road.

"We could go to Point Lookout and see the light," she said. "And the beach at Scotland. The Chesapeake is like the ocean there."

He saw it was inevitable, and he knew that a priest, bluntly and rightly, would have counseled him to leave Jane now, as simply as that. But the picture of himself fleeing was too ridiculous. He didn't speak as she turned the car south, and was still silent as they passed the junction with No. 5, the last chance to go north and to Calverton. The wind came across the bull-pine and the cedars. They could smell the trees faintly, even in the closed car.

"You're quiet tonight," she said after they had passed the side-road to Scotland.

"It's been a tough day," he said.

"That killing was terrible, I know. The boy used to work for papa."

That was only part of it, but there was no way of telling her, although he wanted to tell her. From the Scotland turn-off the road was bad. It was full of holes and ran close to the shore. They drove slowly over it, the sound of small waves on their left. The light at Point Lookout hung motionless over the joining of the river and the bay. Nothing moved in its radiance, and when Jane cut the motor they could not even hear the waves on the bay but only the faint, dull hurry of the river. The flatness of the land, the circle of moony light could make them think they were on an island.

"Saturday night," Cosgrave said. "You'd think there'd be more visitors here to admire the view." For a little while he could stand apart in spirit and be ironic. He felt both pity and scorn for himself. "The view is certainly terrific," he said. "Wouldn't you say so?"

She looked at him, not knowing whether to smile or not. He saw that she was young—it was always an effort for him to think of her as such—and that irony was still beyond her. "A very pitiful lady, very young." He didn't know why Dante's words should occur to him now.

To the left and south he could see the lights of boats on the Chesapeake. In that stillness, on the pallid edge of light, the noise of waters was at once subtle and urgent. He had begun to shiver involuntarily. When he kissed her she was not responsive, but moving a little away from him, lay back against his arm, looking at him. She appeared to be faintly amused.

It seemed to him that his hands had a separate volition and, even, intelligence. They were devious and sly, tentative as his mind had never been. So that she was amused by him, he saw, but not unkindly. "I like you," she said. "I like you a lot."

What clarity his thought still possessed was gone now. He was not aware of any stages between love and lust. If she 'liked' him, why? He did not like her. Or did he? Anger at himself was sullen and he turned from her a little.

She began to drive again, back over the bad road along the shore. In the moonlight breaking through the scud he could see, at the junction with the Scotland road, the monument to the Confederate soldiers who had died in the prison camp. Their deaths were suddenly a burden upon him; he prayed for them. He was calmer, he thought. The skirt of her polo coat was turned back and he saw that she wore white again, a sort of white or very light-gray tweed. He had misjudged her, he told himself with relief; she was young and fresh and not knowing, unconscious of the effect of some of the things she did.

A kind of joy beat through him, an indescribable relief. It was he who had been wrong, he knew now, his own lustful mind seeing slyness where there was none. He was glad that he knew her, even if he did not love her. She had turned right at the monument, instead of left and up the main road. The road to Scotland Beach was worse than that going to the Point, and all but impassable. Quite near them a wave broke and the water flooded under the car in a dark, thin sheet.

"The tide's coming in," she said.

She turned the car onto the sand and they got out. The wind blew brokenly from the southwest, over the land. Crab-grass had gathered in thick lumps and ridges on the shore. The few, old wooden hotels and boarding houses behind them were closed for the winter and blank.

"It's lovely here," he said.

"I like it. I come here alone at times, but it's better with someone."

He was disturbed and turned to her in the lee of a small boathouse. She had loosened the belt of the button-less coat, and he slipped his hands around her waist under the coat. It was good, kissing her like that, the wind to either side of them, they as if in an island of quietness and stillness near the weathered little house. Lust was gone, he felt sure. Then he knew he had be-trayed himself. Her hands touched him incredibly and he gasped. In anger that was only the simulation of itself he bent her to the sand. His hands were again not his own and he saw that everything she wore was white. He did not seem awkward to himself because she had anticipated that.

"I'm sorry," he said, presently.

She didn't speak. He moved slightly and she said, "You're a good boy. You're very nice." Her voice was heavy and slurred a little.

"What do you mean?"

"You're not angry—or disgusted."

"With myself I am."

"But not with me?"

He hesitated. "No. Why should I be?"

"I don't know. Some boys are—for a while."

Jealousy wrenched at his guts like pain, and passed. His body was too quiet for it to stay. "You mean— mortal sin?" he said.

"No." She shook her head once. "It seems something else. Not sin. They don't think of that. It seems dirty to them. I don't know why."

He knew why. He knew all their Jansenistic history, from Cromwell in Ireland to a boy named Haggerty in a nigger whorehouse in Washington. The same Haggerty that was with Mary Larkin tonight and would be afraid to touch her breasts, not because it was a sin but because she wasn't 'that kind of a girl.'

Cosgrave stood up and turned away from her for a moment. The wind touched the moisture at his temples. There was no disgust; he felt relaxed and clean. He had committed a mortal sin, but that was something else. That was intellectual. He did not confuse the sin with a sense of defilement or physical disgust. Grace would always work strangely in him. Of his time and of his people he was one of the lucky ones.

They drove in silence back to the rectory and he got out of the car, turning to face her through the open window of the closed door. He didn't know what to say.

"Call me soon, John."

"I'd like to," he said, "but do you think we should?"

She turned from him and didn't speak. She might have

been crying; he didn't know, as she drove away. Watching the car-lights move slowly between the two rows of holly trees, he began to want her again. "Christ!" he said. The only light in the rectory was the red sanctuary lamp in the chapel. He went toward it wearily, a little hopefully.

13

IN the morning Cosgrave went to late Mass at the church near Great Mills. He hesitated to go to Mass at St. Patrick's. It had occurred to him that, since he had been in the habit of receiving Communion each Sunday, Father Cornish was not above asking him—with fine jocularity, to be sure—why he had not been to Communion that morning.

The church at Great Mills, like most of those in the County, was in bad repair. It needed paint within and without, and many of the long, narrow strips of wood that formed the ceiling were loose at one end and hung down close to the heads of the parishioners when they stood. Cosgrave had never been to any church in the County except St. Patrick's. Because of the proximity of Kane's church, no Negroes attended St. Patrick's. Now, a little surprised at the crowd of people in a church in such poor condition, Cosgrave did not at first notice how the Negroes were segregated in the last four pews.

The Mass went through its opening movements: Christ prayed and broke into a bloody sweat: a friend betrayed Him and another friend did violence to defend Him: only a little later the violent one also betrayed Him: Pilate quibbled: a bearded king and his women laughed while thorns were pressed about His head.

The priest paused in the Mass and turned to read in English the day's gospel. After that he gave his sermon. Like many of the priests sent down to the County by the provincial, he was not a well man. In his case, the strenuous life of a Jesuit had been a little more than even the sacrament of Holy Orders could cope with. Like most nervous priests he inclined to err on the side of zeal rather than that of prudence.

"Yesterday," the priest began, after the announcements, "there was a very unfortunate accident downcounty. There will be a tendency to blame all colored people for the faults of a few." The priest paused and Cosgrave, standing halfway down a side aisle in the crowded church, heard a man near by whisper, "There goes the son of a bitch again."

"Now, none of you have to be told," the priest went on, "that the lot of the colored people down here is an unfortunate one. You have helped to make it so yourselves."

The congregation was very still; no one even coughed. Cosgrave, himself suddenly uneasy, turned and saw the Negroes, sharply segregated in the last four pews. For a little while after, he could not hear what the priest was saying.

"Many of you," he finally heard the priest say, "do not know what the Doctrine of the Mystical Body of Christ is. When Christ said, 'I am the Vine, you are the branches,' He meant that we were all part of one another in Him."

"Sounds like a lot of crap," someone near Cosgrave whispered. He turned slightly and saw the man who had been with Jimmy Gordon yesterday. Cosgrave remembered his being pointed out before: Pete Calvert,

187

a game-hog who made his living by petty lumbering operations.

"This being so," the priest said, "we cannot hurt anyone else, regardless of race, creed, or color, without hurting ourselves in a very real way. We cannot hurt anyone and still continue to call ourselves Christians. Therefore—"

In his own anger, Cosgrave could still feel some embarrassment. He saw that this priest and Cornish believed in bluntness as Kane believed in subtlety. And he knew finally that he was living among strange people. And yet, he wondered, were they more strange than the puritanical Irish of New York and Georgetown, than the Catholic manufacturer he knew, who wouldn't have thought of taking a mistress, who had a large family, and who paid his workmen sixteen dollars a week? Who were the Christians? Cosgrave wondered, and grew a little sick. And what was a Catholic? He remembered what a man at Harvard had said, in indifferent jest, "A Catholic is someone who thinks that the only two mortal sins are sex and murder, in that order."

The Mass had reached the Consecration before Cosgrave could follow it again. He wanted to receive Communion and watched, a little jealously, those others who went to the rail. There were no Negroes at Communion. And then he saw them coming down the aisle, again following the whites.

He had to go outside the church, bumping into people as he went toward the door. Near his own car he stood a moment to steady himself before driving. Jane Saunders came out of the church and hurried toward him. "You looked bad going out," she said. "I thought you might be sick."

He shook his head. "I know," Jane said, "you're worrying about that Negro that killed a man yesterday. You don't have to. They never hang anyone for murder in this County. They just put the Negroes away and the whites hardly ever get anything much, because they've always got relatives on the jury."

"I'm all right," he said. He stared outwardly. With her near him, any girl solicitous, he could feel heroic. "I was just thinking," he said, "of a conceit someone expressed once: supposing God is a Negro?"

He heard her gasp. "Oh, you're strange!" He turned slightly away.

"I tried to get here early," she said, "to go to Confession before Mass so that I could go to Communion. But I was late."

"You're a good girl," he said. "I like you a great deal. Maybe—maybe we could see each other and not—"

She looked up quickly. "Oh, please. I love you."

He felt tears come behind his eyes. "No, you don't. You just think so." They couldn't speak or look at each other. He heard the people begin to come out of the church. "Goodbye," he said and opened the door of his car.

"Goodbye."

He saw Mrs. Saunders, her face puzzled, coming toward them, and he got into the car and drove away.

The Bible in George Blair's office had dust on it. He noticed it as he drew the book from the case, and supposed that somebody could have wangled a parable out of the dust on the Bible. He was just plain lazy, he told himself again. He drew less satisfaction out of telling himself this than he ever had before. Something cold had fastened in his mind and would not go away. He had always been proud of his laziness, of people's saying he could be a great man if he really wanted to be, if he didn't prefer quietness, if his son hadn't died. Lately, the truth had come to him, quietly. He had been reading Sigrid Undset and she had written that of the seven deadly sins, the deadliest was sloth. He had sat still for some time after reading that. It explained his whole life to him, he had realized; why he hadn't even wanted to be Attorney General of the United States. Not modesty, not indifference, not even a real liking for the horses. The name of the thing was sloth. The word had been in him ever since. He could not justify himself; there was no argument. It was simple as could be. And always he had worried over the things like being honest, like being faithful to Martha and having a good name: with sloth in him like a cancer he would never know about until he was too old to fight it.

They still came to him, though, when they were troubled, he knew. Two of the new priests down-county had been running off at the mouth about the niggers again, and people were disturbed and angry. Some had spoken to him about it and more would, he knew. So he would refute the priests out of their own book, the Bible. The older priests down here knew better than to talk about the niggers. He would put the new ones in their place by giving some of the boys quotations to use on them. There were no elections this year but next year he wanted to be in the driver's seat again and the boys would remember what a clever fellow he had been to give them quotations to confound the priests. He wanted to turn that damn cuckold, Dabson Morgan, out of office and put Mr. Dave Camalier in. Next year.

He would start now by helping the boys get back at the new priests. Some people were always trying to take advantage of the Church, he knew, to advance their crackpot theories about race and whatnot.

Someone knocked on his door and he called, "Come in." John Cosgrave entered, dressed in rough clothes. Blair stood up. He was rather pleased. People were starting to come to him again. "How are you, Mr. Cosgrave? Thought you'd be up long before now to see me. How are things down your way?"

"We've been pretty busy. Right now, though, we're sort of between oystering and fishing, and I managed to take the afternoon off and come up here to buy a shirt or two."

"You won't find much in this town fit to wear. Sit down. You look thin, as though they haven't been treating you right down there."

"Oh, we eat well. Better than I expected to in a rectory." They both laughed.

"Sit down," Blair said, when the young man remained awkwardly standing. "I don't see many intelligent people." He grinned expectantly, always avid for the quick response to his flattery.

"Thanks." Cosgrave sat down laboriously, as though he were older and heavier than he was. His glance evaded the older man's, and Blair noticed this.

"How is all that foolishness of yours and Father Cornish's doing down there?"

"It's getting along. We might have an oyster-shucking house before winter sets in. But I guess you know that."

"No, I didn't. Some of those foolish northerners giving it to you, I suppose?" He grinned to show he was in jest; well, mostly in jest. Cosgrave noticed how like

191

a death's-head the face seemed when it grinned. He felt sorry for George Blair and yet it was so hard to judge the man: you never knew whether he was a faker or someone so mysteriously tragic as to be greatly pitied.

"Something like that," Cosgrave said. "It'll give some of the colored people work without their having to go up to Calvert or Anne Arundel Counties."

"What about the whites?" Blair said, some trace of the grin remaining. "By the Lord, the world and this County in particular are run for the benefit of white people." He let the smile come to his face; it was half-quizzical, half-defiant, almost wholly designed; it was to let the young man know he wasn't serious. Well, not entirely so.

"The whites will have a local place to shuck and market their oysters for them without dealing with a middleman. That's a considerable advantage to them. But that's a terrible thing for you to say. God made the world for all people."

" 'And fixed the bounds of their habitation'!" Blair said triumphantly. "I and Lincoln. We both quote it. Right out of the Bible." He laughed happily and taking off his pince-nez polished them with a clean handkerchief. "By the Lord, you're a holy terror, young man. I don't know that I'm either seeing or hearing you right when you say things like that. Georgetown never taught any of the people I know anything like that when they went there."

It occurred suddenly to Cosgrave that he might be something of a hypocrite himself; here he had committed fornication and he was moralizing to someone else. "What I came up for," he said, "was to ask you if you couldn't say something in the *Torch* about—well, more

192

amity between the races. One or two priests in the lower County haven't been very diplomatic and there seems to be an increase of bad feeling." He paused, suddenly mindful of how awkward, how inadequate the formal phrases were.

"They certainly haven't been diplomatic," Blair said. "But it's not those we ought to be afraid of. It's people like Father Kane," he said pleasantly. "He never pops off. He just goes about his business, giving the niggers down there ideas, and first thing we know they'll be running the place."

Despair in Cosgrave became anger. "You're not really serious, Mr. Blair? You couldn't be and remain a Christian. Why—"

"Oh, yes, I could. I believe in individual interpretation of the Bible. That's where the Protestants were smart. Look, let me show you, right here now." He only had to turn to what he had just looked up. "Genesis, the ninth chapter, the twenty-fifth verse, 'Cursed be Chanaan, a servant of servants shall he be unto his brethren.' Now, we all know Chanaan was the son of Cham, and all the niggers descend from Cham. So what more do you want? It's right there in the Bible."

"I've never heard that that was the Church's interpretation of that particular passage—"

"It's mine, by God!"

"And even if it were to be interpreted literally it would give us no license to abuse and injure Negroes. St. Ambrose or one of the theologians says that servants, in the order of our obligations to those close to us, are to be classed with such relatives as cousins, aunts, nieces, and so on."

"Very vague," George Blair said, stretching. "Very

193

vague. Anyhow, who said anything about abusing them? I guess a few people do, but I don't. Why—"

"How about some of the select citizens around here who pay them three dollars a week?"

"Hell's fire, man, a nigger can live on fifty cents a day. And Mrs. Dabson Morgan and Mrs. Lee Raley, the banker's wife, they pay them two and a half a week. 'Course, Mrs. Morgan isn't much good personally, but Mrs. Raley's a right respectable woman."

"She'll be in Purgatory so long she'll smell like smoked beef."

Blair laughed, a little too loudly. "I'd say you sounded like Savonarola except you have a sense of humor." More quietly, he added, "Offhand, I'd say it'll save you, maybe save your life."

"You're just trying to change the subject."

"By the Lord, you're all right, even if you are a nigger-lover. Isn't anyone sassed me back in years around these parts." His laughter became the grin again. He wondered if Charles would have grown up so? Charles had been a good boy. Charles Carroll Blair.

Cosgrave sat there, seeing that something moving went on in the other man. He himself was puzzled but principally weary. The past ten days had had their own desperation: he wanting badly to go to Jane and not going because she was the occasion of sin. He had written to Mary almost every day, and heard from her once. And Kane, to whose serenity he usually looked for an example, had been oddly strained and silent at their meals together while Cornish talked on. On his own grounds, with his own weapons, Cornish was undefeatable, Cosgrave realized. He wondered again whether Cornish was brave or ignorant. His lip turned oddly as he remembered when he had first begun, as an under-graduate, to realize how many other things were called courage. In one of the flashes of insight that character-ized his thinking, he knew finally that he did not like Cornish.

George Blair misunderstood the change in Cosgrave's expression. "Come, come," he said. "We mustn't quar-rel. You'll see it the way we do, after you've been here a while. Right now, let's forget about it. I'd like to buy you a drink. What do you say? We'll go over to John Raley's and play a game or two of pitch. Or don't you know how to play it?"

"I've been to Raley's several times and I've seen them playing it down-county. We call it High-Low-Jack-and-the-Game farther north."

"The same," Blair said, putting on a topcoat. "Just as soon kill time at that as at anything else."

Cosgrave turned from the death's-head grin and went out the door. Leaves from the beech trees were caught in the yews that spread in front of the house of Blair's mother, and more leaves blew aimlessly on the court-house lawn. The fox-hounds, Patuxent and Charles County, looked mournfully at the men leaning slightly against the wind, looked with dulled hope; it was too late in the day to begin the running of foxes. Just west of town, a thin, early wedge of ducks flew over St. Clement's Bay. Early, Blair thought, seeing them, but scaup were always the earliest down here; not this early, though. He would have to take the boy ducking, get his mind off the niggers; living with a couple of priests was enough to drive anyone crazy.

People greeted them as they walked.

John Raley was in his bar. Cosgrave felt relieved to

find that Jimmy Gordon wasn't there. He had been in the bar once since he had seen Gordon arrest the Negro at Ridge but they had hardly spoken. Gordon had served him his drink and moved off to watch the pitch game at the other end of the bar. Today it was a little early for the usual late afternoon drinkers and Raley was alone. He came toward them behind the bar, greeting Blair loudly, Cosgrave politely.

"Thought we might scare up a little pitch game," Blair said.

"The boys'll be in soon and we can get enough for a couple games. What you having?"

They stood there drinking, Raley and Blair talking politics, Cosgrave standing quietly by, enjoying not the taste of the liquor, but for the first time the feeling the drink induced in him.

The door burst open and a noisy group came in, their hunting coats heavy with rabbit and quail. Talk and laughter hushed slightly as they saw Cosgrave and someone yelled, "By God, I smell niggers! Get your guns, boys!" Their laughter came back at them from the ceiling. Jimmy Gordon, Pete Calvert, Luke Havenner, the great, squat mechanic, were among those in the group. No one spoke to Cosgrave.

"Let's get that pitch game started," Blair said. "There's enough people here for two games."

"I'll play but I don't want to be in the same game with no nigger-lover," Luke Havenner said. He tried to indicate he wasn't wholly serious. The others laughed half-heartedly. Blair said, "Mr. Cosgrave is no nigger-lover. He works with white people down there. Don't you?"

"Sure," Cosgrave said. "That's right."

"No one minds what that Fawther Cornish is doing down there," Pete Calvert said. "Ain't never going to do no one no good, but ain't never going to hurt no one, neither. Just so long as no niggers ain't being made uppity. Here, have a drink on me. John, give this young feller a drink."

It was a little too much for Cosgrave. He mumbled something about having an engagement and went toward the door. He heard the peculiar silence form as he left them. Christ, he thought, I am so dirty, I stink.

Driving south, he was going fast without knowing that he was. He slowed for Great Mills. Figures moved near the schoolhouse and on a sudden impulse, he turned the car into the drive in front of it. He didn't know yet that emotional disturbance of any sort made him want to be near a girl; and he had set himself to avoid Jane.

Rose Camalier came down the steps of the frame schoolhouse to greet him. She was not able to conceal all of her eagerness and Cosgrave felt, suddenly, aimless and destructive. He asked himself why he had come here and couldn't find an answer.

"It's very good to see you," she said. Her hand was a woman's, even though, standing before him, she was fairly taller than he. "I didn't think you'd get down. I know you've been busy, though."

"Not so busy. I've just come from drinking with some of the citizenry in Calverton."

"Oh, they'll teach you any bad habits you don't happen to have."

"I can't think of any."

She seemed pleased out of all proportion that he should even attempt humor with her. "Won't you come in?

We're not exactly elegant here, and there's no parlor, but it might be a little warmer."

He went with her into the classroom. "My assistant is gone," she said, to explain its emptiness. "She had to go up to Calverton to get some mail off. She'll be back later to pick me up. I had some work to clear up here."

"I can take you home," he said. "I have nothing to do today. I'm very gallant," he added.

"That's too much trouble," she said, but he saw she was pleased.

"No, it isn't. I've wanted to meet your father, too." How considerate I am, he thought; but saw that she took nothing he said as clumsy or hurtful.

"Papa hasn't been so well lately," she said as he helped her into her coat. "And he won't go to the doctor's, so we have to have Doctor McKay up to see him. I suppose you know Doctor McKay?"

"I've heard the priests talk of him. He seems sort of their official physician down here."

"He scandalizes them—on purpose, I imagine. Then they keep him as their doctor because they think they have to save him."

They were outside and she noticed the car his father had given him for his graduation from Georgetown. "That's an awfully prosperous-looking car for the manager of a poor co-op to be driving."

"It is deceiving, isn't it? But I had it when I came down. At one time, my father was fond of me—until I came down here instead of going to law school."

"How is the co-op doing? I've gotten permission to mention co-ops in the high school until someone objects, and no one has yet."

"They will," he said. He had intended, as much as

he had a conscious intention, to make the remark lightly, but something in his tone shocked her.

"You sound cynical."

"I don't think I am," he said. "I guess I just like to talk that way."

After a little while, she said, almost indistinctly, "I imagine the worst cynicism is that which comes on us unaware, and isn't a pose or a rationalization."

He was not sure he had heard her clearly and was afraid to speak. A kind of anger formed in him and obscurely he wanted to hurt her.

"I suppose," she went on when he didn't speak, "that I shouldn't say such things to a comparative stranger, or to anyone."

"It's all right," he said thickly. His anger became sorrow effortlessly. "I'm just a punk kid."

"Oh, but you're not. You're a very fine person to be doing what you're doing. Without any future in it or—"

"No." He shook his head. "It's selfish like everything else. I just don't know anything else I want to do. And I suppose—since we seem so concerned with obscure motivation—that I get pleasure out of shocking my lace-curtain Irish friends by doing something such as I am doing instead of going to law school and then into politics and marrying my rich girl-friend."

"She'll wait," Rose said quickly. "If she loves you, she'll wait."

"You think so?" he said in surprise that was only partly forced. "I guess I'm just tired," he added before she could speak.

"You turn here," she said. "The Medley's Neck road."

"Did it derive the name from couples parking along

it?" he said. He forced humor as though the process were a vital one, like the transfusion of blood. Her smile was confused. "Over yonder," she said. "The white house near the trees."

Nearer the house, she said, "Doctor McKay's here. You and he and the bankers are the only ones with such expensive cars."

"You seem worried over my car," he said. "Jane Saunders has one as good or better."

"You know Jane?" Rose said after a little hesitation.

"Yes, I know her." He stopped the car and got out. As he helped Rose out he saw that she avoided his glance. Going up to the house, he began to think of Jane. That he should still like her, that he could think of what they had done as something not unclean, that her having been with other men should bother him only as a jealousy that was sharply physical—these things were wonders to him. And, in his hands, her breasts, solid as fruit.

As with Kane, weariness was now his norm; but unlike Kane that weariness could lead Cosgrave to accept things that in strength and clearness of mind he would perhaps not have accepted.

Wathen McKay stood up as Rose came into the big room, and David Camalier also as Cosgrave followed his daughter in. David's courtesy, an anachronism in its quiet sincerity, embarrassed Cosgrave for some reason. McKay said, "You're another one they're trying to make into a lay Jesuit. I don't know why they don't form some kind of a third order, like the Franciscan tertiaries, and be done with it."

"Never thought of it that way," Cosgrave said. "I'll

resist their attempt to make me one, though." He was surprised that he could make them laugh.

"Sit down, Mr. Cosgrave," David said. "What'll you have to drink?"

"He's another one of them northerners," McKay said. "You'll have to crack out that bottle of Scotch you keep for Father Kane."

"It will be a pleasure," David said.

"Anything at all," Cosgrave said.

"Wathen, you talk too much," Rose said.

"Got to have some relaxation from working so hard, trying to get people like your father and such to take care of themselves. Don't know which is the worse, that or trying to get nigger-women to take care of themselves during pregnancy."

The other smiled uncertainly. In the silence, McKay said recklessly, "What are you and Father Kane doing with them niggers down there, Cosgrave?"

"I have practically nothing to do with them."

"By God, news gets around here, though. You and Kane are supposed to be making the niggers uppity. And then you get this priest at Great Mills popping off. There'll be trouble first thing you know."

"Now, don't you believe him, Mr. Cosgrave," David said. "Wathen's always saying things to see their effect on people."

"Not this time," McKay said. "Coming on for winter, those boys in Calverton ain't got much to do."

"Wathen, you're an alarmist," Rose said. She turned to Cosgrave. "Pay no attention to him, Mr. Cosgrave. He delivers all the colored babies free. He just likes to try to shock people."

"Sure," McKay said, "I deliver them free because I

wouldn't get paid anyhow. I deliver them on the floor. When I get there, they're always on the floor, waiting, so they can save the bed and not get it mussed. I deliver all nigger babies on the floor. It's what you call a strictly indigenous problem in obstetrics: how to keep the baby's head from bumping on the floor."

David Camalier moved uneasily and Rose wet her lips but didn't speak. Cosgrave saw the doctor was a little drunk. Were the others embarrassed, he wondered, at the reference to the mechanics of birth or by the implications of a terrible poverty? He felt the tension in him again and he wondered how long he could stay in the County. "There was something said," he said, to break the silence, "of your giving a few talks at the Institute, Mr. Camalier. Father Kane mentioned it offhandedly. I was wondering if there was any message you'd like me to bring him?" Cosgrave felt cheap immediately after speaking; he knew then that some part of him had tried deliberately to embarrass the old man.

"I, ah, don't think I'm going to be able to, Mr. Cosgrave. There was some slight talk earlier in the year, but—"

"I, as his physician, won't let him," McKay said.

Cosgrave sensed how strange the silence was: he felt suddenly hunted and betrayed. Rose said, "Have another drink, Mr. Cosgrave. Father really hasn't been well. He's always tended to overwork."

Where truth ended and prejudice began, Cosgrave didn't know, and perhaps no one knew. He suspected, with his usual suddenness, that he was becoming something of a fanatic. He wondered, too, if they were right in New York, if they were even right here? Something about the dual nature of man, he guessed. His weariness came up in him like sickness. McKay rose to leave and Cosgrave got up, too.

At the car he said to Rose, "I'd like to see you again. Sometime." His own general vagueness alarmed him.

"Do you feel all right?" she said. Her hand on his own seemed natural. He leaned toward the window and kissed her in the failing light.

She seemed to realize it was almost impersonal. "You—you mustn't judge us too harshly," she said. "I want to do something about the colored people. I—I don't know. I simply—"

"I know," he said. His voice had the shape of calmness, of quietness. "You're at least honest, whereas I'm probably a faker. I'm always suspicious of do-gooders. So many of them are just trying to gain a feeling of importance from helping poor people, that they aren't talented enough to gain in some other activity, like law or the arts. So, I'm probably a faker, too."

He was surprised at her tears, barely visible in the light almost gone, and he drove away because it seemed that neither of them could speak.

14

ALL night Cosgrave moved uneasily, trying to sleep. His thoughts seemed to possess no order, and always he came back to Jane, the details of her body. Once, on the edge of sleep, he was able to picture someone with her body and Mary Larkin's face. Then sharply, the image was all Jane. After a while he got up. It was an old trick, learned at school, but now seemingly not as effective as then. He still wanted Jane. He knelt and began to pray. It was better and after a while he could sleep.

Both Kane and Cornish were at breakfast. Cornish seemed displeased over something, and Cosgrave thought of how little he himself had seen of Kane since coming here. "How are things going at the Institute, Father?" he asked Kane.

"They're getting along. I think I see enough money to take us through next year, too. And Samuel is going to stay as dean. After that killing last month I was afraid he wouldn't last. But he's not only going to stay, he's going to marry Miss Bartrow, our domestic science teacher."

"I'd like to see more of him," Cosgrave said. "We've only met once."

"I can't say that I approve of Samuel's marrying," Cornish said. "To involve women in the kind of work we're attempting is—well, I don't know."

"We couldn't very well have a man teaching domestic science," Kane said gently.

"I suppose not," Cornish said. After a moment of silence, he said, "We haven't seen you at week-day Mass as frequently as we did when you first came here, John? And the last two Sundays you haven't been at Communion?"

"I just haven't been able to get to sleep at night, and so I sleep later in the morning."

"Ye-es, but we need the grace of the Sacraments in this work, you know."

"I don't think you get enough recreation," Kane said. "You ought to get up to Calverton occasionally to a movie."

"I bought a shotgun," Cosgrave said. "But you can't do much bird or rabbit shooting around here without a dog."

"I'll have Mr. Hebb take you duck-hunting one of these days," Kane said. "It's a little early yet but the first time we have bad weather north of us for more than a day at a time, will bring the blackheads and canvasbacks down. Mr. Hebb has a blind set up in the Potomac, just off the Institute's land.

"That would be good."

"You know, John," Father Cornish said, smiling, "I introduced you to some of the best people, the Saunders, so that you wouldn't lack suitable company. And I expected that through them you'd meet the Raleys, the banker's family. They have a model farm next the Saunders. And Mrs. Saunders comes from one of the oldest families down here. She's a Calvert and you know, of course, that it was Calvert, Lord Baltimore, who founded this community as one of Tolerance."

"I thought we were against the banks?" Cosgrave said. He tried to smile but couldn't quite manage it. To his surprise, he saw that the priest understood his remark, the smoothly broad athlete's face coloring slightly.

"Well—" Father Cornish said and grinned.

"I must get along," Kane said. "Come over to the Institute any time you have the chance, John."

"I was thinking, John," Cornish said, after Kane had gone, "that since today is Saturday, you might go up to Calverton or even Washington. Just for the day. I'll ask John Mattingly to mind the co-op for a while."

"I'd rather go hunting, if I am going to take the day off."

"Do whatever you wish. One thing, only, though, John. We mustn't be really opposed to the banks. I sometimes think that Father Kane is going a little too far. Why, three of his credit unions are already functioning. The first thing he knows, the bank will crack down on the mortgage they have on the church."

"What will the bank do with a church? Especially one located in the middle of a lot of Negroes?"

The priest laughed. "I never thought of that. I guess they could do something, though." He went out of the room, smiling fondly.

Moving slowly through the long grass of the dun-colored fields near Point No Point, Cosgrave began to feel better. The lack of people or houses, the noise of the Chesapeake's waves to the east seemed good things. He moved through grass and the thicker cover of brush, but flushed no quail. Once grass moved and parted slightly, to his left, but, the gun almost to his shoulder, he could see nothing.

206

Each little thicket, each pile of cut brush or wood was a possibility, but neither birds flushed nor rabbits ran. The tension grew in him. The constant expectancy of rising birds, of a rabbit's bounding course through grass, and yet never getting a shot was, he realized, like making love to a girl and never reaching a climax. After a while it was almost unbearable.

He shouldered the gun after unloading it and walked home sullenly. No one was at the rectory and he drove up to Calverton. It was mid-afternoon and farmers were in town in old cars and wagons. The day had turned damp and he heard, on the corner in front of Clement's Drug Store, Bert Greenwell, the Saunders' tenant farmer, talking to another man. "Think I'll run back," Greenwell was saying. "It's turning wet enough to strip tobacco."

Cosgrave made himself think of why tobacco was stripped on a damp day: because the leaf handled easier and didn't crumble and crack as on a dry day. He considered with a sort of aimless irony how much he had learned about fishing, farming, and oystering since he had come to southern Maryland. And how they would smile in New York. He wondered why he always thought of what his former friends would think? He also considered getting drunk. The idea repelled him; and he realized that what was repellent was the thought of losing control of his mind for even a little while, rather than losing control of his body. That body he had once been so proud of, slender, wiry, the far-striding legs; nurtured carefully to grace and pain as others were nurtured to comfort. And now quick sudden in memory the track at Soldiers Field, Chicago, and the three of them coming down the long stretch and the Purdue man in gold and his own legs rising each time a little less high so that it was a long stumble to the tape and the desperation at the body's failure—the body had always betrayed him, he could believe—and the fall, the cinders cutting into the flesh, and the finish line under his body and the gold jersey ahead of him. But he had known that later, that he was second. He had been blind when he fell and the taste of cinders on his lips strange and harsh.

He shook his head slightly as though clearing it after a blow. When he had been with Jane that night at Scotland Beach, there had flashed ridiculously to his mind's eye runners running, himself among them. He had forgotten about it afterwards, but it returned now. He felt chagrined and sardonically amused. Christ, he thought, do all Catholics grow up so late?

He stopped outside Raley's Bar. Over the curtain covering the lower half of the window he could see the crowded bar, farmers and hunters drinking at it or playing pitch or the slot machines. Both Gordon and Raley were busy behind the bar. *All right*—he was virtually talking to himself by now—*go in, but for God's sake keep your mouth shut!*

Inside it was warm and stank of the crowd. Talk and laughter made a steady, almost even sound. No one who recognized Cosgrave saw him come in. Some farmers made room for him at the bar and Jimmy Gordon came along, not seeing it was Cosgrave, as he mopped up the bar. "Yes sir. What'll it be?" Then Gordon looked up and saw it was Cosgrave. "By Christ, what're you doing up here with the white folk?" He grinned unpleasantly to temper his words.

"All I want is a drink. Supposing we keep the conversation on that basis."

"That's all right with me even if I don't know what the hell you're talking about."

"Give me some Scotch and soda."

"By God, you would make me open a bottle. Why in hell can't you take rye and bourbon like the men down here?"

"You don't mean I'm not a man, friend?"

"I don't know. I guess maybe you are. Can't never tell about no nigger-lovers."

"All right. How about that drink?"

"Okay, just hold your water, though. By God, down at Ridge you and that Father Kane are so polite to the niggers you forget to be polite to white folks."

"I haven't got a damned thing to do with any niggers down there or any other place. And all Father Kane is trying to do is make them decent."

"Decent, my eye. He ought to have his ass kicked."

"Did anyone ever tell you you were a son of a bitch?"

"Not and get away with it," Gordon said.

"Well, I'm telling you."

Gordon put one foot on the cooling tub under the beer-spigots and stepped onto the bar. People fell back a little and someone yelled hoarsely in the growing silence.

"No nigger-loving bastard says that to me," Gordon said, "and gets away with it." He jumped down at Cosgrave who stepped backward. Gordon's swing missed him. The thing that was like fear, but wasn't fear—that he had always known before a race—twisted, ball-like, in Cosgrave's belly. Gordon swung again at Cosgrave coming in to clinch and the blow took him glancingly on the head. The feeling went—that was the way it was; he had forgotten. He ripped upwards with his free fist and it went along Gordon's chest and was lucky enough to catch him full on the chin. Gordon stepped back, surprised.

"What the hell goes on?" John Raley was yelling, but couldn't get through the ring of people. Gordon came in again and Cosgrave couldn't get away from the clumsy swing. The knuckles cut his lips against the teeth. The taste of blood and pain—after so long—surprised him. He swung heavily at Gordon and hit him twice, right, left, too high on the head, and hurt his hands. They clinched, wrestling, and the crowd gave way and the fighters went against a slot machine. It fell and the box broke and dimes scattered in the little cleared space. Some of the men kneeled and began to scrape the nearer dimes up and the fighters slipped on the smooth metal.

They broke and on the break, Gordon caught Cosgrave with his crooked elbow. Cosgrave thought he had been hit with a fist. He was hurt and stunned and thought he must surely lose to anyone that could hit so hard. He wondered what it would be like to be humiliated by being beaten with fists and he knew suddenly why men had preferred death or wounding in a sword- or pistol-duel to being beaten with fists.

Gordon came after him, rushing, and Cosgrave, remembering rudimentary boxing lessons at school, stuck out his left arm. It straightened exactly as Gordon ran into it. Blood spurted from his upper lip and he stopped. Cosgrave, over-eager, went toward him and Gordon slipped inside his clumsy swing. They hung together, their breath sobbing. Thy were both tired already. The difference was that Cosgrave was used to pain. Gordon tried to knee Cosgrave. The knee glanced out off the thigh instead of in. Cosgrave tried the same thing and missed. Only later was he surprised that he had tried to knee someone.

When they broke, Cosgrave saw on Gordon's face that he wasn't used to keeping moving violently while in pain. ". . . to be able to think on your feet while in pain." He remembered someone's saying it was the only real justification of the American intensity toward the playing of games. He knew now that he could win. He went after Gordon and tried to hit the bloody mouth again but missed. Gordon caught him neatly over the eye, cutting the eyebrow slightly. Blood started in a narrow, heavy trickle from it. Then Cosgrave had him against the bar and was slugging with both hands at the belly. Gordon groaned and dropped to his knees. "He fouled me."

"He sure did," said John Raley. "The son of—" He stopped.

"Ah, bullshit," Cosgrave said. "He quit. He's yellow." Not yellow, tired. Don't get tired. Part of him knew the truth but it felt better to call the downed man yellow.

Gordon stayed on his knees, holding his belly well above the belt and moaning he'd been fouled. Cosgrave looked at him and was surprised at the pleasure it gave him.

John Raley said, "And now I'll thank you to leave my bar. This is a gentleman's bar and—"

Cosgrave began to laugh and he saw that the faces around him were both hostile and afraid. "Christ," he said, "you're so phony you're a laugh."

Raley colored and Cosgrave picked his hat off the floor and walked toward the door. Dimes slid and scattered under his feet. He felt proud and good but not happy. The people in the bar not liking him bothered him obscurely. In the street people looked at him and he remembered the blood and began to feel it drying on him. He went into Clement's Drug Store and the youngsters dancing to the music of the juke-box hesitated in their rhythmical swinging and looked at him. The awe in their faces pleased him. He went into a phone booth and called Mary Larkin's number in New York. She was out to a tea dance, her sister told him. He hung up when she asked if there was any message.

Stout Mrs. Clement stopped him as he went toward the door. "My goodness, young man, you're a sight. Let me wash your face."

"No, really, thanks. It's good of you, but—" He was at the door. He couldn't have stood for having his face washed in front of the children, he thought. At least it seemed so to him.

Now, outside, the wet air on his face, he was again and finally angry, remembering the silly legends they told at Catholic schools: how violent exercise was an anaphrodisiac. And he remembered the football players at the whorehouses Saturday nights after the games . . . and the priests still telling the younger students to box or wrestle and so avoid temptation. And now himself wanting to be near, to talk to some girl he knew well. The adrenalin still in the blood. And could he go to Kane and say, "I had a fight because someone said you should be kicked. And now I want to be near a girl. And the only one I can or want to be near now is an occasion of sin. What shall I do?"

How mawkish we are, they made us, he thought, and was driving south. I'll just see Jane, talk to her, he told himself. And the conscious mind mocked him: but if that's all, why not just 'talk' to Rose Camalier?

But he was past the Medley's Neck road. He kept telling himself he simply wanted to see Jane and talk to her. It was a curious process; by it some part of him was convinced that he was not consciously and deliberately going into mortal sin.

In the drive beyond the withered formal garden he saw that her parents' car was gone and hers was there, but that might mean little. If he moved quickly, he knew, he would not think. When she opened the door for him he saw how varying were the weathers of her face. "John, what's happened to you?" The voice dropping in fear.

"Fight," he said thickly. He held her hard against him. While he blanked part of his mind, another part of it knew slyly that she would not let him hold her as he was holding her if she were not alone.

"Let me wash your face."

"No. Not now."

"All right. Here. Come here."

Afterwards, he sat quietly in the kitchen and she washed the dried blood away and put a small bandage over his eyebrow. When she had finished, she stood a little off from him. Looking at her he could believe that he was more grateful to her than he had been to anyone in all of his life. Tears formed at the back of his eyes and he pulled her gently to him, putting his face between the shape of her breasts.

"Do you love me, John?"

"I don't know. I don't know that I love anyone. I think you're awfully good, though."

"Good?" Her laugh wasn't pleasant. "I'm not good. I wish I could be."

"What do you mean?" He looked up and saw her tears and how still her face was.

"I'm glad you don't love me," she said.

He was puzzled and stood up, looking at her, feeling how useless he was to help her.

"Is it because you know I've been with other men?" she said. "Is that why you fought Jimmy? I never . . ."

"I don't know." He had to look away from her. Jealousy shot like pain through his belly. "It once seemed I could love and marry only a virgin. Maybe it's still so. But I'm grateful to you and I think you're good and—oh, Christ, I don't know! I don't know a thing." He turned away almost savagely and went to a window. Below the long slope, he could see the river in the last light, and men rising in a duck-blind and the dark flecks that were birds come in, bank, wheel, two of them wither and fall. Coming in, hard, to death. He smelled her near him and turned. He wanted to ask her certain things but couldn't. They looked at each other and together, without expression or sound, began to weep. The tears were hot on his cheeks and because he was ashamed of them he held her again. Desire was quicker than he had thought it would be and he took her again. But he knew, later, that this time he had given her no pleasure.

He felt depressed. "I'd better go," he said. She looked at him without speaking. Her face seemed tired. At the door he kissed her quietly and because he was sorry for her said that he loved her. She shook her head without speaking and turned away.

Driving home, he prayed—an act of contrition; he had a sudden, morbid fear that he might be killed in an auto accident.

Cornish was at the rectory, eating supper. "You're late, John. And what happened to you?"

"I had a fight in Calverton."

The priest looked at his plate. "With whom?"

"Jimmy Gordon—in Raley's Bar."

The priest shook his head. "That kind of thing won't do. It'll give us a bad name. What was the fight about?"

"Nothing much."

"Were you drinking?"

"I suppose that was it."

They ate in a rather long silence. Finishing his meal before Cosgrave, the priest looked seriously at him and said, "I'll expect you at Confession tonight. Come right after supper and I can hear you before the crowd gets there."

Cosgrave choked on his food. When he could talk, he said, "I'll go to Confession. I'll go over to the Negro church later."

The priest's lips contracted. "That's your privilege." He went out of the room. It's over now, Cosgrave thought, and felt a slight sense of relief. He wasn't quite sure what he meant.

In the dark he walked to the Negro church, crossing the triangle of land that, at Ridge, lay between the Three Notch Road and No. 5, and then up No. 5 to the dirt road that led west to the Institute. The wind had died with the light's passing and Cosgrave moved slowly, enjoying the dark stillness. A fox bounded almost noiselessly across the road behind him, the only noise the sound of its nails on the dirt. Cosgrave stopped but did not turn. He felt quiet and even a little stupid, part of the night.

Lights showed feebly in a few of the buildings, the

convent, the church, and Bernard Hebb's house. It was a little early for confessions, but Kane, opening the front door of the church from within, stood outlined against the dim light of the interior. He was so seldom in a soutane that Cosgrave at first didn't recognize the figure as Kane's, but thought it might be one of the other Jesuits, who frequently came down from New York or Washington on retreat. Neither did Kane recognize the advancing figure. He had not expected a white man.

"Oh, hello, John."

"Hello, Father. Didn't recognize you at first."

"It's me, all right. Did you have a good day? What happened to your eye?"

"I was in a fight in Calverton."

Kane contrived to look at once superior, amused, and pitying. Perhaps it was only the effect of the light that made him seem to, but Cosgrave thought that only a Jesuit could manage to look so. "That's too bad, John. I hope you weren't hurt badly. I suppose you're out taking a walk?"

"Not particularly. I'd like to go to Confession." He saw Kane hesitate awkwardly.

"Oh, yes. Sure," the priest said.

"It's all right to come here to Confession, isn't it?"

"Of course. We've had white people here before, to go to Confession." Kane seemed suddenly to regret his own words and they were both awkwardly silent.

"Perhaps you'd like to go to Confession now," Kane said, "before the crowd comes. The crowd, if any." He smiled.

"If it's convenient for you?"

"Oh, it is. I was thinking—some night you might like to come down and talk to one of the credit unions?"

Cosgrave didn't speak for a moment. "I honestly don't know what I could say to them."

Kane touched his arm and smiled abstractedly. "We'll think of something. I'll be in the confessional when you're ready."

Cosgrave knelt in the last pew. He said the first half of the Confiteor, absently. He had never had to confess before the sin of fornication. Like most American Catholics—to say nothing of American Protestants—he had grown up in the belief that next to murder it was the worst of sins, and now that he must accuse himself of it, he felt dismayed.

The first Negroes were coming into the church and Cosgrave rose and went into the confessional. He heard, in the almost complete darkness of the little booth, Kane slide the wooden panel back. "Bless me, Father, for I have sinned. It is—five weeks since my last confession."

"Yes."

"I took our Lord's name in vain—several times. And used considerable bad language." The petty ones first, he thought. How we flatter ourselves with the confession of petty sins!

"And I was uncharitable in my thoughts and conversation."

Again the pause in which Kane did not move or speak.

"And I took pleasure in immodest thoughts." Oh, we are euphemistic bastards, all right!

"And I gave way to anger and did violence to another person."

Kane moved slightly and Cosgrave expected him to speak. Now he himself had to say it and he couldn't speak. Kane said, "Is that all?"

"No. . . . I committed fornication . . . three times."

After a moment, Kane said, "Is that all?"

"Yes."

"And you're sorry for these and all the sins of your past life?"

"Yes, Father."

Kane, about to pronounce the words of absolution, hesitated. "Is something bothering you, John?"

"I suppose so. I've never—committed fornication before." Oh, sure, tell him what a holy, pious son of a bitch you are!

"It's doubtless a sin, John, but it's not one to be more concerned over than, say, your lack of charity. And our uncharity is so often premeditated, whereas the sin of fornication is frequently unpremeditated. You must remember your grammar school catechism lessons—that for a sin to be mortal, three conditions must be fulfilled. It must be not only a serious matter, but there must also be sufficient reflection and full consent of the will."

"I know."

"Of course, you must try to avoid the occasion of sin."

"I have been trying to, Father." Oh, noble, noble! You are just a noble, tragic bastard!

"That's why it's so terribly wrong to underpay a man," Kane went on. "Because almost invariably it's done in cold blood and after considerable reflection." He laughed a little, apologetically. "We're all so economic-minded these days. It pursues us into the confessional."

He murmured quickly the ancient Latin formula. "Go in peace, John," he said. "Say a prayer for me."

"Yes, Father. And thank you."

Outside, Cosgrave felt fresh and relieved. It was always so after confession. He attributed no mystical origin to the feeling; he knew it was merely psychological.

Samuel Raife and Miss Bartrow, a pleasant-looking young Negress, were coming up to the church. Cosgrave had met each of them once before. They greeted him and paused. They agreed about the weather.

"Father Kane tells me you're being married," Cosgrave said. "I want to congratulate both of you." He could wonder whether they were very brave or very foolish.

"Yes," Samuel said. "We thought it would be a good thing, since we are both interested in the same work."

"And the Institute will be functioning next year, too. It all seems fine," Cosgrave said.

"Yes," Samuel said. "Miriam here has as many domestic science pupils as she can care for."

Sure. Of course. And next year they might even have something to eat. "That's fine," Cosgrave said. "Well, good night and good luck to both of you."

"Good night, Mr. Cosgrave," they said.

Mr. Cosgrave, he thought, walking back to St. Patrick's Rectory. They should call me Mr. Cosgrave. Jesus Christ!

He wondered, walking in the night, if he should also have confessed the sin of despair. And whether, if Jane were an occasion of sin, was not Father Cornish also? For it was the priest, Cosgrave knew, who was the most frequent object of his own uncharity.

219

15

LIKE plants the ducks were thermotropic. Unlike plants, they clung only to the edge of heat. When storms roughened the salt waters of the upper Chesapeake and froze the brackish creeks, the ducks rose without anger and went farther south in great, ragged wedges. Where water ran they flew and where the wild celery grew they settled. Their movements were only gradual, and from the early storms they flew only as far as the lower Chesapeake.

It was the first mass flying of the birds for that region, and on a morning in early December, many of the men of the County went out to the shooting. Blinds stood above Point No Point and men from Calverton took the Three Notch Road there: John Raley, Jimmy Gordon, and the insurance salesman, Joe Tennison, were in one car. Pete Calvert and Luke Havenner in another.

At Dameron, not far from St. Inigoes, where still stood the Jesuit house the British warships shelled in 1812, the two cars bore east over the dirt road that wound about the northern and eastern shores of St. Jerome's Creek. Ridge lay below them and just to the north they heard hounds baying. A fox, leveled out and running hard, went across the road in front of the cars and the cars stopped and the men got out.

"Didn't think Bucky was hunting so far south," Joe Tennison said. "He started for Cedar Point."

"Well, he's here," Luke said. "We might as well follow. I ain't never hunted it much around here."

"I hunted it good," Joe said. "Used to have a nigger wench down here. Had to get rid of her, though; someone give her a dose."

"Bet you were the one," John Raley said. They laughed and Jimmy Gordon said, "Damned if I want to go after any foxes. We come to go ducking."

"Fox is already started," Pete Calvert said. "Ain't as if it wasn't."

Hounds came belling across the road. Their mouths slavered and their eyes were wild. The men stayed carefully out of the hounds' way, even going behind trees until they had passed, then followed them south into the fields on foot, carrying their long-barreled duck-guns.

About the same time, Jane Saunders was walking between the holly trees that led to St. Patrick's Rectory. She had walked all the way from her home, because her mother had taken the keys to both the cars. The girl looked pale and older. She rang the bell of the rectory and asked Melissa, when she answered it, if Mr. Cosgrave were in.

"Ain't none of them in," Melissa told her. "Mr. Cosgrave, he's up in Calverton doing something. Father Kane, he's in Baltimore and Father Cornish, he's in Washington about a lawyer or something. They're getting that oyster-shucking shed, you know, and they got to tend to the business about it."

"I see. You don't know when Mr. Cosgrave will be back?"

"Can't say that I do. He's been going around looking like he was half-dead. I don't imagine he's going to stay here much longer. Your ma phoned just 'fore you come here and said to tell you, if you came here to come right home or she'd be after you."

Jane didn't change expression. "Don't tell her, Melissa. I'm going right on home." She hesitated to give Melissa the note she had in her bag.

"I won't."

The girl went down the Three Notch Road to the post office in Ridge and addressed the note to John Cosgrave, then began the walk up the road. She didn't want her mother to meet her walking on No. 5 and make her get in the car and be driven home. There had been enough humiliations in the past few days. She hadn't been even allowed to phone the rectory. And she couldn't say what she had to say into the boothless phone at the nearby general store. So she had walked to Ridge to see Cosgrave.

North of her she heard hounds belling in the full, frenzied note of the near-kill. City-bred, she knew nothing of hunting and walked on. The noise of hounds sounded pleasant, hardly more urgent than on other occasions when she had heard them.

The quadroon, Loker Abell, rang the bell at the rectory shortly after Jane had and asked Melissa if Father Cornish were in. "I hear they'll be opening a oyster-shucking house right soon," he said.

"Yes, indeed," Melissa said. "They figures to start building it next week. Some rich northern folks give Father Cornish the money. People name Foundation."

"So I hear, Mrs. Maddox. If you'd please tell Father

Cornish I was here asking for a job in it. I guess maybe I'm one of the first."

"You're the very first, Loker, as far as I know."

"Okay, then. Thanks, then, Mrs. Maddox. Hopes you and Mr. Maddox is well."

He went out to the Three Notch Road and began to walk up it to the shack he lived in alone on the northern edge of St. Jerome's Creek. Jane, walking north now from the post office, was only a hundred yards or so ahead of him. Loker recognized her. He followed more slowly, dropping further behind her. Now, he heard the hounds and, beyond Jane, saw the fox cross the road, the hounds only fifty or sixty yards behind, a brown and white and black stream of moving flesh.

The quadroon knew, immediately, what was going to happen: there was a creek beyond the western side of the road and the creek would probably turn the fox, who would double back south and then east, the hounds following, and cross the road near where the girl was. Loker knew that hounds in full cry often ripped at anything in their path, man or animal. He began to run. The girl heard him running and turned. He saw she was frightened.

"Come back," he called as he ran. "Come back out of there or climb a tree. Them hounds." Her fear frightened him.

"Why should I?" she said. "Leave me alone."

"Them hounds," he said, closer and still running. "They'll tear hell out of you. They'll tear you. Get up in that there low holly tree." In his anxiety he grasped her arm awkwardly with one hand. Jimmy Gordon and Luke Havenner came out on the road, Luke almost winded from following the dogs. He screamed, "Leave that white girl alone, you nigger bastard!"

They ran at Loker, who backed away. "I wasn't doing nothing."

"Don't you run or I'll blast you, you son of a bitch," Havenner said. Loker raised his hands and paused. He couldn't control himself and they could see where he was wetting. Jimmy Gordon ran at him and took a free-arm swing as he ran, catching Loker full in the mouth and knocking him, bleeding but conscious, onto the road.

"He didn't do anything, Jimmy," Jane said. "He was trying to get me out of the way of the dogs."

"You're no goddam good, anyway, Jane," Gordon said. "Get the hell along."

She choked, crying, and turning, began to hurry along the road as the other men came out of the woods. Below them on the road, only a scant twenty feet from where the quadroon lay, the fox crossed, doubling, holding now his own against the hounds.

"What the hell goes on here?" Joe Tennison said.

"This black bastard was going after a white girl," Havenner said.

"Why, the dirty son of a bitch." Tennison went quickly over to the quadroon and kicked him in the ribs. Loker gasped and said, "My God, man, don't!"

"Shut up, you dirty black son of a whore," John Raley said. "I'll teach you to talk back to a white man." He jumped up in the air and came down with both feet on Loker's belly.

"Don't fool around," Pete Calvert said. "Got to teach the bastards a lesson. Cut his nuts out."

"Take him in the woods," Tennison said. "We could fool with him there."

"I was trying to get her out the way the hounds," Loker managed to say. "Them hounds'd—"

"Shut up, you black bastard."

"Maybe he was," Jimmy Gordon said. "Them hounds run awful close."

"Jimmy," Tennison said, "when the hell were you born, yesterday?"

"Carry the black son of a bitch into the woods," Luke Havenner said. "We'll fix his wagon."

"Carry him hell," Calvert said. "Make the bastard walk?"

They pulled Loker Abell to his feet and kicked him until he started to gimp toward the woods. To the south and east the hounds bayed along the creek-shore and northward they heard Bucky Maddox sounding his conch-horn, not in recall but in sheer jubilation over the belling dogs.

"Butterflies," George Carroll Blair said. He liked to twit the serious young man. It had become a pleasant diversion these past ten days or so, since the young man had come up to see him more often. "I'm just a butterfly. By God, you just shouldn't take life so seriously, John. Why should I put something in the paper about the co-op oyster-shucking shed? It'll just get people against me. And next election I'm really going to be top-boy. But I'll need every vote."

"I guess I can't talk to you, Mr. Blair." Cosgrave stood up. His face showed strain.

"Sit down, boy. You just take life too seriously." Looking at Cosgrave, it seemed to Blair that there was a resemblance between the young man and his dead son, Charles. There was no real resemblance. But Blair thought him like Charles. He would like to please the young man, but he couldn't back down now. He watched Cosgrave turn and leave without saying good-bye. He admired spirit, Blair thought; he leaned back in his swivel-chair and stared dully at the certificate of the Sons of the Confederacy.

The telephone rang and a girl's voice asked for Cosgrave when Blair answered. "He just left the office. I could probably catch him if there's a message."

"This is Jane Saunders, Mr. Blair. I thought I might catch John at your office."

Something in her voice made him ask, "What seems to be the trouble, Miss Jane? If there's anything I can do?—"

She hesitated. "You know that nigger, Loker Abell? Used to be Mr. John Mattingly's nigger? Well, some of the men from Calverton have him in the woods above Ridge, right off the Three Notch Road near that rise that's covered with holly trees, and I don't know what they're going to do to him. They think he was bothering me and he wasn't, he really wasn't." She was crying. "I—I thought John might be able to do something. I called Corporal Small at his house and he's out some-where. If you'd tell John, I know—" she cried again.

"Sure, sure," George Blair said. "I'll tell him. You just calm yourself. I'll tell him. He'll probably be right down there." He hung up. "Like hell," he said, out loud.

It seemed to him that the room grew peculiarly quiet. The wings of the butterflies were very blue, the color of the sky in a barroom mural. "Christ," he said out loud after a while, "what the hell am I supposed to do—save a goddam nigger's hide?" He knew who had gone hunting down that way this morning; he knew their habits and the way they thought. If thought was the word, he corrected himself.

The Attorney General of the United States had said, "For God's sake, Blair, you're honest and you're intelligent and you're not too much of an egomaniac, and that combination doesn't happen too often in the same man. Why do you want to go back to your country weekly?"

And Henry Mencken had written to him and what, if anything, did the certificate of the Sons of the Confederacy mean?

It was all sentimental, he told himself, and he simply would not be swayed by sentiment. To hell with it, to hell with all of them.

He had gotten up without knowing it and was walking back and forth in the narrow office. He was too old, he told himself, even if it was worth saving a jig's life. They'd hardly kill the nigger. It wasn't that they wouldn't have liked to but that they didn't have quite the guts to kill a man. Although twenty years ago some of them had, on a Sunday morning after attending Mass. But he was goddamned, though, if he'd do anything. Nobody'd hang, even if the nigger was killed; they never hanged a white man in this county. Why, they never even hanged niggers. The niggers just didn't know when they were well off.

Sentiment, he told himself—he had forgotten momentarily about sloth—it was sentiment that had brought him back here from Washington. He wouldn't let sentiment move him, and that was that.

The only thing, though—if that Saunders girl hadn't

believed him and had kept the operator trying to get John Cosgrave and did get him at a bar or the drugstore, and sent the damn fool kid down-county to rescue a nigger. . . . George Carroll Blair, whose father had fought at Chickamauga and whose mother had seen Sidney Lanier asking for water and whose great-granduncle had been an archbishop, picked up a paper-weight and threw it at the door. He said, aloud, "Of all the stupid sons of bitches." Bitch, he thought, a little bitch. He began to remember that there had been stories about her.

He put on his coat and, without conscious effort, began to compose himself. *Gun wouldn't do. And it mustn't be as though deliberate.* A kind of sick grin came onto his face. He would just go down there and kind of accidentally break it up, that is, make them go to a place where young Cosgrave wouldn't find them if that little bitch sent him down there to the rise where the holly grew. The grin was terrible on the death's-head as he took from a high, narrow closet a butterfly net and walked out with it into the December morning.

By now they had the quadroon stripped. They had bound his hands and feet with running cedar—they used it to festoon the churches with at Christmas—twisting five and six strands of it together so that it would hold. And they had broken branches off the holly trees—the idea was Joe Tennison's—and laid them in a thick mat on the ground; and then they had rolled the naked man over the thorny mass. He was no longer yelling—he was too frightened and besides Luke Havenner had hit him across the windpipe. A thin slime of blood was beginning to cover him from the hundreds of tiny holes in his skin.

"First thing you guys know," Joe Tennison said,

"he'll pass out and then there won't be any more fun. Take it easy with him. Draw it out. And if you're going to cut his nuts out, you'd better do it now, while he's still conscious."

"Kill the bastard and get it over with," Havenner said. "And we'll go ducking."

"That's what I say," John Raley said. "Did we come to go ducking or not?"

Hounds belled to the south, near Ridge.

Gordon jumped up from where he had knelt. "Hold off, Luke. Someone's coming."

"Shoot him, too. Ain't no one's business but ours."

They could all hear someone coming through the brush and they were all looking at the same place, all of them still, and holding themselves tight. George Blair came out of the brush and they were relieved. No one spoke, although Luke Havenner mumbled something to himself. "By the Lord," George Blair said, "I never expected to find you boys here. Thought all of you'd gone ducking." He came closer, bearing, like treasure, his sick grin and the butterfly net.

"December's a hell of a time to be going butterflying," Havenner said. On the ground, the quadroon lay still, his blood-red eyes watching George Blair steadily. Blair saw the eyes watching him and looked back at Luke Havenner.

"Tree-moths," Blair said. "There's a species of tree-moth that's on holly trees in December." He grinned. "By the Lord, you're certainly doing a job on this nigger. Isn't he kin to John Mattingly in some way or other?"

"Don't care if he's kin to Jesus Christ," John Raley said. "White women down here got to be protected."

"They sure do," Blair said, "but I didn't know one had been bothered down here in twenty or thirty years. Not in my memory, leastways."

"Say, George," Pete Calvert said, "you down here to spy on us or hunt your goddam butterflies?"

George Blair smiled foolishly. It had just occurred to him that a man named Calvert, Lord Baltimore, had founded this place they lived in as a community dedicated to tolerance. "Why, you boys know I wouldn't be doing any spying. I'm just down here after butterflies."

"We ought to beat hell out of you, George."

"I don't know why? I was thinking, though, that maybe someone saw you come in here, the girl this nigger was bothering, or someone. . . ."

"What of it?" Havenner said. "And how you know he was bothering her around here?"

"Only that someone'll talk," Blair said hastily. "We'll get a bad name in the County if it gets in an outside newspaper. Understand, I'm all for putting the niggers in their place."

"Oh, sure . . . you son of a bitch."

It so happened that Blair had never been called that before and now he grew suddenly afraid. They were all, except Jimmy Gordon, looking at him and no one spoke. He began to sweat and of the grin there remained only the lips pulled back from the teeth.

"George, you snaky bastard," Joe Tennison said, "you done told people and they're coming after us. If anyone shoots, I'm going to get you first."

Blair began to tremble, and couldn't speak.

"How did you know we were here?" Raley asked. He was white. "They know in town," he said to no one.

"I don't know about you birds," Joe Tennison said,

"but I'm getting to hell out of here. These priests down here ever hear of this, my business will be ruined."

"All right," Luke Havenner said, slowly, his eyes closed to slits in the fat face. "I'll go. Only one thing. That goddam nigger leaves this County. You promise me he does, George, you slippery bastard, or I'll kill him now and like to see any St. Mary's County jury hang me! I got relatives all over. Promise." He leveled his automatic shotgun at Loker's belly and the quadroon began to shake and make water again.

"All right, I'll get him out," Blair said. Relief left him sick and weak. He watched Tennison and Raley go. The others followed them, heavily, cursing.

"All right," Blair said to the quadroon. "Get dressed." He saw then that Loker's wrists were bound and he leaned and cut the knotted running cedar. He wondered why anything as light as the running cedar could hold a man bound. Loker had trouble getting up but Blair didn't help him. He just turned away; Loker looked too bad. What he minded most, George Blair knew, was his not being able to save Loker. Whatever had saved Loker, he hadn't. It came rather suddenly to Blair that God worked in strange ways at times, but the thought did not please him and he put it away.

"If I was to get to the bay and wash, Mr. Blair," Loker was whispering brokenly.

"Any goddam thing you please. Only hurry."

"Yes suh."

Four shots sounded out near the road, fired slowly and with apparent deliberation. They seemed to have a strange quality to them. "Hurry," Blair said. "They might be changing their mind."

Still naked, and carrying his clothes, the quadroon

231

began to follow George Blair eastward toward the Chesapeake. They moved without speaking. There was no sound but the noise of their passing. Blair didn't look behind him but headed as swiftly as he could walk for the water. Some panic, nameless and shapeless, was in him. It was the first time his pride had been so completely broken and the effect was similar to that of physical shock in another man. He moved, quite literally, as though dazed. The Negro followed dumbly after, in pain and stumbling. They were both breathing hard.

Holly and blackberry bushes caught at Blair's clothing, tearing it, and finally he had to stop and rest. He could hear the Negro's pained breathing behind him but didn't stop to look at the man. Then, as their breathing grew quieter, Blair heard, not far off, feet coming toward them, breaking through the underbrush.

"We'd better run," he said. "They maybe changed their minds." He was badly afraid and didn't know he had said 'we.' "Take one of those skiffs they have for the duck-blinds, you, and row to Calvert County. And don't ever come back." They were already moving as he spoke the last words.

The quadroon's walk became a run. He did not run well, stumbling and veering. Blair began to run, too, blindly. He found it an effort to keep from screaming. He could hear the feet, running also. He tripped and fell, earth going into his open mouth. He got up, crying pettishly like a child, and kept running. Loker was ahead of him, almost out of sight in the heavy brush. The taste of brass was in Blair's mouth and it had become important that he not lose sight of Loker. When he couldn't see Loker, panic came up in him and he began to yell hoarsely as he went toward the water with stumbling run.

A voice some ways behind him, called, "I think I saw one of the sons of bitches then." They'd kill him, Blair was sure; and nothing would be done to them. He was absurdly grateful that he was out of shotgun range. He knew none of them had rifles. When he stumbled he was already reconciled to death, part of him that was always quiet was. Sand was in his mouth this time instead of dirt, and he saw that what had tripped him was the soft sand of the beach. He saw Loker at the water's edge, trying alone to get a crabbing skiff down into the water. Blair ran toward him. He hadn't run in years and now, toward the end, in the soft sand, the agony was slow and bitter enough to be that of a dream.

"Hurry," he called. His mind moved frantically trying to decide whether to go with Loker or to stay and hope that nothing happened to himself. Together they tried to move the light boat but they were so weak that it slid only a few inches at a time in the sand. Blair felt insane: running now with a hunted nigger, hunted like him, hating him, he, George Blair.

Figures showed at the edge of the wood and Blair turned, his hands coming up as though to defend himself. Then he began to cry in relief. There were only two figures, those of Cosgrave and Blair's cousin, Fenner Ridgel, carrying shotguns. Blair sat on the gunwale of the skiff and the sobbing of breath in his raw throat was audible to the men coming over the sand. Loker stood near by, still naked, the blood dried on him in a kind of dirty film.

"Where's them bastards, George?" Fenner said. "We thought we was following them and it was you."

"Gone," Blair said. "Forget it." He could hardly talk.

Fenner began to curse and say what he wanted to do to Raley and Calvert and the others. Cosgrave looked at Blair and said, levelly, "You didn't try very hard for to find me, did you, Mr. Blair?"

"Grow up, bub." Blair didn't look at him. Even now he could think how curious it was that the boy had used the word 'for' so oddly, as in the County. Then Blair turned away and began to vomit.

"Where the hell you going, Loker?" Fenner said.

"Away fum here," Loker whispered. He had washed the blood from his body with the cold salt water and was dressing.

"Like hell," Fenner said. "You stay here and work for me. I ain't going let no one be run out of this County. You're going to stay."

"No, I ain't," Loker said. He pointed to his throat. "Hard to talk, Mr. Fenner. Let's keep quiet."

They watched him dress. Once Loker looked at John Cosgrave and in his own trouble, could think how strange the young man's face was.

"How much money you got, Cousin George?" Fenner said.

"I can give him five dollars."

"I got three," Fenner said.

"Here's ten and some change," Cosgrave said. "It's all I've got."

"Gimme five more than you were going to, George," Fenner said. "You're a rich man."

"God, for twenty-three dollars I'd leave the County myself," Blair said. No one laughed.

"You stay here, Loker," Cosgrave said. "We'll get the

law." He spoke weakly, as though convinced of Loker's intention.

"No suh," Loker said. He shook his head. They helped him pull the boat to the water and he launched it without speaking to them or thanking them in any way. He began to row in a northeasterly direction. No one waved or moved. They watched him for a while without speaking. He had to row twenty miles, the last part of it across the mouth of the Patuxent River. He had the tide with him now, but they knew it would be against him before he reached Drum Point in Calvert County. It would be coming fast out of the mile-wide estuary of the Patuxent.

Cosgrave waved impulsively as they turned to go, but Loker kept rowing. Walking in silence through the woods, except for Fenner's grumbling threats, they headed for where Blair had parked his car. Blair himself felt less weary. He could believe now that he had prevented people from being killed. He knew what would have happened had Cosgrave and Fenner come upon the others when they had Loker. Some of the old sense of power stirred in him; it stimulated him like whiskey; he grew confident and even optimistic. When people knew that he had prevented white men from killing each other, they would be for him next fall instead of against him. He would elect Mr. Dave Camalier and turn Dabson Morgan out. He shivered slightly. Damned if he wanted Dab Morgan hanging over his grave with a pair of rosary beads a yard long.

Blair could see his car before they came to it. It looked odd. Closer, he stopped and looked at it. Havenner and the others had blown all four new tires open with their shotguns. Blair sat on the running board. "I'm not well," he said, clearly. "Will one of you get a car or a doctor or something?"

Mid-afternoon now and the longer shadows, like the air, thin and cold. Cosgrave came slowly up the drive between the hollies, the still loaded shotgun on his shoulder. He hesitated before the church and then decided not to go in. At almost the same moment he saw the big car with the New York license on it and he went toward it. He knew whose it must be.

Mary Larkin, Jimmy Haggerty, and another young man and woman stood on the little walk before the rectory talking to Father Cornish. The priest was smiling pleasantly and had apparently just arrived himself and was about to invite the visitors into the rectory.

"Ah, the hunter," Haggerty called to him.

Cosgrave saw them laugh. When he was closer, Mary Larkin said, " 'Home is the sailor, home from the sea, and the hunter home from the hill.' " She smiled and Cosgrave felt unwillingly something not quite passion stir in him, lifting, reminding him in a single flash of a happier time when you kissed a girl on a terrace in the dusk outside a tea dance.

"Been hunting, eh, John?" Father Cornish said.

"Yeah, been hunting."

"Any luck?"

He hesitated. "No. No luck."

"I bet you saw plenty and couldn't hit them," Haggerty said.

Cosgrave ignored him and greeted the others, then Haggerty.

"You look tired enough to have killed a couple of bear," Mary said.

"Or big game, anyhow," the other girl said pleasantly.

He saw their smiles, even Mary's, fading; and he knew how dramatic he seemed. "We certainly wanted to kill big game," he said. "We were after it. Some of the boys from Calverton. Me and Fenner Ridgel." He knew there was something wrong with himself and he saw the faces change, Haggerty's retaining something of a smirk. Cosgrave wanted to hit it. He began to walk toward the rectory. He heard Father Cornish say, "But there's no big game in this County. I don't know what's the matter with John."

In the rectory Cosgrave went up to his room. He stood the loaded gun in a corner and lay on the bed. He was so tired that it was as though his body slept while his mind remained conscious. In a few minutes he heard Cornish come in and up the stairs. The priest stood in the doorway of the room. He looked disapproving. "I don't think you're very well, are you, John?"

"I suppose not."

"Yet I think you could have been less rude to your friends. They're going to go now, but Miss Larkin said that she'd like to see you for a moment. She can't come up here because it's cloistered, so you'll have to go downstairs."

Cosgrave got up slowly and moved toward the door.

"What's the matter, John?" the priest said, not unkindly.

"Why—they've just been trying to kill Loker Abell and he's not here any more and—and George Blair is in the hospital and—oh, Christ, I don't know." He went down the stairs slowly and heavily. Mary was in the little reception room or parlor across from the chapel. She was good-looking, all right, he thought. "I'm sorry," he said, and tried to smile, but smirked instead. "It's been a tough day."

She did not approve, her face told him. "You've been rather rude, John, and we're going to go. But I thought I'd best tell you what I came here to tell you. Jimmy and I are engaged. We wanted you to know and to tell you ourselves so there wouldn't be any bad feelings. We wanted to still be friends, although now—"

He was staring at her incredibly and she misunderstood him, her face softening. "Now, please try not to feel badly, John. I—we—"

He shook his head. "That's not it. I can't understand why in God's name you came down here to tell me."

Since she wasn't sure why she had herself, since even the pleasure it gave her was nameless and obscure, she felt even more annoyed with Cosgrave. "I think you're a boor, John. You—"

"I know," he said. "Run along now. I hope Jimmy does as well by you as he has by some of the people in Washington. But I doubt that he will, I doubt it very much." He turned slightly toward the door.

"I don't understand what you mean," she said, but he saw that she understood a little.

"It might be just as well if you never do," he said. His voice trailed and wandered. He went slowly up the stairs, hearing the door close behind him. I can certainly think of cheap things to say, he told himself.

In his room he saw the note Jane had mailed to him and which she had mentioned in their hurried phone conversation. It read: "I have to go away, John. Dr. McKay has finally made mother think so, too. I don't know where I'm going to be, but I'll write you when I get there, if I'm able. I love you. Jane."

He sat on the edge of the bed and, without urgency or excitement, contemplated the gun in the corner. He thought—academically, it seemed to him—of what it would be like to put the muzzles in his mouth and pull a trigger. He couldn't tell exactly why he should do this or why he wanted to do it. The desire seemed even academic and certainly without emotion or heat. He laughed for the first time that day. He said, aloud, "Jesus Christ, I am one of the few goddam Irishmen in this country that knows a temptation can be something else besides sex."

He rolled on the bed, laughing until the tears came in streams down his face.

16

THAT night Cosgrave waited a long time in the hospital in Calverton to see Wathen McKay. The small sounds and half-tones of a hospital at night seemed appropriate to the time. The pleasant young nurse came into the reception room again and told Cosgrave the doctor was still busy with Mr. Blair. She wore a faint but definite and heady scent. She was pretty and when she asked him if there was anything she could do, read easily the dark, strained face and blushed, leaving the room before he could speak. Someone ought to tell her about using scent in a hospital, he thought. He wondered what it would be like to be in bed in the hospital and have her flitting in and out of the room, with her faint, virginal smile and heady odor.

It was after ten o'clock when McKay finally came into the reception room, closing the door behind him. He looked tired and annoyed. Cosgrave stood up. "How's Mr. Blair?"

McKay shrugged. "He's no worse. You never know what's going to happen with one of these neuro-cardiac cases. He might live. What do you want?"

"I suppose you think I'm a nuisance coming in at this time and—"

"I think you're a son of a bitch, if you want to know. Now what's on your mind? I haven't much time."

Cosgrave saw the little man was quite serious. He, himself, felt no resentment. "I had a note from Jane. She said you had her mother send her away. I think that, well, perhaps I have some right to know why."

McKay's lips turned a little. "I like almost to believe you. That's a great act you're putting on. If you're worried about her being pregnant or your being implicated, you needn't be. Now, why don't you run along."

"I came here to ask you a question, not to get a lot of cheap abuse. Why did you have Jane sent away and where?"

"Why don't you ask her mother or her father?"

"I don't think they maybe actually know why Jane had to go away."

"They're clucks, all right," McKay said. He looked at Cosgrave. "I recommended she be sent away, be put in some sort of nursing home. I recommended it a while ago, too, but her parents aren't the kind of people who understand euphemisms. I finally had to tell them in words of one syllable. I did it because lately Jane seemed more disturbed than usual by some sort of line you handed her." He paused, seeing Cosgrave's face. "I've always wanted her taken care of at some other place than her home, until a thorough study of the psychological and physiological factors involved, could be made."

"Why?"

"Because there are too many bastards like yourself who don't mind shooting the sitting pheasant."

"I still don't get it."

McKay looked at him. "Let's see, like myself, you went to Georgetown, didn't you? It's unlikely then that you know much about anything practical. All right, I'll tell you. Some people would call it nymphomania."

Somehow, McKay had expected violence, not this slow collapse of the young man, his face in his hands. The doctor stood for a moment, looking at Cosgrave, then sat in a nearby chair. "All right," he said. "That's enough. Look up. I didn't say *I'd* call it that. Come on, snap out of it."

Cosgrave bit his upper lip to control it and looked at McKay.

"You liked her, then?" McKay said. "That's tough. I know people I could send you to and they'd give you a lot of advice, all bad. If you want to listen to me I'll tell you that there's nothing much you can do about it, about yourself, except maybe pray—and even then, don't expect anything to happen very suddenly."

"But I ought to be able to see her. If—"

"No. It wouldn't be much good for either one of you. Sometime, she'll be better."

"You've got no right. She—"

"She's not being forced or coerced into anything. And where she is—it's run by one of the more intelligent orders of nuns—it's a pleasant place with gardens. It's simply that there are no men there. In time I expect her to be all right. It seems to be mostly physiological."

"I'm sure that if we were—she'd be faithful. She—"

McKay drew in his breath, perhaps impatiently, and let it out. "Look. Maybe you're right. Maybe you are. See? But all I have to go by is my experience as a doctor. I'm not trying to be smug, but my knowledge—such as it is—is special. And I think you'll agree with me that I'm capable of more objectivity than you are? At least, in this matter. And I'm not trying to be nasty or hard when I tell you that I don't think she could, now, as she is, be faithful to anyone. If she remained here, too, there's always the possibility of disease." Seeing Cosgrave's face change, McKay went quickly on. "She's going to be all right. I'm performing a minor operation on her in a few days and I honestly think she's going to be all right, then."

"Truly?" Cosgrave said.

"Truly," McKay said, nodding once, his eyes briefly closed. "In this sort of thing physiological causes and psychological ones are almost invariably mixed. My own feeling is that Jane is or can easily be made normal, psychologically. The operation I expect to take care of the rest."

"And you'll tell me when she's all right?"

McKay nodded. "Keep in touch with me. Although I don't imagine you'll be staying around here much longer?"

"Not much longer." Cosgrave thought he felt better. It seemed to him that, clearly and now without passion, he loved Jane. Enough to marry her when she was well. But a quality of remoteness seemed to inform her and their future. Where he was and what had happened today, what still, he felt, might happen, were the realities. For a little while love and gentle things would seem unreal to him.

McKay looked at him, pitying him. The nurse came in, trailing her scent. "I think Mr. Blair needs you, doctor."

McKay stood up. "You have a drink, Cosgrave. Don't go into any of the bars down in the village, though. I'll have a drink sent out to you here. And I'll give you something so you can sleep. I'll send them both out with Miss Drury."

Cosgrave didn't move as they left the room. Sitting

there, listless, he could hear them going down the hall. He wondered why his love for Jane seemed cool, dispassionate, remote. He made himself believe it would be intense again. He knew suddenly that it was not good for violence to be the only thing that seemed to possess reality. Sitting there, their footsteps sounding outside the room, he knew he was bound to try to change his thought, but an iron lethargy was on him.

He heard McKay talking to the nurse. "Miss Drury, don't you know perfume should not be worn in a hospital? A whorehouse maybe, but not a hospital."

Cosgrave thought that he smiled at McKay's words.

Kane wasn't at breakfast; Cornish had almost finished when Cosgrave came down. "Good morning, Father."

"Oh, good morning, John."

Cosgrave wasn't hungry and poured himself some coffee. He felt the priest's eyes on him. "You know, John, I've been thinking. We'd best have a talk. You, well, haven't been well, very well, lately."

Cosgrave nodded without looking up.

"While I know that yesterday's events were rather trying, what with your search for Loker after the people from Calverton had, ah, abandoned him—still you might have been more courteous with our visitors. And then the fight in Calverton some days ago. If this goes on, we'll lose good will. This place will never be a second Antigonish."

Cosgrave continued to nod. "I know. I'm sorry."

"I, too, have my problems," the priest went on. "I was badly disappointed when the governor said he could not come to the high-school graduation in January. And I had met him when he was campaigning down here.

I've been thinking, John, that maybe you could go on retreat for a while. If you don't want to go to one of the regular retreat houses, you could go to Woodstock or to Chaptico. Father Mattingly at Chaptico was once our master of novices at Woodstock."

Cosgrave shook his head. "I don't want to go on retreat. I got some pretty bad advice at one once, and I didn't get over the effects of it until recently."

The priest was silent and portentous. "I can't conceive of anyone's getting bad advice in a retreat-house. At least not from a Jesuit."

"It was a Jesuit."

"Even so," the priest said, troubled, "it doesn't mean that you must necessarily get bad advice at one."

"I know. I just don't want to go to one."

"I must say that your attitude isn't exactly a respectful one."

Cosgrave didn't speak; he was looking down, his head moving slightly; he was not unlike a man out of his senses.

"And however much we may want to help the Negro," the priest went on, "I must say that a performance like yours yesterday repeated will ruin the co-op if it hasn't done so already."

"Are we opening an oyster-shucking plant to help the Negroes or what?"

"To help the whites and the Negroes both. And we must tread carefully."

"I can't tread carefully, any more. If you want to know, Fenner Ridgel and I were going to kill people yesterday if we had to."

The priest went white. "I've felt for some time that you were about to leave the Church."

Cosgrave looked at the floor to his left before answering. "No, I'm not going to leave it. If I were a bastard-twirp of a would-be intellectual I'd have left it at Harvard where it was fashionable to leave it. It's too easy to leave the Church and stand outside it and write stark novels about how the brave, young man shook off its medievalism and grew up to be emancipated. And I imagine it would give a lot of people pleasure if I left the Church; but I'm not going to."

"To whom would it give pleasure?"

"My friends in New York, some of my former teachers. Yourself, perhaps."

"Now you're becoming impertinent."

"I'm becoming more than that. I think I'd better resign as manager of the co-op."

"Why?"

"Because I don't know whether I'm coming or going and I might do something I regret."

"You have already . . . done and said things you should regret. Your language and general attitude toward myself have certainly lacked respect."

"For you, as a priest, I have respect."

Cornish reddened and couldn't speak for a moment. "It's an attitude like yours that can lead to anti-clericalism."

"I'm aware of the possibility. I think I can guard against it."

"I don't think you have."

Cosgrave felt himself beginning to shake. He left the table and went to his room. He lay on the bed awhile and then got up, knelt and said, in English, the *De Profundis*. He felt no different when he stood up. It was part of their warped heritage, he realized, that they in-

246

variably expected immediate and obvious answer to prayer. He packed his two bags and carried them down to the car. The tightness went all through him and he tried to laugh when he told himself: this is what it feels like to be a neurotic.

No one was in sight when he left the rectory. He drove only as far as the grounds of the Institute and took the muddy, little road that led to Bernard Hebb's house. Mrs. Hebb, a woman bony and yellow, like, though darker than, her husband, came out of the house and looked at him suspiciously. She did not smile when she recognized him although her voice was pleasant.

"Is Mr. Hebb at home, ma'am?"

"He out shelling corn. I'll call him."

Cosgrave waited, leaning against the car, until the tall, yellow man came around the house. Mr. Hebb was pleasant although his eyes did not smile. "How are you, young man? What brings you here?"

"I was wondering, Mr. Hebb, if you'd mind if I stayed here with you a few days?"

The yellow man didn't change expression. "You seen Father Kane?"

"No. I wouldn't mind, though."

"He busy now over at the school. Them nuns—the young ones, not the mother s'perior—feeling right bad about yesterday's happenings. Two of them want go back to the big house they got in Baltimore. What for you want to stay here with me?"

Later, remembering this, Cosgrave recalled the fear in the yellow man's eyes; but now he could not see it. "You see, Mr. Hebb, it's this way. Father Cornish and myself haven't been getting along. It's my fault, of course." He felt as patient as an old man; there seemed a great need for patience and so he possessed it, speaking slowly and with what he knew must be great logic. "And besides," he went on, "I feel like killing people. I thought it might be best if I stayed here where I wouldn't see people for a few days."

Mr. Hebb wet his thick lips and looked up, scratching his head as if thinking of what to do. He had known immediately what he was going to do. "Lemme see—you ever been duck-hunting, young man?"

"No. I've been meaning to go but just never got around to it."

"All right, suppose you and me go now? Ain't shot over my blind in three, four days now. You wait here. You got a gun?"

"In the car."

About ten minutes later Mr. Hebb came out of his house carrying a burlap sack full of wooden decoys, his gun and several boxes of shells.

"I have shells," Cosgrave said.

"What you got, number 6's?"

"Yes, I think so."

"They ain't big enough for duck. You wants number 4's or 5's like I got here."

"All right, but let me pay for them."

"We settle that later. Important thing now's to get out there in that blind."

They began the walk down the long slope to the river. The grass was sere, all the trees dull but the cedar and bull-pine. Sharp against the leaden river, these trees held their green against the cold. Far out, in midstream, thin wedges of birds like smoke flew. To the south one wedge was of bigger birds, white. "See them swans," Mr. Hebb said.

"Will we get any shooting, you think?"

"Ought to. If that wind roughens up a little. I certainly hopes we get some."

South, just off the Institute's land, they could see tobacco patches, the stumps just above ground, a few withered grown plants that had been left to reach maturity for their seed.

"I notice there's no tobacco on the Institute's land."

"Father Kane, he just wants eating crops raised. Tobacco keeps poor people poor. Mos' the white folks that raise tobacco down here they live as poor as colored people. Don't even know enough have a bean patch in case it's bad year for tobacco."

At the shore, the wind blew steadily in their faces. They got in a skiff and Mr. Hebb rowed steadily out to the blind about a hundred feet offshore. Sitting in the stern, the bag of wooden ducks at his feet, Cosgrave felt no less strange. Mr. Hebb watched him carefully.

In front of the blind they scattered the decoys on the water. The wind from Virginia turned the wooden ducks toward the pull of their little anchor-weights and they were all facing southwest to Virginia when the two men had hidden the boat and climbed into the blind. The wind came stronger and Mr. Hebb said, "Load up, now. They apt to come in any minute on that wind."

"I am loaded."

"What you mean?"

"I had the gun loaded in the car."

"You ought know better than carry a loaded gun in a car." When Cosgrave didn't answer, Mr. Hebb said, "What for you do that?"

"I don't know." Right now, he really didn't know.

They were silent for a while, half-sitting, half-crouching behind the bull-pine boughs of the blind.

"We got be patient," Mr. Hebb said. "See 'em out 'ere on the river?"

When the waves bobbed them, they could see the ducks, dark spots, all pointing in the same direction.

"Some white-backs there," Mr. Hebb said. "Hope we get some. All we been getting so far's blackheads, though they's good eating, too." Cosgrave felt stolid, even stupid; he wanted to shoot the gun. Mr. Hebb said, "Down! Down! Here they comes!"

"I can't see them."

"Never mind. Just rise when I does."

Cosgrave peered through the pine boughs but couldn't see anything. Then he saw them, low and coming hard, against the Virginia shore, only their white sides showing at first, then the quick-beating, narrow wings. They came in, six of them, flying faster than he thought birds could fly, the wind quartering on their tails, their necks craned straight.

"Now," Mr. Hebb said and rose in the blind. The ducks banked vertically, wheeled, lost speed, tried desperately to gather it again. The guns went off. First Mr. Hebb's, then Cosgrave's twice, then Mr. Hebb's again. Two birds crumpled and fell, one among the decoys, one farther out. The other birds were flying fast up the river.

"You got both of them, I guess," Cosgrave said.

"No matter. You just takes your time next time and covers them good, with a good lead. Try not to get excited."

"What are they, canvasbacks?"

"No, blackheads. Scaup, some calls them. Some say

bluebills. We better get them 'fore the tide takes them downriver."

They rowed and retrieved the birds. The feathers were smooth, dry, and finely patterned in an irregular design. One bird bled slightly and the other one fluttered when Mr. Hebb picked it out of the water. He gave it to Cosgrave. "Here. Knock its head against that gunwale," Mr. Hebb said.

Back in the blind, waiting, Mr. Hebb said, "We should have brought a drink along. Just forgot to. That wind's roughening."

Birds flew far overhead. "Let's get down," Cosgrave said. "They may circle and come in."

"Not them. Them's mallards. They don't decoy."

A little later, Mr. Hebb said, "Now down!" He waited. "Is only two. You takes the one on the left and make sure. Now up!"

The birds banked, wheeling downriver toward the south. Cosgrave covered his bird and missed with the first barrel. Between the first and second shots he remembered to lead the bird. He swung the twin muzzles ahead of the duck and saw it crumple. Mr. Hebb had gotten his with the first shot and then watched Cosgrave.

"That was nice," Mr. Hebb said. "That was a long shot for a brush-gun. Your barrels ain't long enough for ducking."

Rowing after the dead birds, Cosgrave remembered for no reason he could think of, the lines, "Between the stirrup and the ground, something lost and something found."

He knew which duck was his, it was farther downstream than Bernard Hebb's. When he had the dead bird in his hands, he looked at it. It gave him pleasure.

"We got hurry back that blind," Mr. Hebb said. "They be coming in steady now."

The tide coming up from the Chesapeake met the river's flow in a long riffle not far from the blind. As far as they could see across the river, the water was roughened. The wind crossed harder. On every side, ducks were flying. Blackheads came in again and the guns sounded, the noise flattened and hollowed by the wind against the guns. Three birds fell. "Too bad you can't get a double," Mr. Hebb said.

They were wet getting back to the blind. They had hardly crouched when the Negro said, "Now they come! Now the whitebacks! Git you two!"

Cosgrave saw them, bigger birds with whitish bodies and dark wings and heads, twice as big as the blackheads. Coming in hard now. Hard and quick to death.

He rose as the birds banked, wheeling before settling. The thought of their coming in so hard to death stirred Cosgrave strangely. Standing up he was calm, though. He led each of the big birds, separately and slowly. When they fell it was in a vertical line, their heads into the wind. Pleasure came up in him, diffusing itself through him. The birds floated in the dark water. One of Mr. Hebb's fluttered, righted itself and dived. "We got chase him."

They gathered the three dead ducks, which the stronger wind was blowing toward the shore. "Now stand you in the bow," Mr. Hebb said, "and brace steady."

"But it's your bird."

"Ain't no matter. You git him."

Mr. Hebb rowed. Cosgrave, standing in the bow, braced himself against the wind, the motion and the first rain. The duck showed almost a hundred feet ahead. Cosgrave's shot pitted the water over where it had dived.

"He probably come up nearer shore," Mr. Hebb said. "He hurt bad."

The duck showed not so near shore as Cosgrave was looking, but his shot, the gun already to his shoulder, struck it. The body half-dived, following its last instinct or will, then floated quietly, the wind ruffling the dry feathers, white above the water.

Back in the blind, Cosgrave trembled, waiting. Swans flew overhead, almost in gun range, great white birds, fantastic, reaching east to the Chesapeake.

"Wish there weren't no season on them," Mr. Hebb said. "Like to get one of them. Like shooting something important."

Cosgrave shook. Coming in, like himself, to death, he thought. He saw the canvasbacks flying, gray-white in the rain against the Virginia shore. Coming in on the wind, coming in to death. He rose and shot twice, seeing the banked birds crumpling, the unhit birds moving out as silently as they had come. He did not know Mr. Hebb had not shot. The wind was blowing the dead birds shoreward.

"You stay here," Mr. Hebb said. Cosgrave hardly heard him and did not see him row the boat to the shore.

Still unheeding, the wind behind them, the ducks came in to death. Cosgrave hardly crouched now; standing motionless and in the rain the birds could not see him until too late. Once whistlers came and now, hearing the faint, pulsing pipe of their wings, it was almost too much for him. They were only a pair and when they fell, the wings limp, the piping stilled, there seemed a silence in the storm.

He had forgotten about Mr. Hebb, the boat, retrieving the birds; but stood, the gun-barrels warm in his hand, to give the death the birds came in so seeming eager to seek. He missed more than he hit, and on the shore Mr. Hebb gathered the dead birds blown in by the wind.

They came now, all but continually, now low and driving from the north, now higher and with a lighter, floating motion from across the river, wind-borne. The wind was under their wings and, seeking food and shelter, they came, sudden calm, on death. Geese passed overhead, high and honking. Cosgrave emptied both barrels at them but they were too high for the short brush-gun. He watched them pass southward, their wedge unbroken, their wing-beat impervious, immutable; he felt a hunger and a longing, even envy.

Mr. Hebb was standing next to him again. "We go now." Cosgrave turned, surprised. He had not been aware until now of the illusion of never-endingness. It had been similar when he had been with Jane.

"Why?"

Mr. Hebb laughed as though pleased. "You done shot your limit, the rest of my limit and one over. We gotta go."

Cosgrave felt heavy and slow now, as though coming out of deep sleep. They gathered the decoys and began the walk up the long slope, Mr. Hebb carrying the bag of decoys, Cosgrave the bag of ducks. They didn't speak going up the slope in the rain. They were more than halfway up when Mr. Hebb said, "You feel any more like killing people?"

"No. No more." Shame was sudden in him and he couldn't look at Mr. Hebb.

254

They didn't speak again until they had reached the house. Coming into its warm dimness, Cosgrave saw Kane rise from where he had been sitting near the wood-stove, and come toward them. It was as though he had known Kane would be there. "Are you all right, John?" the priest said.

"Yes, I'm fine. Now."

"Sit down."

Cosgrave saw that Mr. Hebb had gone, that he and Kane were alone. Kane looked at him. The priest's face seemed calm, almost apologetic. "I—I hear you weren't feeling so well a while ago," Kane said nervously.

"Who told you that—Father Cornish?"

"No. I haven't seen Father Cornish today. Mrs. Hebb told me."

Cosgrave felt sullen and couldn't look at Kane.

"You didn't really want to kill anyone?" Kane said.

"I'm afraid I did."

"Whom did you want to kill and why did you want to kill them?"

"I think you know without my telling you. The people . . . from yesterday."

"Yes, I know." Kane looked down, himself apologetic. "That was a terrible thing yesterday. And I'm afraid today's news is pretty bad, too."

"What?"

"Mr. Blair died this morning at the hospital and about the same time one of the oyster-patrol boats picked Loker Abell up on the Chesapeake, almost dead from exposure. He died on the way in."

"Sure, and I'm next."

"Now, John," Kane said gently, "try not to be the-atrical."

"I'm not." He knew he was, though, and couldn't face Kane. "The other day in my room I wanted to put the shotgun in my mouth and pull the trigger."

"Why?"

"I don't know. It seemed something vague like curiosity and was soon gone."

"Despair?"

"I guess I was despairing enough, but the despair seemed to have no connection with what I wanted to do with the gun."

After a moment Kane said, looking away, "I get tired at times of apologizing to my liberal friends and the observers who come here, for the existence of the Devil."

"I suppose there is a tendency to forget about him."

They didn't speak. Cosgrave looked at Kane's face, turned away, and saw how the flesh sagged in weariness where it was not drawn tight over bone. The only sound was that of the rain on the roof.

"At first," Kane said, "Mr. Blair didn't want to have a priest before he died. But he saw one, later."

"Why didn't he want to have a priest?"

"Pride, I imagine. What's wrong with almost everyone today that holds public office or responsibility?"

They were still again. Cosgrave felt quiet, had even begun to grow a little sleepy in the warm room after the cold air. "I'm sorry about wanting to kill anyone. I don't think maybe that I really wanted to."

Kane nodded abstractedly. "I'll hear your confession presently—if you want me to."

Again the silence and then Cosgrave asking, "Why do you Jesuits stay here, in this County? It amounts to

256

ministering to a heresy. Or—or something worse, unnameable."

Cosgrave sensed the priest's discomfiture. "You—you mustn't judge them all by the toughs that hurt Loker yesterday," Kane said. "Most of those don't even attend Mass any more."

"I'm not thinking of them. I'm thinking of the head of the Catholic Daughters, the banker's wife, that pays her Negroes two and a half a week. And of the ones who say they'd stop going to church if the niggers weren't made to sit in the back of the church."

Kane was very nervous. "You—you see, I'm the lucky one of our Order down here. I'm not strong and they give me the easy parish, the Negroes. The difficult parishes are the white ones. What protects the whites down here is their invincible ignorance. It's a theological term, a very providential one, the same sort of term that saves the followers of Father Coughlin in the eyes of the Church.

"Oh, I don't know," Kane went on, aimless and distracted. "I think we're here out of habit, because we were here at the beginning with Calvert three hundred years ago and it's been our mission ever since." It was the closest he had ever admitted to despair. "Then again," he went on, "you must remember that we're the youngest of the five major Orders of the Church and we ourselves are still trying to get adjusted. Our attitude has been, for the four hundred years of our existence, an essentially negative one because we were founded as a counter-reformation movement. We are only learning to take a more positive attitude."

"But sooner or later," Cosgrave said, "you Jesuits here will have to tell the whites that they are deliberately and continually doing things that are not only contrary to Christian teaching but to dogma. And then?"

"I don't know," Kane said. "I really don't know. We mustn't despair. Yesterday I saw Amish farmers from Pennsylvania in Calverton. They're here to buy farms for their sons. I happened to remember that the Amish are originally heretics. These are good people, not decadent. Probably I'm tired, but it seems almost as though God has tired of what the local people have been doing, the way they have let the land run down, and is going to see to it that the Amish inherit it."

It was darker outside. They could see each other only dimly in the little kitchen. Kane said, "What are you thinking?"

"I was thinking that Dabson Morgan will have his rosary beads out and be hanging over George Blair's grave at the burial. Blair didn't live long enough to turn Dabson out of office. And of how Dabson's wife will be with Joe Tennison in Washington about the same time Dabson is getting votes at George's grave."

"Be charitable, John, and try to be less morbid. You were going away, weren't you?"

"Yes, now."

"I think that's the best thing."

"I'd like to go to Confession before I leave."

"All right."

Cosgrave knelt on the wooden floor. Kane bent slightly toward him.

"I wanted to kill myself," Cosgrave said.

"I don't think you really did . . . but go on."

"And I wanted to kill other people. I hated them."

"Yes."

"And I was uncharitable in word and thought." He paused.

"Is that all?" Kane said.

"I think so. I was disrespectful to a priest."

"Is that all?"

"Yes."

Kane paused only briefly. "Now, for your penance I want you to pray for your enemies, for the people you wanted to kill."

In the faint light that escaped through the chinks in the stove, Kane saw the sweat start on Cosgrave's face. "I can't."

"You must," Kane said.

"I wouldn't be sincere."

"Sincerity of that kind needn't be emotional. It may be intellectual. And you have a will."

After a moment, Cosgrave said, "All right."

Kane waited outside, the lee of the house sheltering him. Presently Cosgrave came out. The light was gone now. "It was very difficult," Cosgrave said.

"I know. You're a good boy, John."

Cosgrave didn't speak. He was tempted to say something unpleasant.

"Do you know where you're going?" Kane said. "I mean home or—"

"I can't go home."

Kane looked toward the river, invisible in the gloom. "Look," he said, quietly, "would you, as a personal favor to me, go up to our house at Chaptico? Just for a few days? Zeke Mattingly is there and he used to be our novice-master at Woodstock. It might be good to talk to him for a few days."

"If you think there's any chance of my entering a seminary, that's out."

"No, it isn't that. They wouldn't take you in the state of mind you're in now. You're too nervous. If Zeke should mention it to you, you can slow him down by asking him about the time he had one of the seminarians design a new building at Woodstock. You know that story?"

"No."

"Zeke sent the plans for the dormitory to Rome for approval and some old, crusty monsignor there who had charge of such things, sent them back with just three words of comment on them, *'Qui sunt angeli?'* Are they angels? The seminarian had neglected to provide any bathrooms in his plans."

Cosgrave smiled, even laughed a little. "I suppose," he said, "that the remarkable thing is not that the ones like you stay here, but that the ones like Father Cornish stay."

"You shouldn't talk like that about a priest, John."

"I know. I'm sorry."

"And look at Samuel Raife. He's not only staying here but is going to marry."

"And I'm quitting."

"I would have had to insist on your going, anyhow. And, such as I am, I am Father Cornish's superior here."

"I don't think he would be for my staying. Well, it's been good to know you."

"Goodbye, John, and God bless you."

In the rain, Cosgrave drove north. He thought of stopping at McKay's office and trying to make the doctor tell him where Jane was; but his stomach turned before the conscious thought that, as he was, neither he nor Jane could help each other. But his love for her, its possible fulfillment, did not seem remote. He realized, for the first time, how close to madness he had come. Or so he thought. He had another reason for going to the house at Chaptico, he knew.

Driving in the steady rain, the dead were with him again: Loker, George Blair, the old ones at Point Lookout. He prayed for them and hurried on.

In the rain he could see the house, a lighter bulk in the dark, a few of its many windows lit. He went up the muddy drive, the car-wheels slipping, and swung in next to the lighter, cheaper cars of the priests.

A tall, thin man in a white shirt and old pants was standing in a lighted doorway, waiting. The doorway was level with the ground. "Hello, Cosgrave," he said in a dry, indifferent voice. "I'm Father Mattingly. Laurence Kane phoned to say you were coming up. Come on in."

Cosgrave stood outside the doorway in the rain. "Thanks, but before I go in I want to settle something. When a man is what might be called slightly unorthodox in his belief and the Church isn't sure whether he's a faker or not, they give him the test of obedience, don't they?"

"I guess so."

"Well, I'm here. Father Kane told or asked me to come here. And I'm here." It was why he had come to Chaptico, to make this obeisance.

"My, my, Cosgrave, you mustn't take yourself so seriously. Come in. Have a drink. You're just in time for dinner. Like all Jesuits, we eat well."

Cosgrave entered the little hall between the kitchen and the dining room. Three young priests and an old one were at dinner. They were all strangers to him, but as he entered the room they rose with grave, bright faces to greet him.

That day was the first Friday in December. After Cosgrave had left him, Kane ate supper with the Hebbses and then went over to the church to prepare for Benediction.

There were a few more people at Benediction than usual. Kane felt he must say something, but just what he did not know. After they had said the Rosary together and before proceeding with the simple movements of the service, he turned to them. There was a phrase of opening or greeting, borrowed from the epistles, some priests used to their congregations before talking. Somehow, Kane had never used it before. Quite spontaneously he used it tonight.

"D-dearly beloved—" he began.